SONIC ™ THE HEDGEHOG

FALLOUT!

Facebook: **facebook.com/idwpublishing**
Twitter: **@idwpublishing**
YouTube: **youtube.com/idwpublishing**
Tumblr: **tumblr.idwpublishing.com**
Instagram: **instagram.com/idwpublishing**

COVER ART BY
TYSON HESSE

SERIES EDITS BY
JOE HUGHES
AND DAVID MARIOTTE

COLLECTION EDITS BY
JUSTIN EISINGER
AND ALONZO SIMON

PRODUCTION ASSISTANCE BY
SHAWN LEE

ISBN: 978-1-68405-327-8   22 21 20 19   4 5 6 7

Originally published as SONIC THE HEDGEHOG issues #1–4.

Chris Ryall, President & Publisher/CCO
John Barber, Editor-in-Chief
Cara Morrison, Chief Financial Officer
Matthew Ruzicka, Chief Accounting Officer
David Hedgecock, Associate Publisher
Jerry Bennington, VP of New Product Development
Lorelei Bunjes, VP of Technology & Information Services
Justin Eisinger, Editorial Director, Graphic Novels and Collections
Eric Moss, Sr. Director, Licensing & Business Development
Rebekah Cahalin, General Manager
Tara McCrillis, Director of Design & Production
Jud Meyers, Sales Director
Anna Morrow, Marketing Director

Ted Adams and Robbie Robbins, IDW Founders

Special thanks to Anoulay Tsai, Mai Kiyotaki, Aaron Webber, Michael Cisneros, Sandra Jo, and everyone at Sega for their invaluable assistance.

LETTERS
COREY BREEN

COLORS
MATT HERMS (#1 & 4)
ADAM BRYCE THOMAS (#2)
HEATHER BRECKEL (#3)

INKS
JIM AMASH (#1)
BOB SMITH (#1)

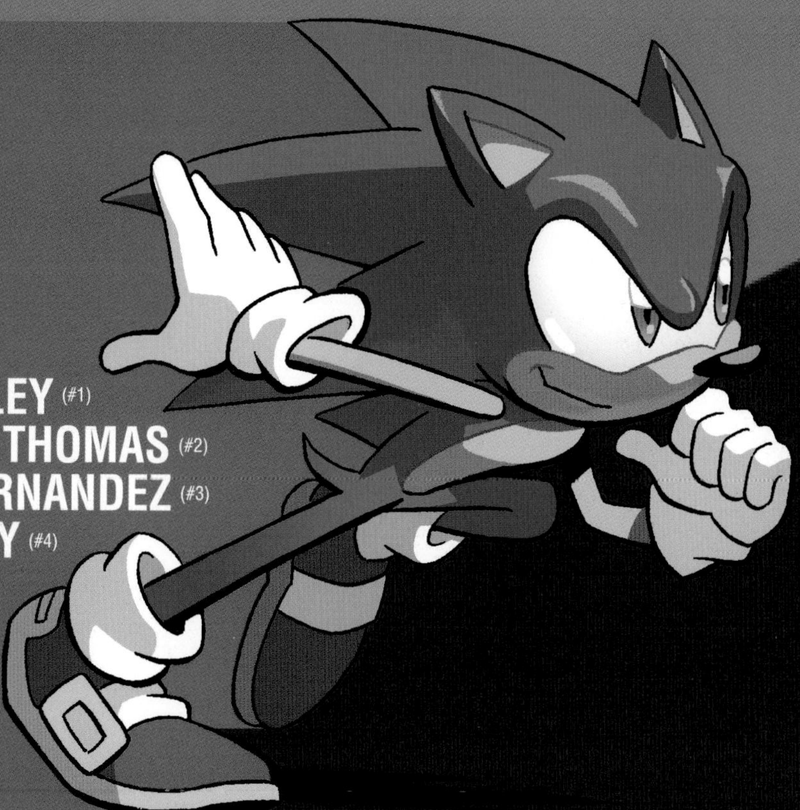

STORY
IAN FLYNN

ART
TRACY YARDLEY (#1)
ADAM BRYCE THOMAS (#2)
JENNIFER HERNANDEZ (#3)
EVAN STANLEY (#4)

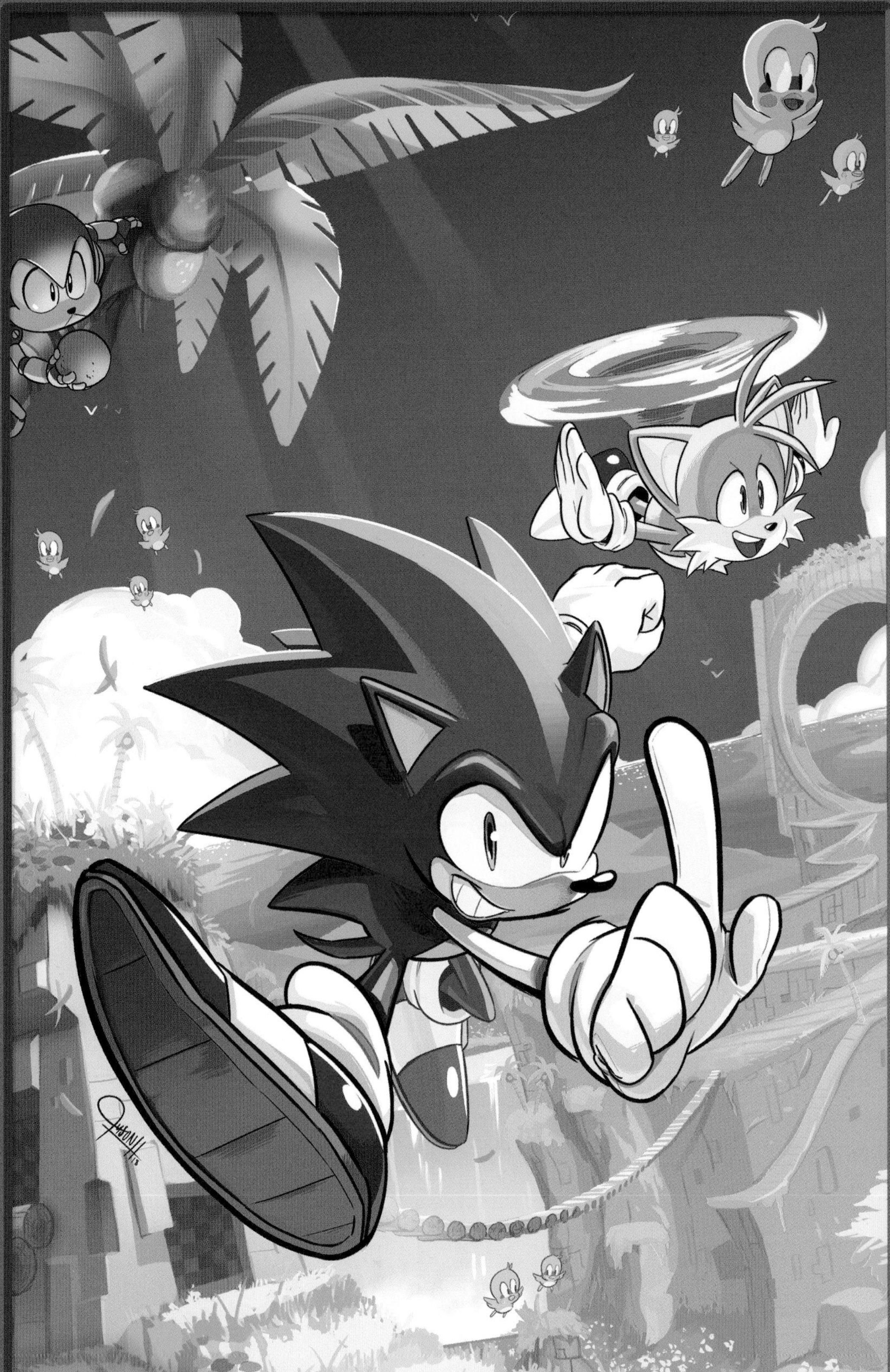

ART BY TYSON HESSE

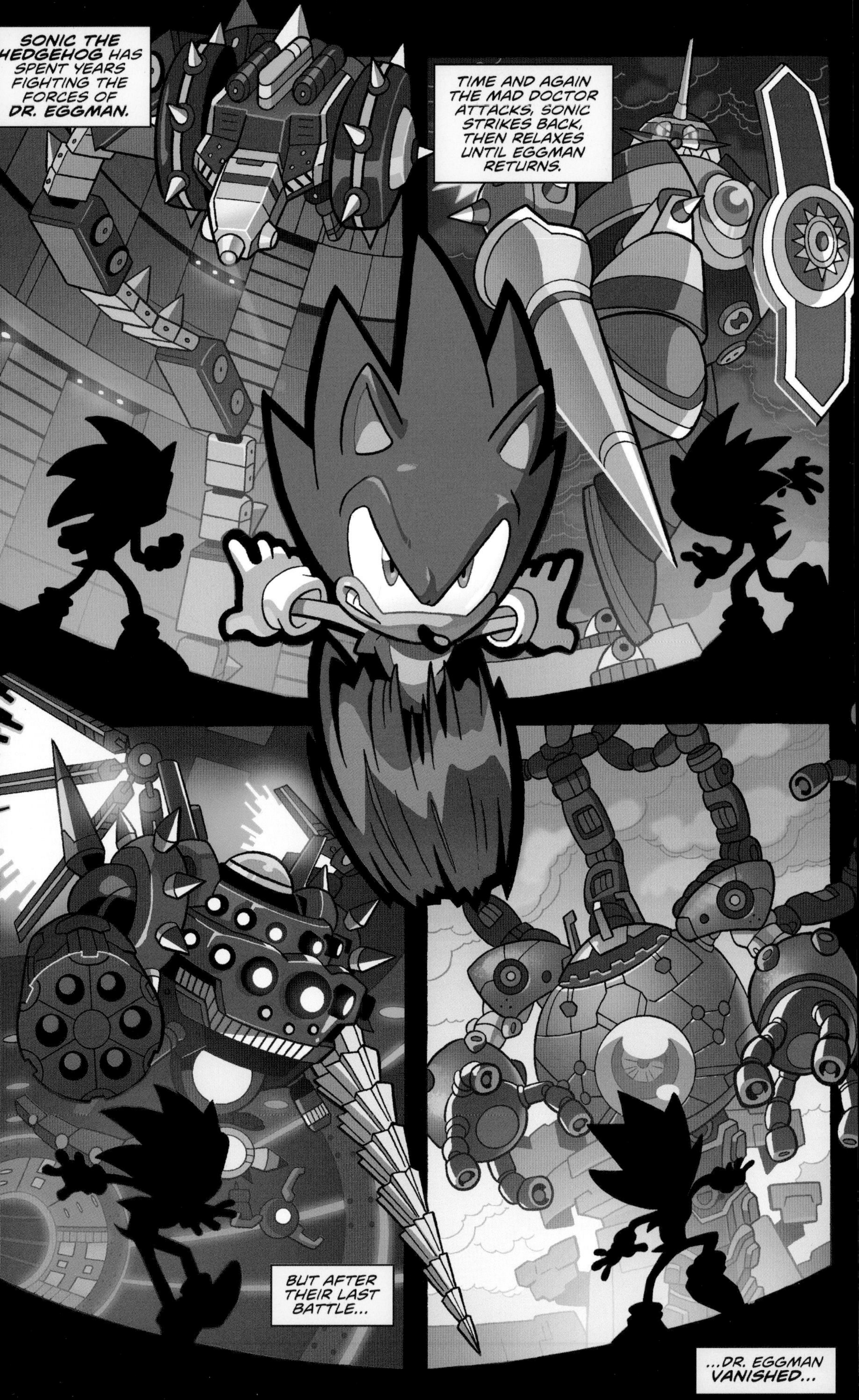
SONIC THE HEDGEHOG HAS SPENT YEARS FIGHTING THE FORCES OF DR. EGGMAN.
TIME AND AGAIN THE MAD DOCTOR ATTACKS, SONIC STRIKES BACK, THEN RELAXES UNTIL EGGMAN RETURNS.
BUT AFTER THEIR LAST BATTLE...
...DR. EGGMAN VANISHED...

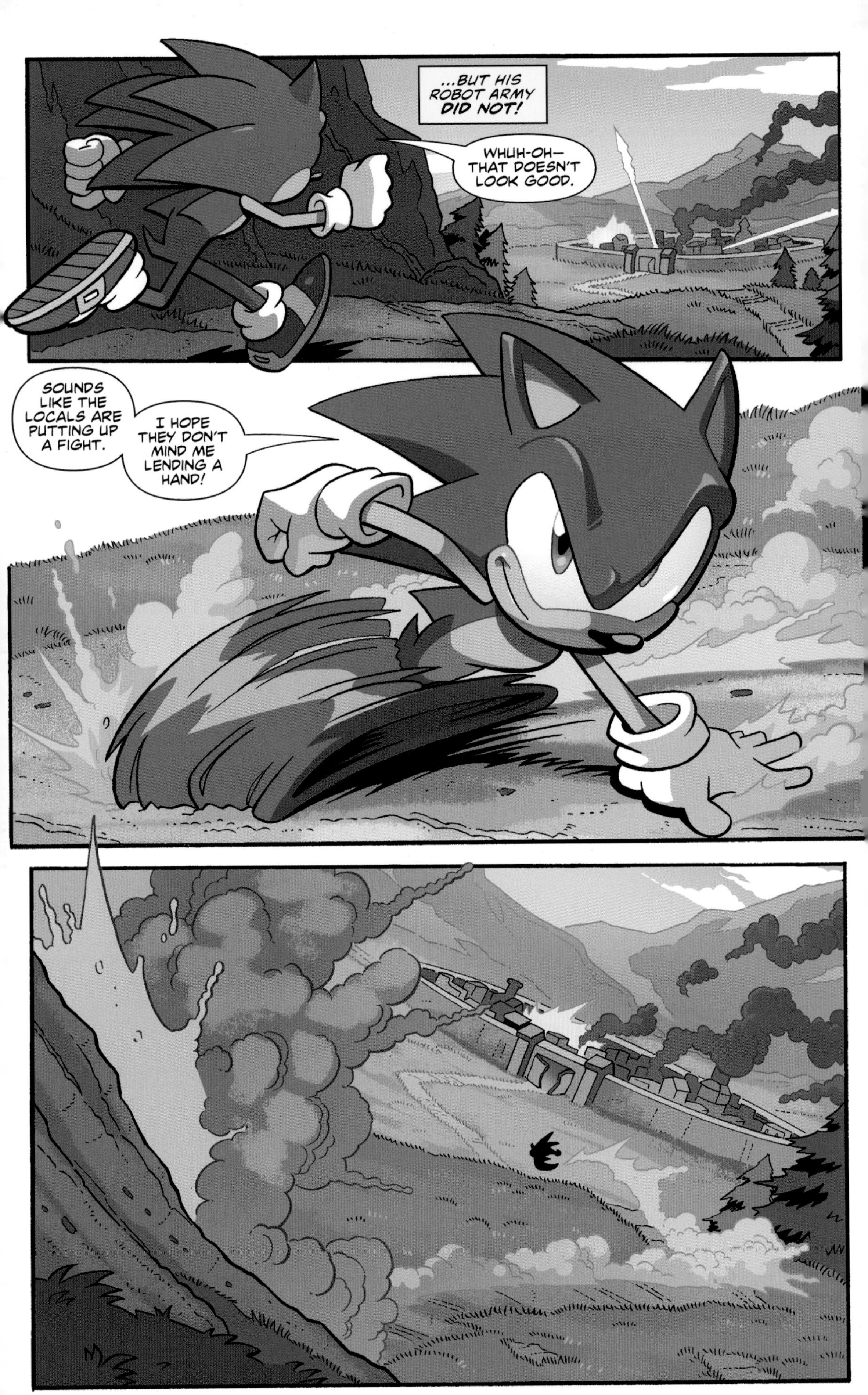
...BUT HIS ROBOT ARMY DID NOT!
WHUH-OH— THAT DOESN'T LOOK GOOD.
SOUNDS LIKE THE LOCALS ARE PUTTING UP A FIGHT.
I HOPE THEY DON'T MIND ME LENDING A HAND!

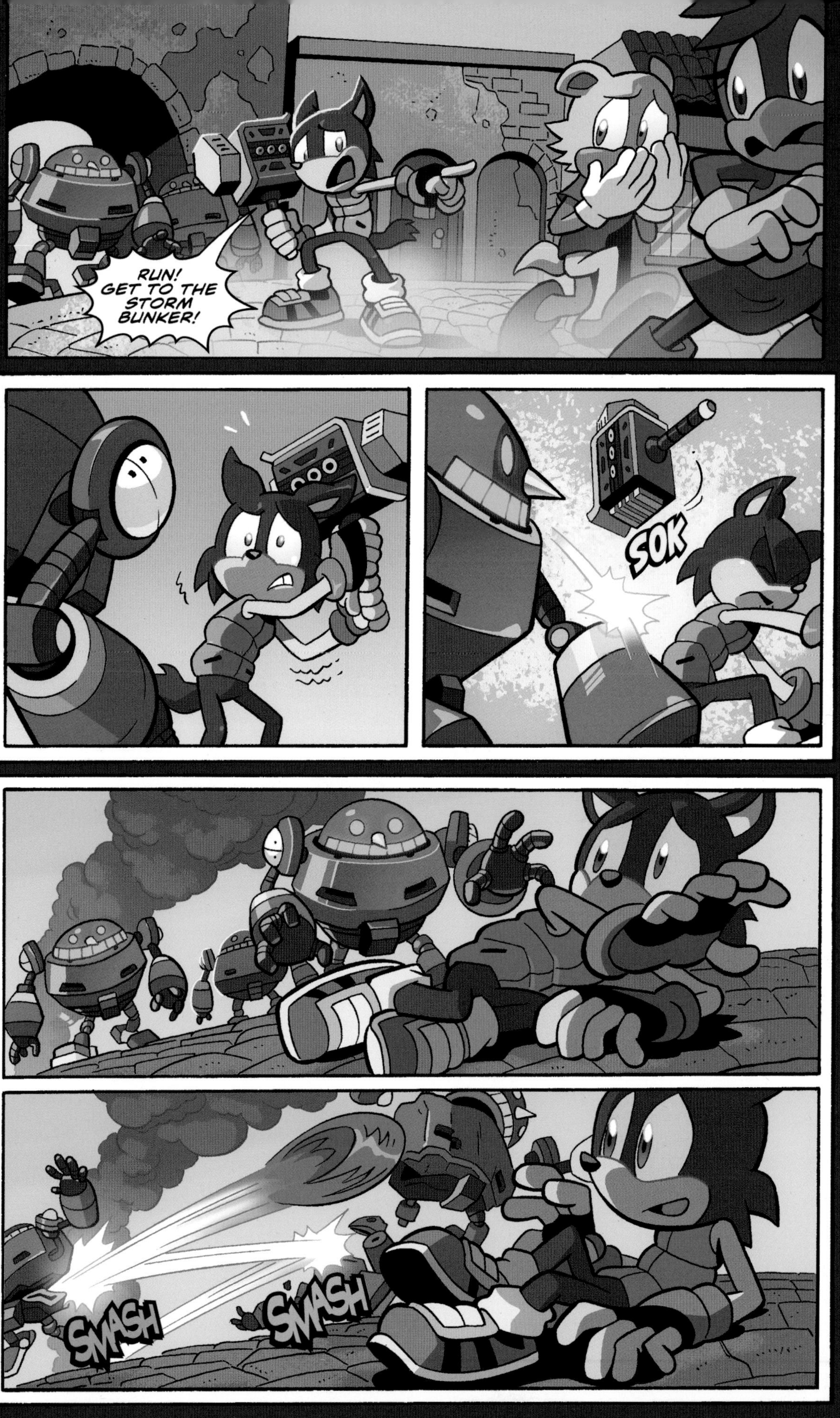
RUN! GET TO THE STORM BUNKER!
SOK
SMASH
SMASH

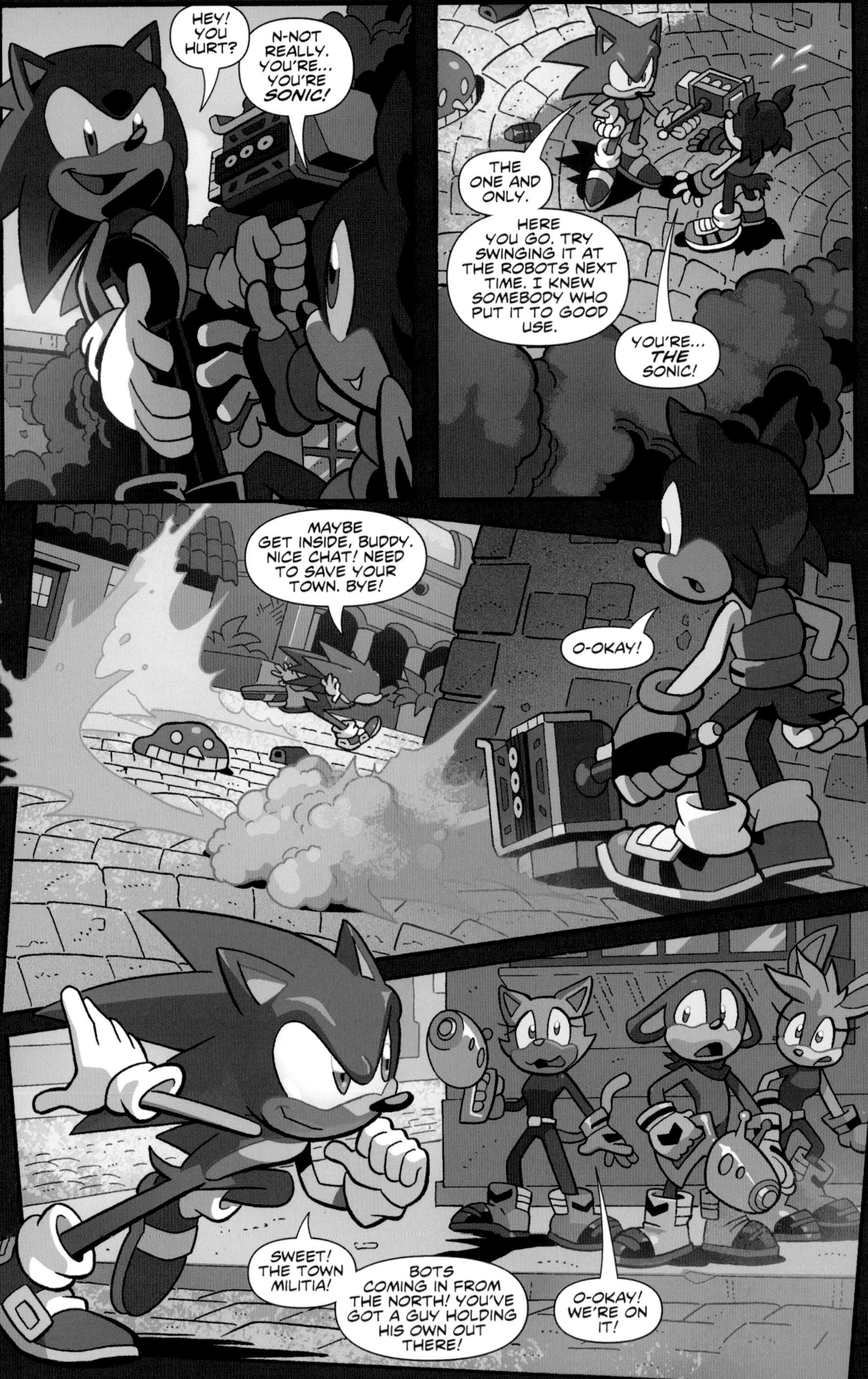
HEY! YOU HURT?
N-NOT REALLY. YOU'RE... YOU'RE SONIC!
THE ONE AND ONLY.
HERE YOU GO. TRY SWINGING IT AT THE ROBOTS NEXT TIME. I KNEW SOMEBODY WHO PUT IT TO GOOD USE.
YOU'RE... THE SONIC!
MAYBE GET INSIDE, BUDDY. NICE CHAT! NEED TO SAVE YOUR TOWN. BYE!
O-OKAY!
SWEET! THE TOWN MILITIA!
BOTS COMING IN FROM THE NORTH! YOU'VE GOT A GUY HOLDING HIS OWN OUT THERE!
O-OKAY! WE'RE ON IT!

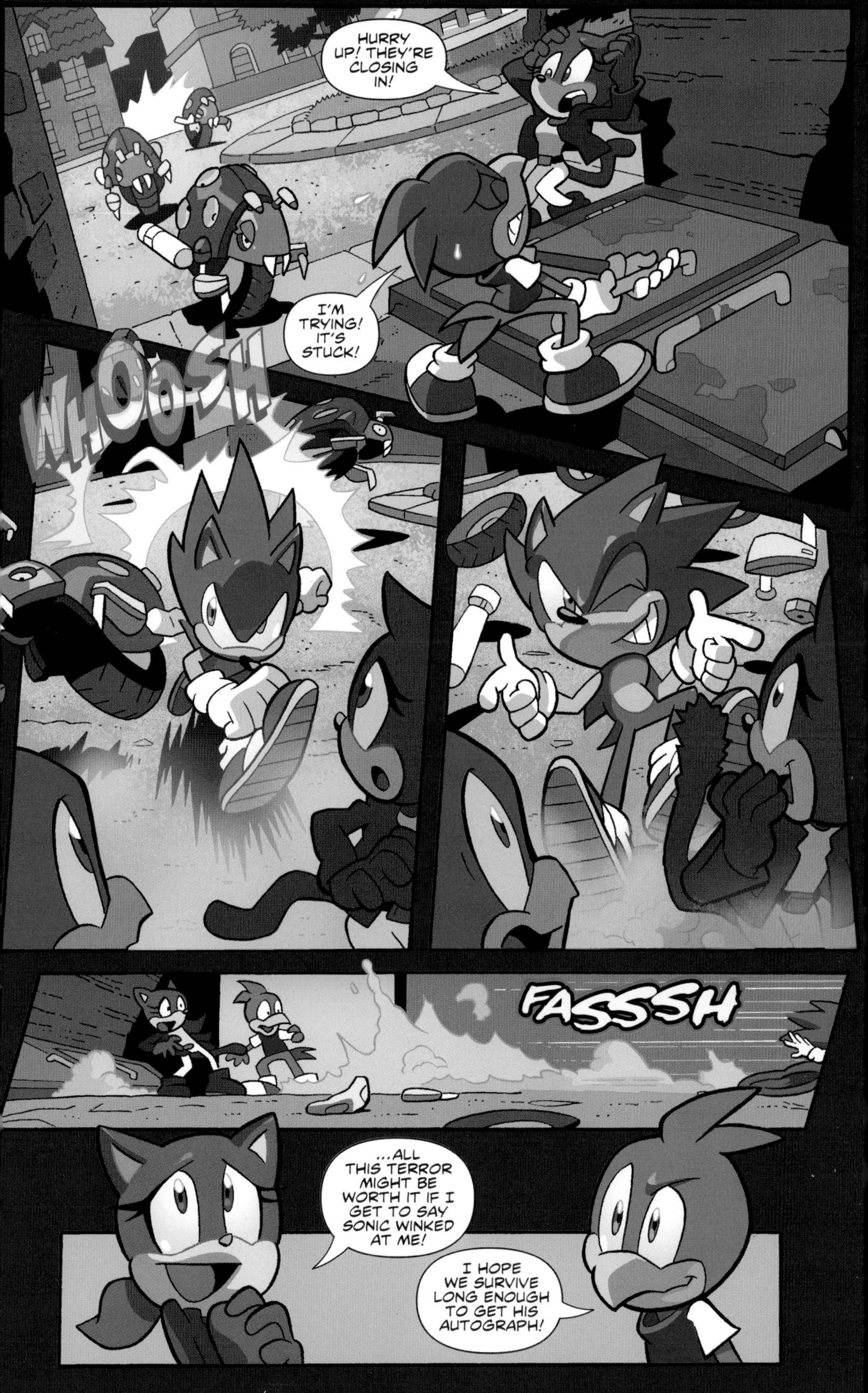
HURRY UP! THEY'RE CLOSING IN!
I'M TRYING! IT'S STUCK!
WHOOSH
FASSSH
...ALL THIS TERROR MIGHT BE WORTH IT IF I GET TO SAY SONIC WINKED AT ME!
I HOPE WE SURVIVE LONG ENOUGH TO GET HIS AUTOGRAPH!

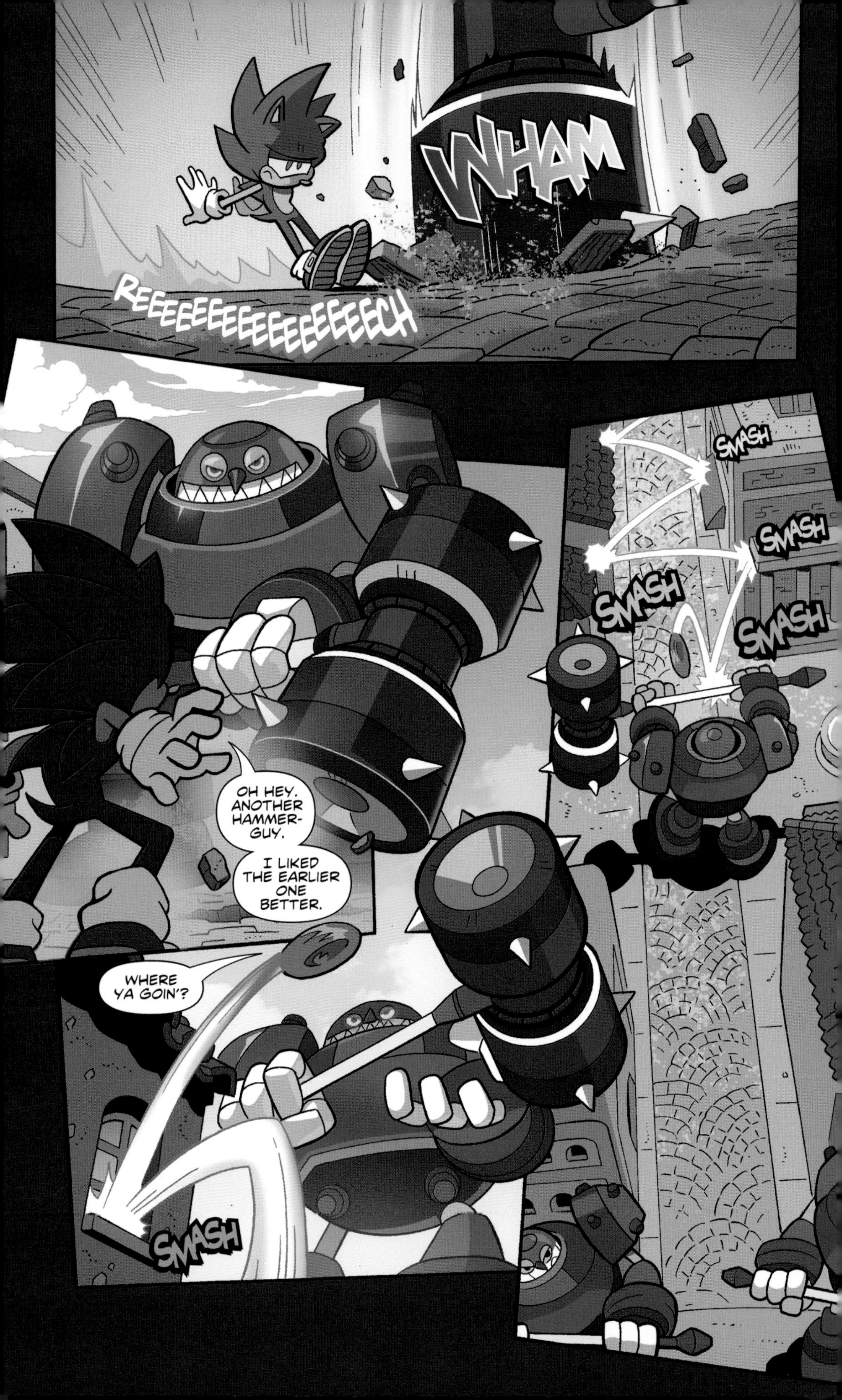

WHAM
REEEEEEEEEEEEEEEEEECH
OH HEY. ANOTHER HAMMER-GUY.
I LIKED THE EARLIER ONE BETTER.
SMASH
SMASH
SMASH
SMASH
WHERE YA GOIN'?
SMASH

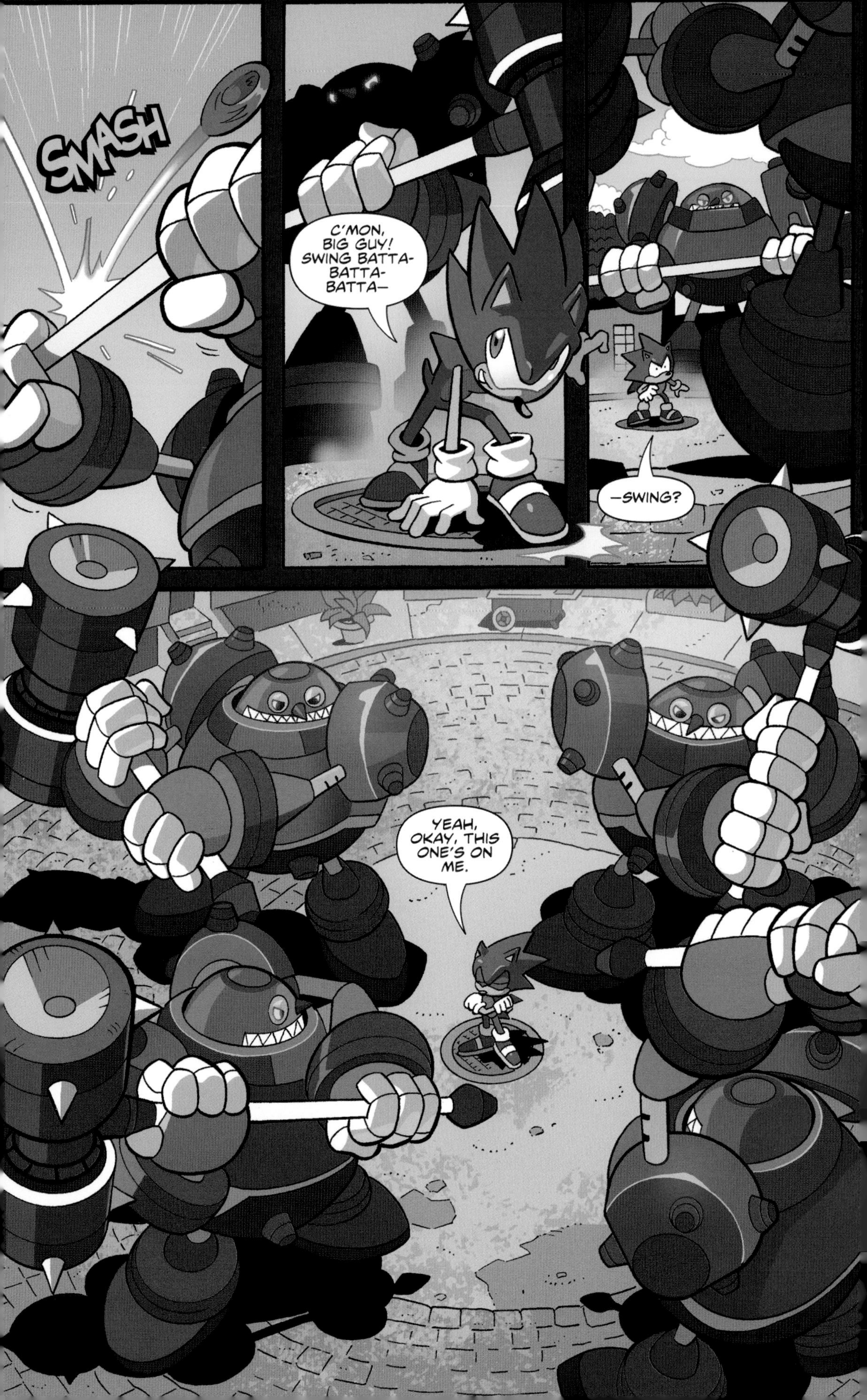
SMASH
C'MON, BIG GUY! SWING BATTA-BATTA-BATTA—
—SWING?
YEAH, OKAY, THIS ONE'S ON ME.

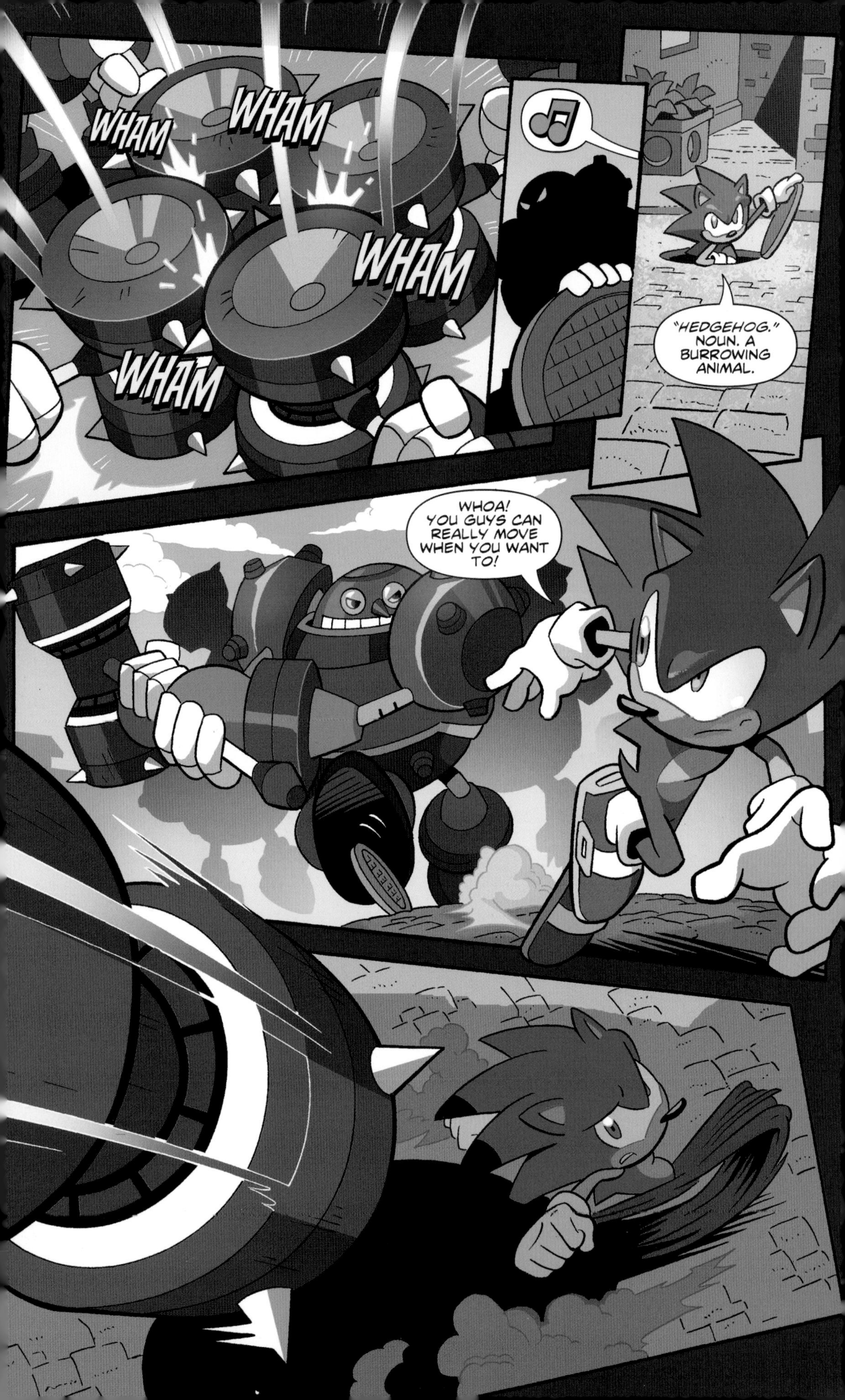
WHAM
WHAM
WHAM
WHAM
"HEDGEHOG." NOUN. A BURROWING ANIMAL.
WHOA! YOU GUYS CAN REALLY MOVE WHEN YOU WANT TO!

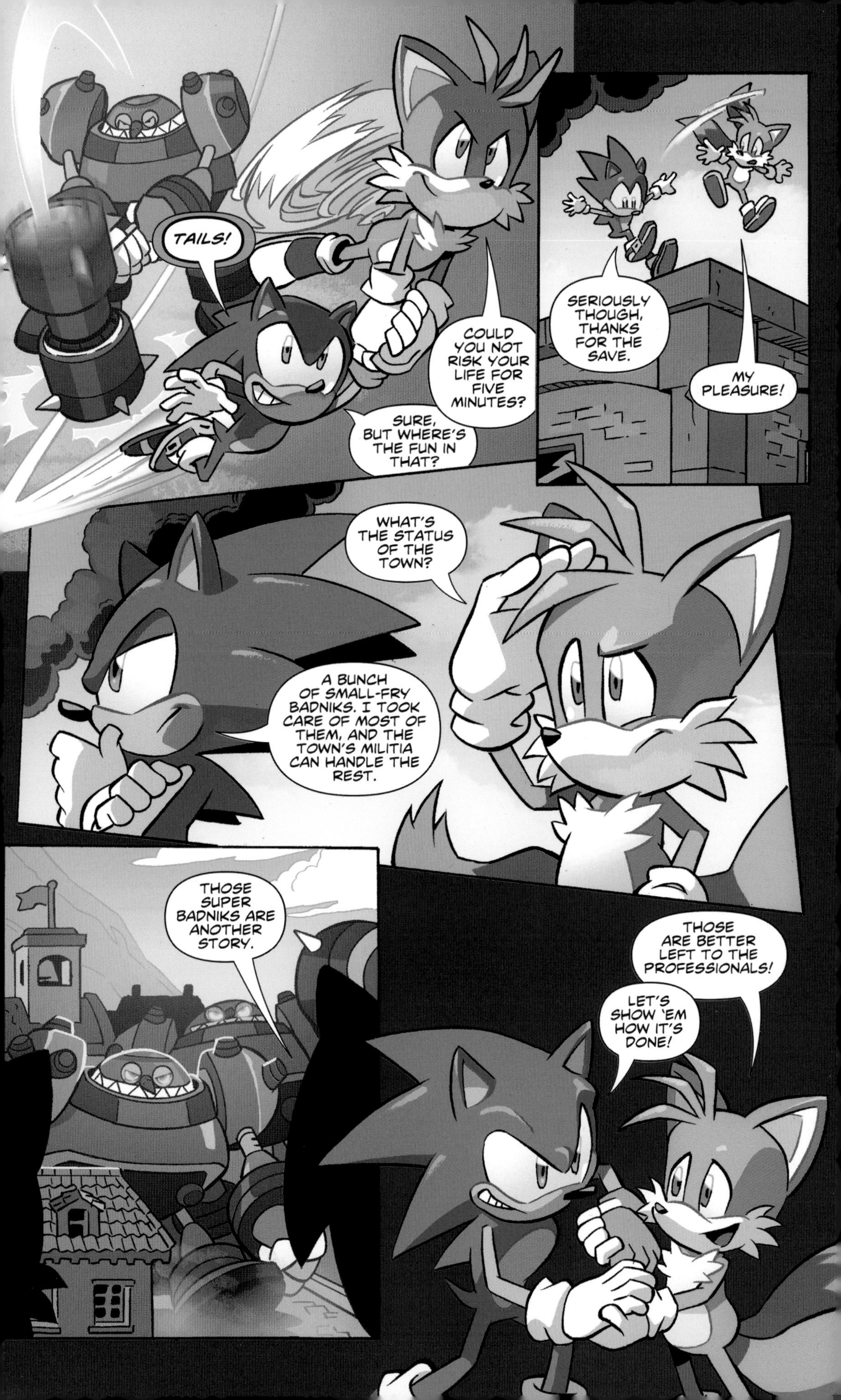
TAILS!
COULD YOU NOT RISK YOUR LIFE FOR FIVE MINUTES?
SURE, BUT WHERE'S THE FUN IN THAT?
SERIOUSLY THOUGH, THANKS FOR THE SAVE.
MY PLEASURE!
WHAT'S THE STATUS OF THE TOWN?
A BUNCH OF SMALL-FRY BADNIKS. I TOOK CARE OF MOST OF THEM, AND THE TOWN'S MILITIA CAN HANDLE THE REST.
THOSE SUPER BADNIKS ARE ANOTHER STORY.
THOSE ARE BETTER LEFT TO THE PROFESSIONALS!
LET'S SHOW 'EM HOW IT'S DONE!

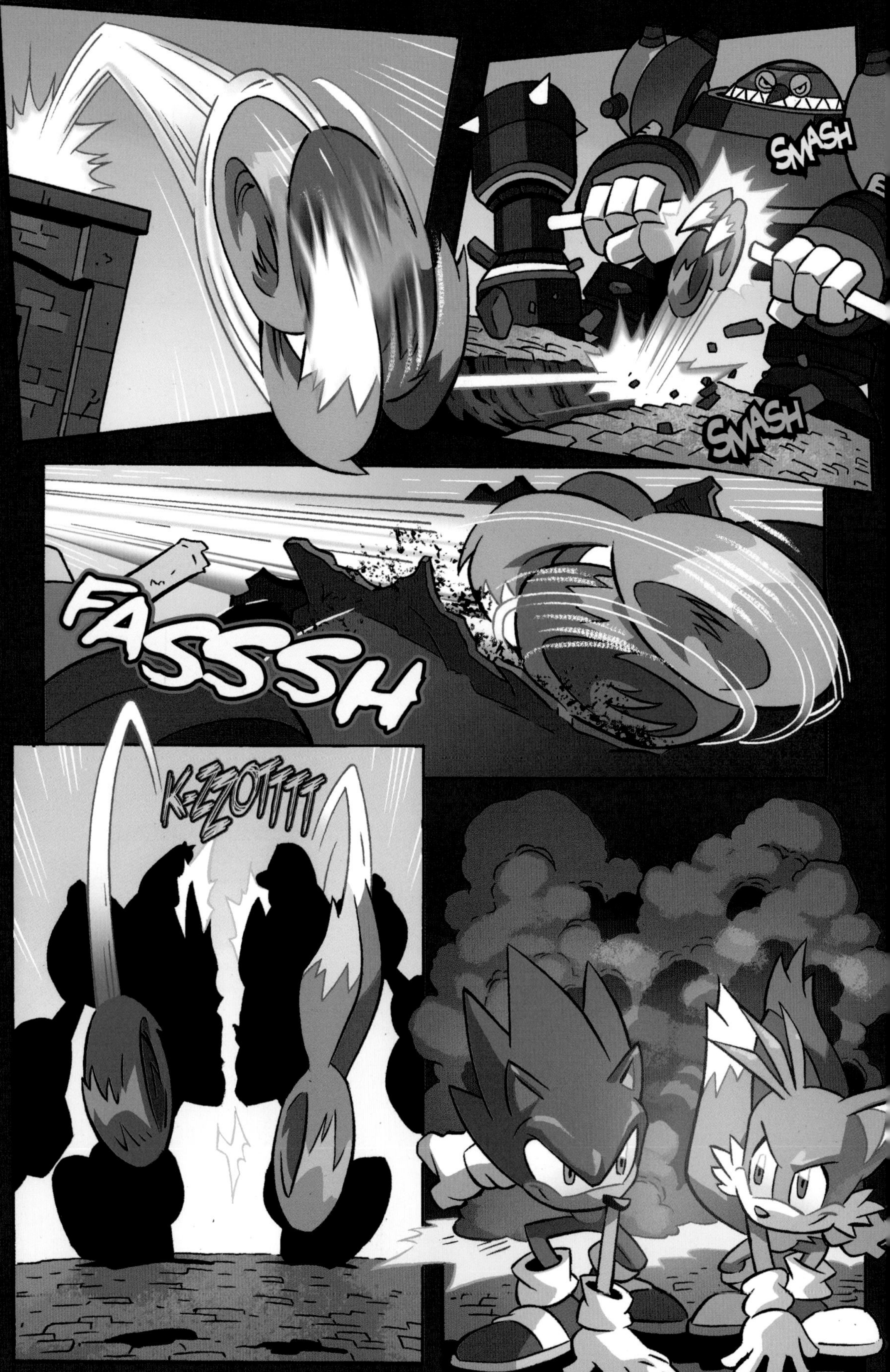
SMASH
SMASH
FASSSH
K-ZZOTTTT

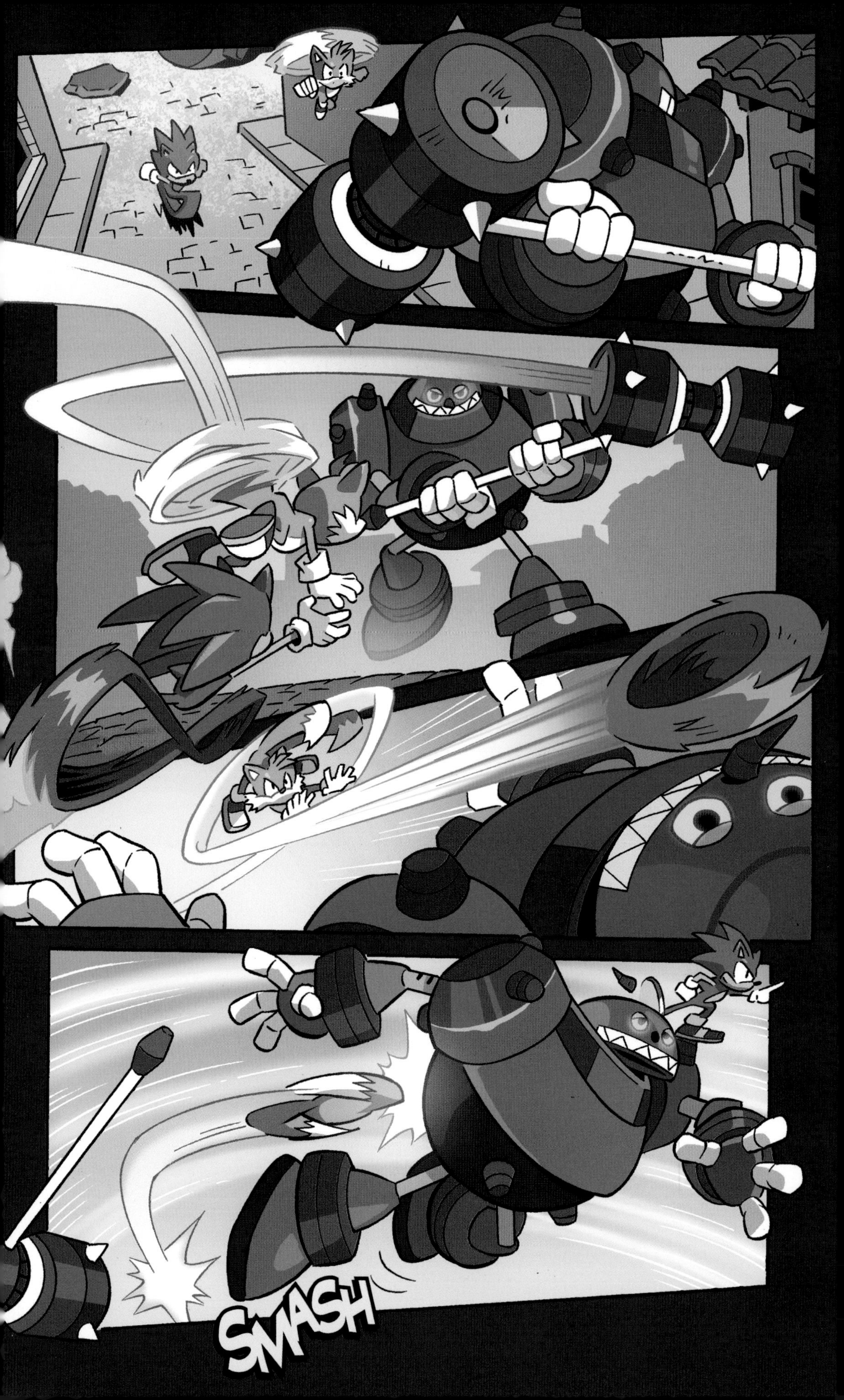
SMASH

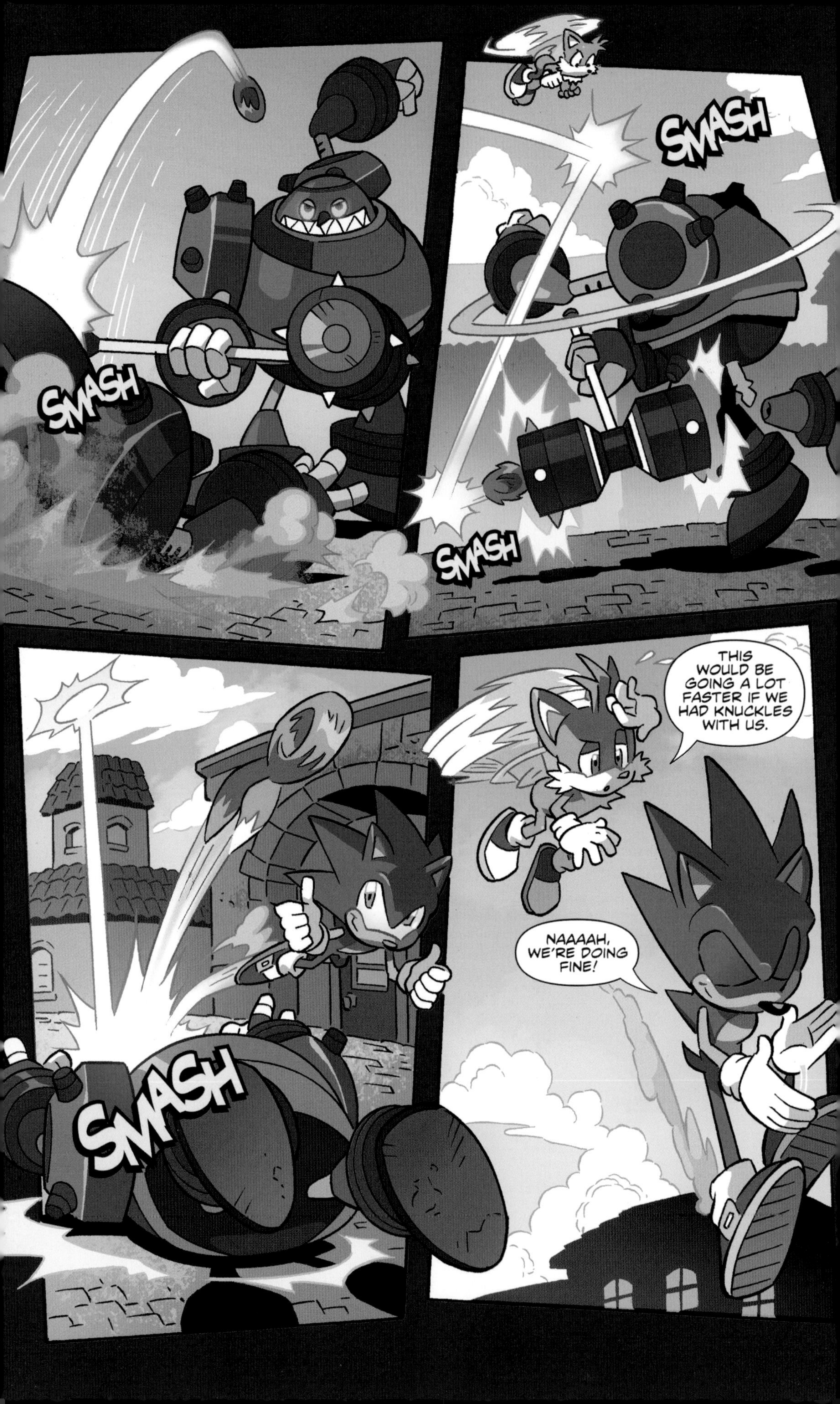
SMASH
SMASH
SMASH
SMASH
THIS WOULD BE GOING A LOT FASTER IF WE HAD KNUCKLES WITH US.
NAAAAH, WE'RE DOING FINE!

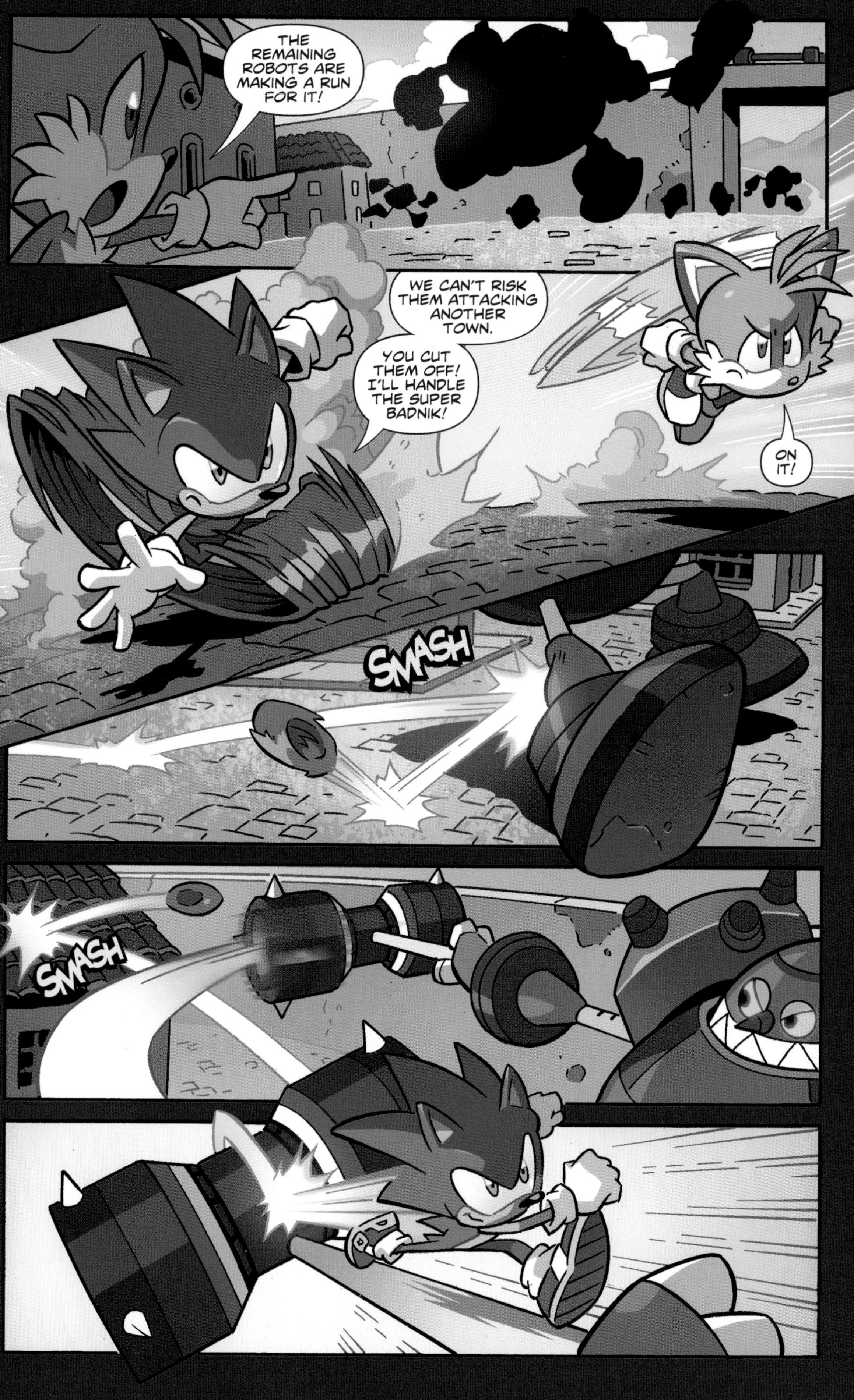
THE REMAINING ROBOTS ARE MAKING A RUN FOR IT!
WE CAN'T RISK THEM ATTACKING ANOTHER TOWN.
YOU CUT THEM OFF! I'LL HANDLE THE SUPER BADNIK!
ON IT!
SMASH
SMASH

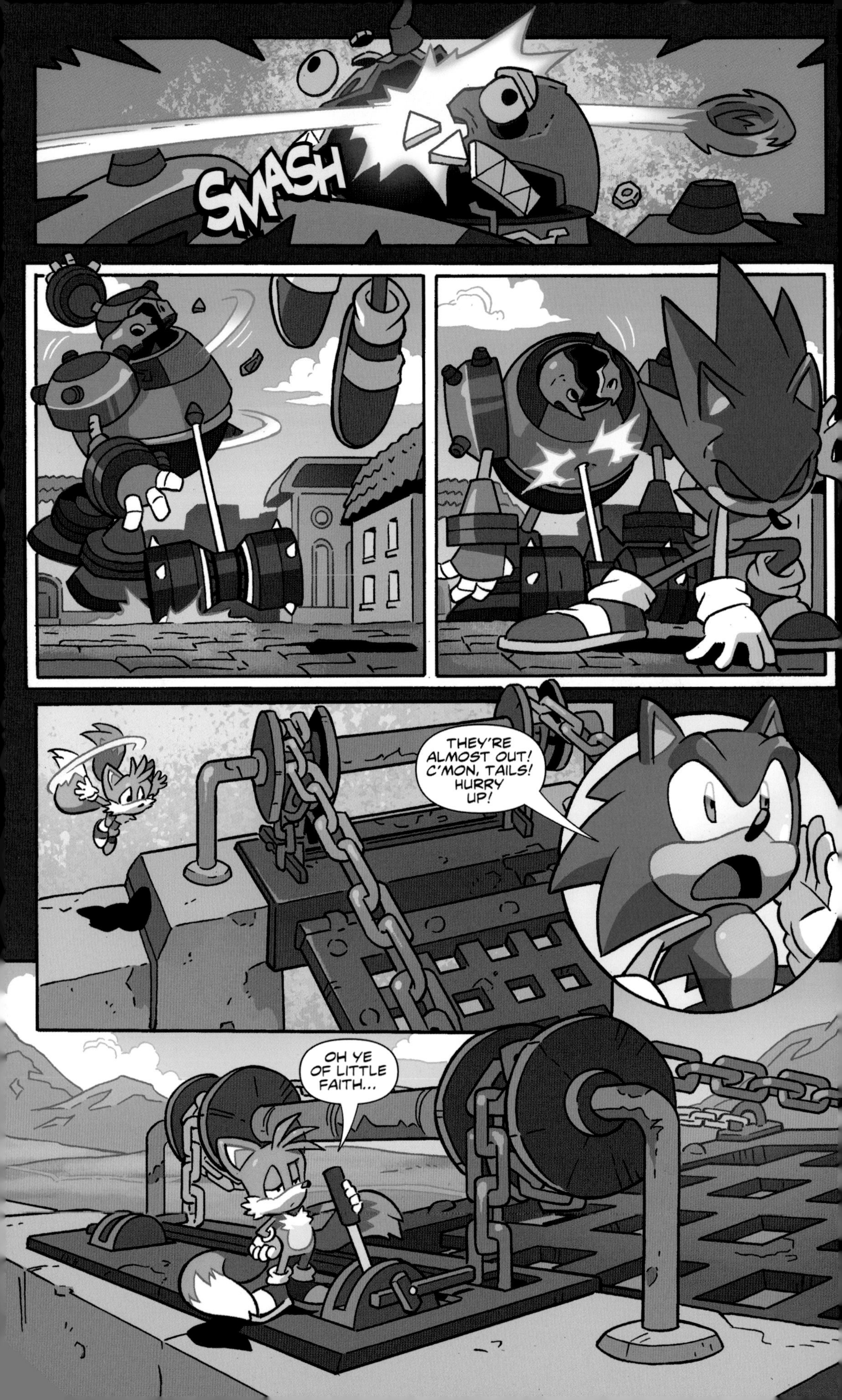
SMASH
THEY'RE ALMOST OUT! C'MON, TAILS! HURRY UP!
OH YE OF LITTLE FAITH...

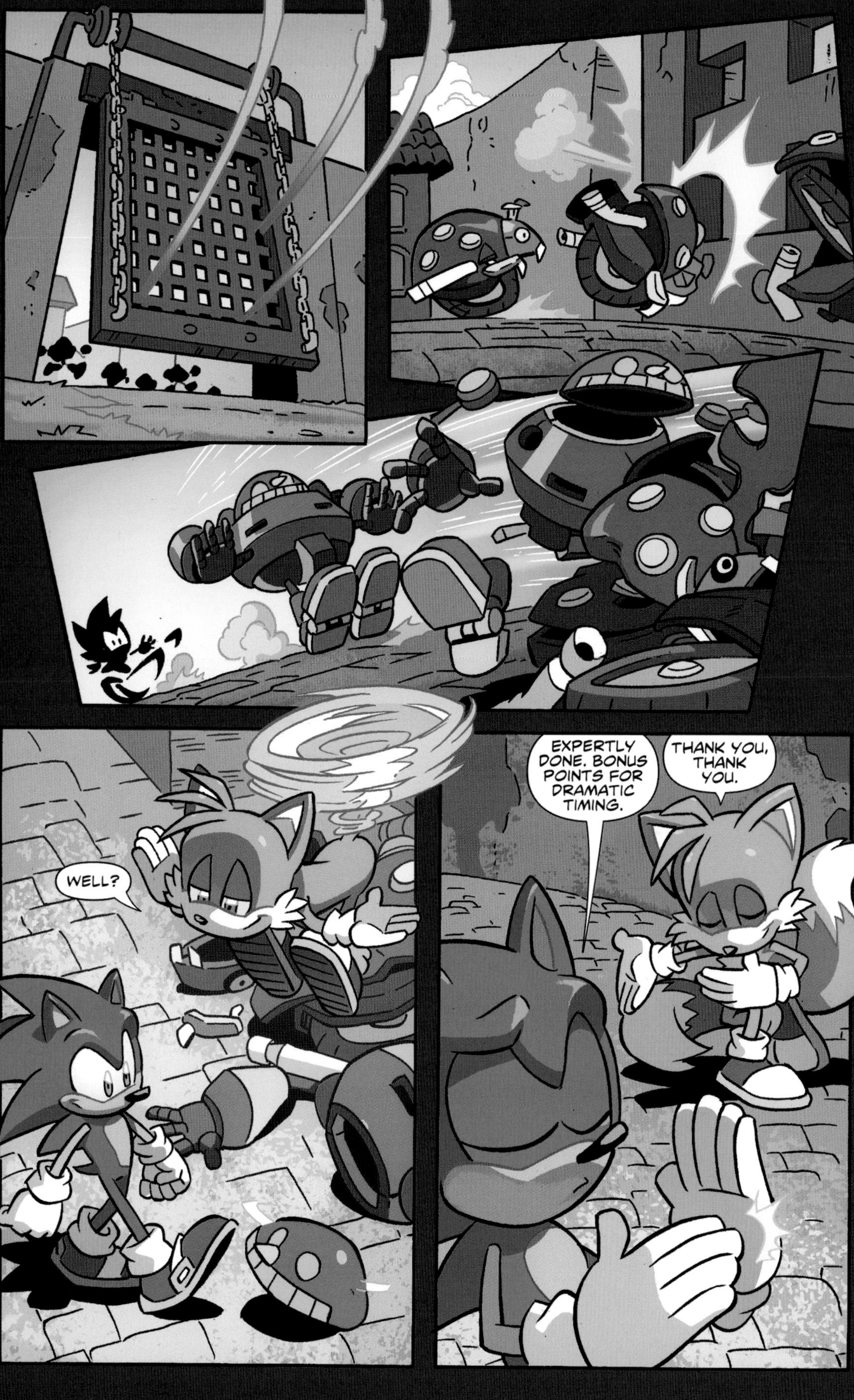
WELL?
EXPERTLY DONE. BONUS POINTS FOR DRAMATIC TIMING.
THANK YOU, THANK YOU.

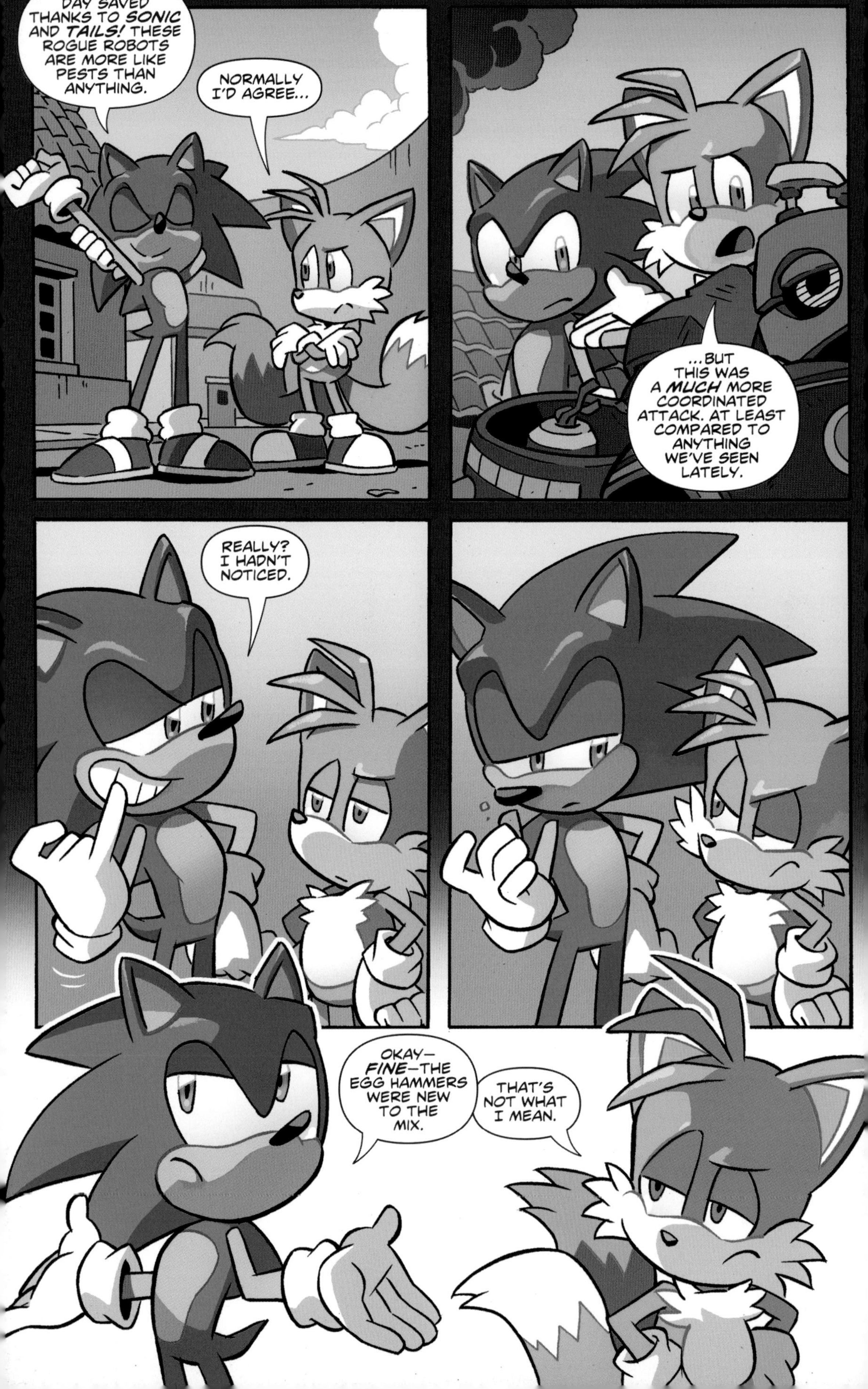
ANOTHER DAY SAVED THANKS TO SONIC AND TAILS! THESE ROGUE ROBOTS ARE MORE LIKE PESTS THAN ANYTHING.
NORMALLY I'D AGREE...
...BUT THIS WAS A MUCH MORE COORDINATED ATTACK. AT LEAST COMPARED TO ANYTHING WE'VE SEEN LATELY.
REALLY? I HADN'T NOTICED.
OKAY—FINE—THE EGG HAMMERS WERE NEW TO THE MIX.
THAT'S NOT WHAT I MEAN.

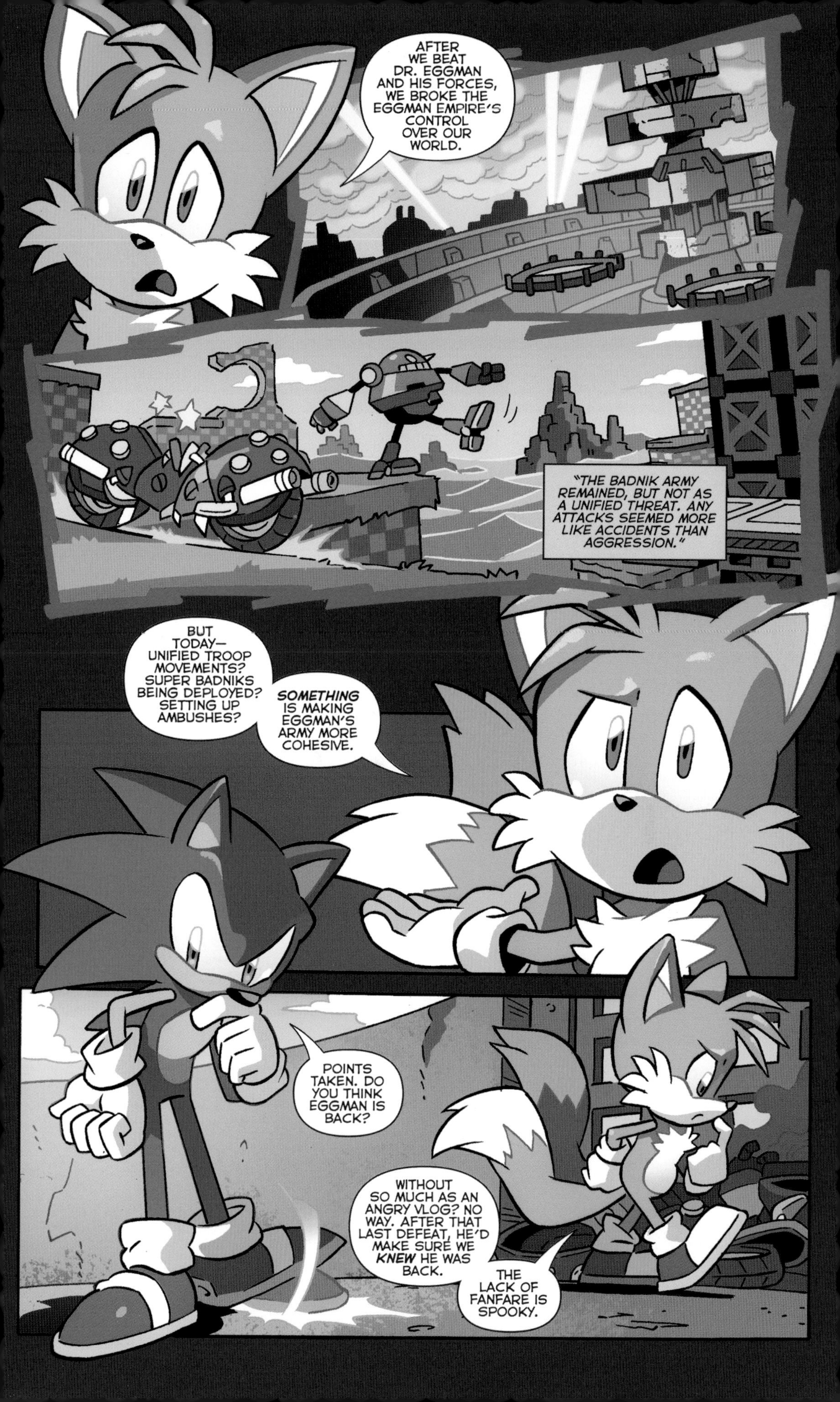
AFTER WE BEAT DR. EGGMAN AND HIS FORCES, WE BROKE THE EGGMAN EMPIRE'S CONTROL OVER OUR WORLD.
"THE BADNIK ARMY REMAINED, BUT NOT AS A UNIFIED THREAT. ANY ATTACKS SEEMED MORE LIKE ACCIDENTS THAN AGGRESSION."
BUT TODAY— UNIFIED TROOP MOVEMENTS? SUPER BADNIKS BEING DEPLOYED? SETTING UP AMBUSHES?
SOMETHING IS MAKING EGGMAN'S ARMY MORE COHESIVE.
POINTS TAKEN. DO YOU THINK EGGMAN IS BACK?
WITHOUT SO MUCH AS AN ANGRY VLOG? NO WAY. AFTER THAT LAST DEFEAT, HE'D MAKE SURE WE KNEW HE WAS BACK.
THE LACK OF FANFARE IS SPOOKY.

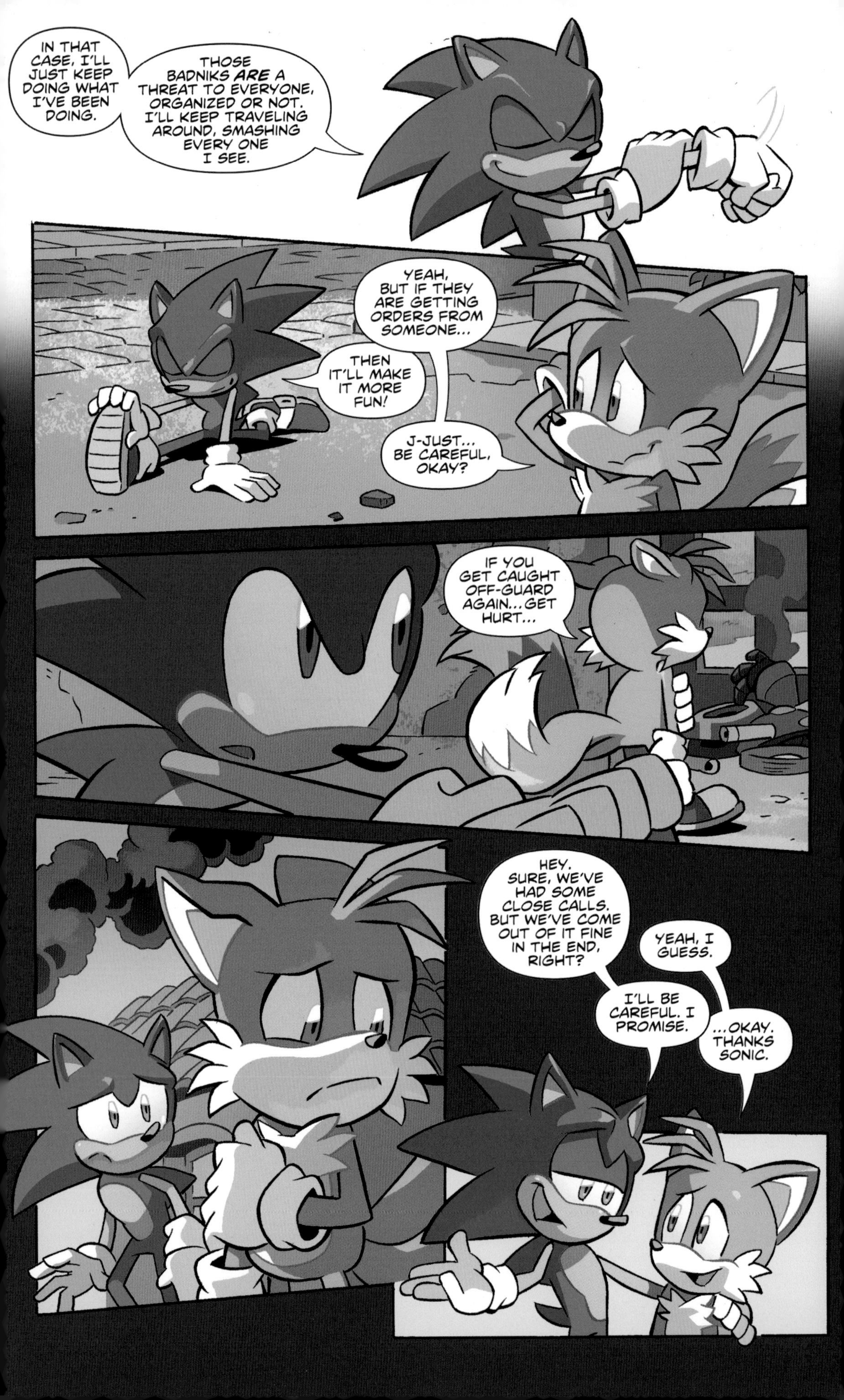
IN THAT CASE, I'LL JUST KEEP DOING WHAT I'VE BEEN DOING.
THOSE BADNIKS *ARE* A THREAT TO EVERYONE, ORGANIZED OR NOT. I'LL KEEP TRAVELING AROUND, SMASHING EVERY ONE I SEE.
YEAH, BUT IF THEY ARE GETTING ORDERS FROM SOMEONE...
THEN IT'LL MAKE IT MORE FUN!
J-JUST... BE CAREFUL, OKAY?
IF YOU GET CAUGHT OFF-GUARD AGAIN... GET HURT...
HEY. SURE, WE'VE HAD SOME CLOSE CALLS. BUT WE'VE COME OUT OF IT FINE IN THE END, RIGHT?
YEAH, I GUESS.
I'LL BE CAREFUL. I PROMISE.
...OKAY. THANKS SONIC.

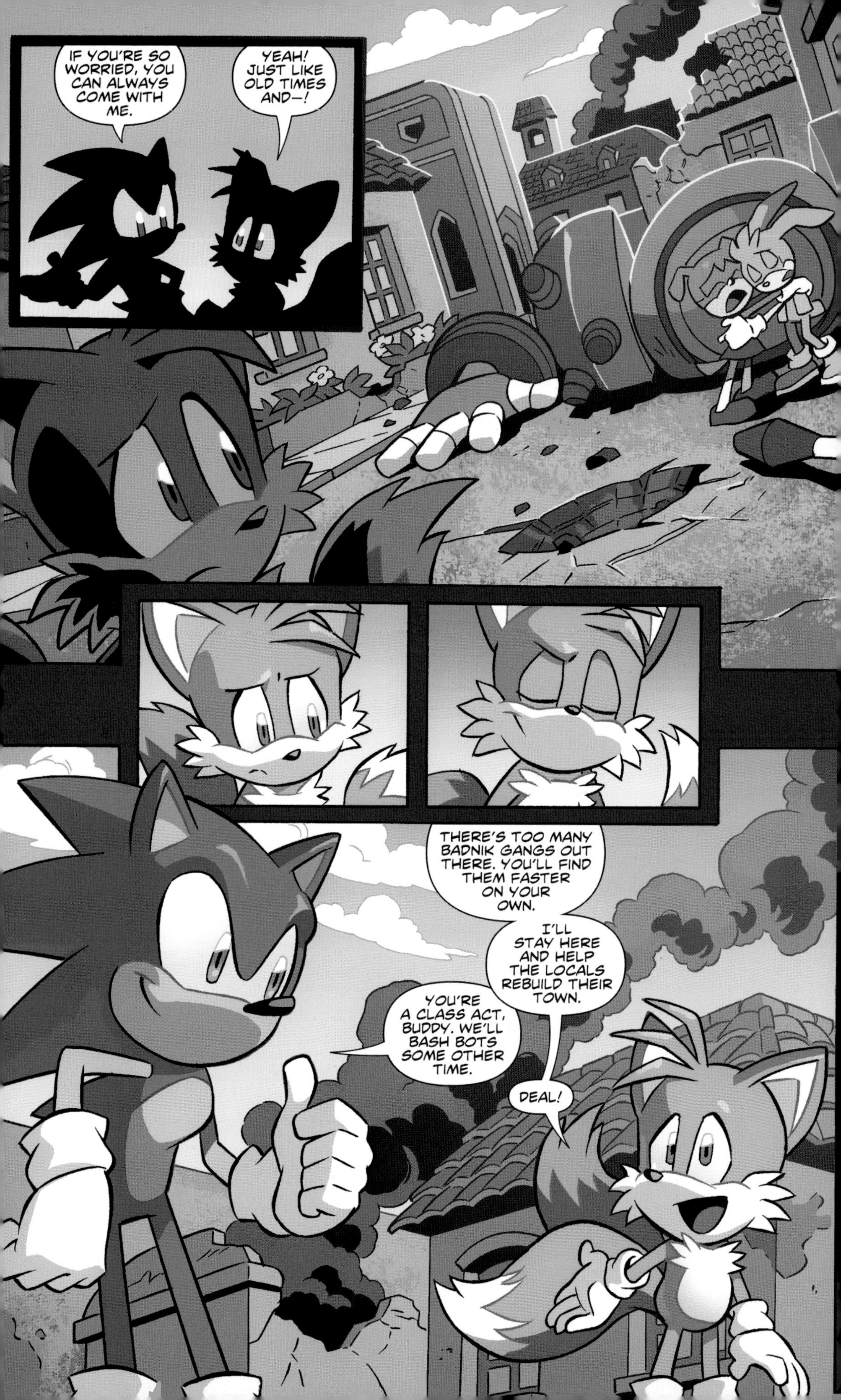
IF YOU'RE SO WORRIED, YOU CAN ALWAYS COME WITH ME.
YEAH! JUST LIKE OLD TIMES AND—!
THERE'S TOO MANY BADNIK GANGS OUT THERE. YOU'LL FIND THEM FASTER ON YOUR OWN.
I'LL STAY HERE AND HELP THE LOCALS REBUILD THEIR TOWN.
YOU'RE A CLASS ACT, BUDDY. WE'LL BASH BOTS SOME OTHER TIME.
DEAL!

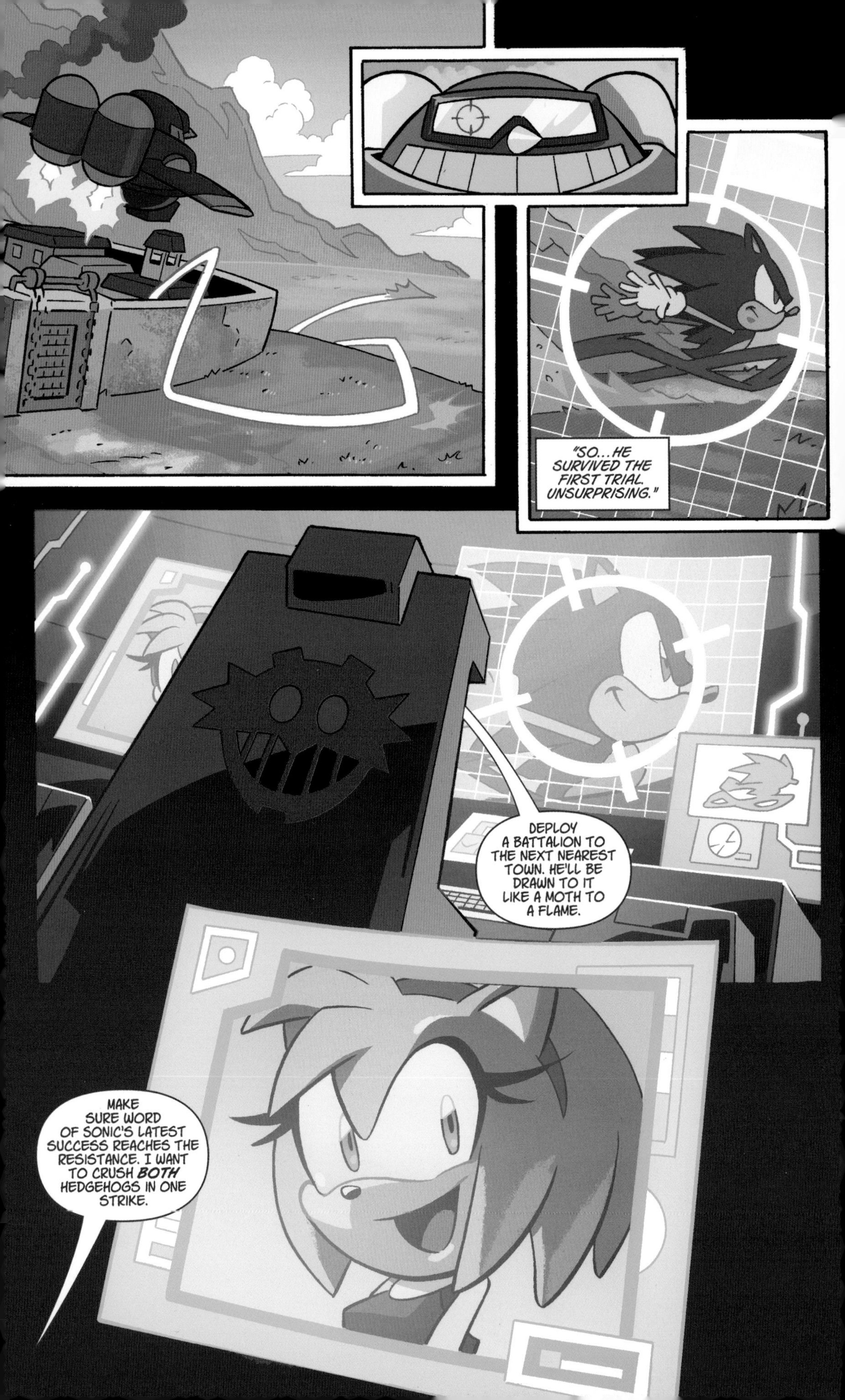
"SO...HE SURVIVED THE FIRST TRIAL. UNSURPRISING."
DEPLOY A BATTALION TO THE NEXT NEAREST TOWN. HE'LL BE DRAWN TO IT LIKE A MOTH TO A FLAME.
MAKE SURE WORD OF SONIC'S LATEST SUCCESS REACHES THE RESISTANCE. I WANT TO CRUSH *BOTH* HEDGEHOGS IN ONE STRIKE.

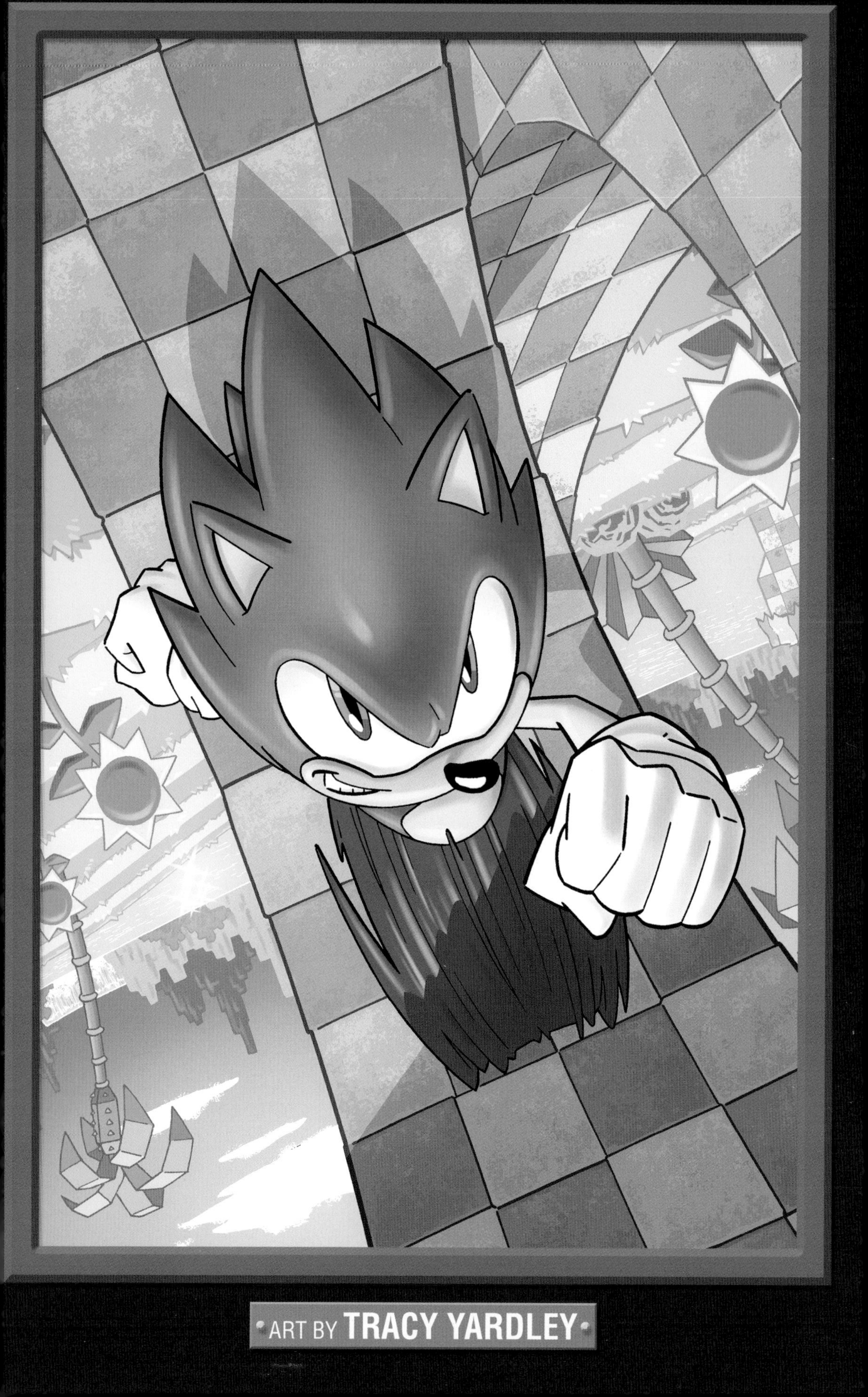

ART BY TRACY YARDLEY

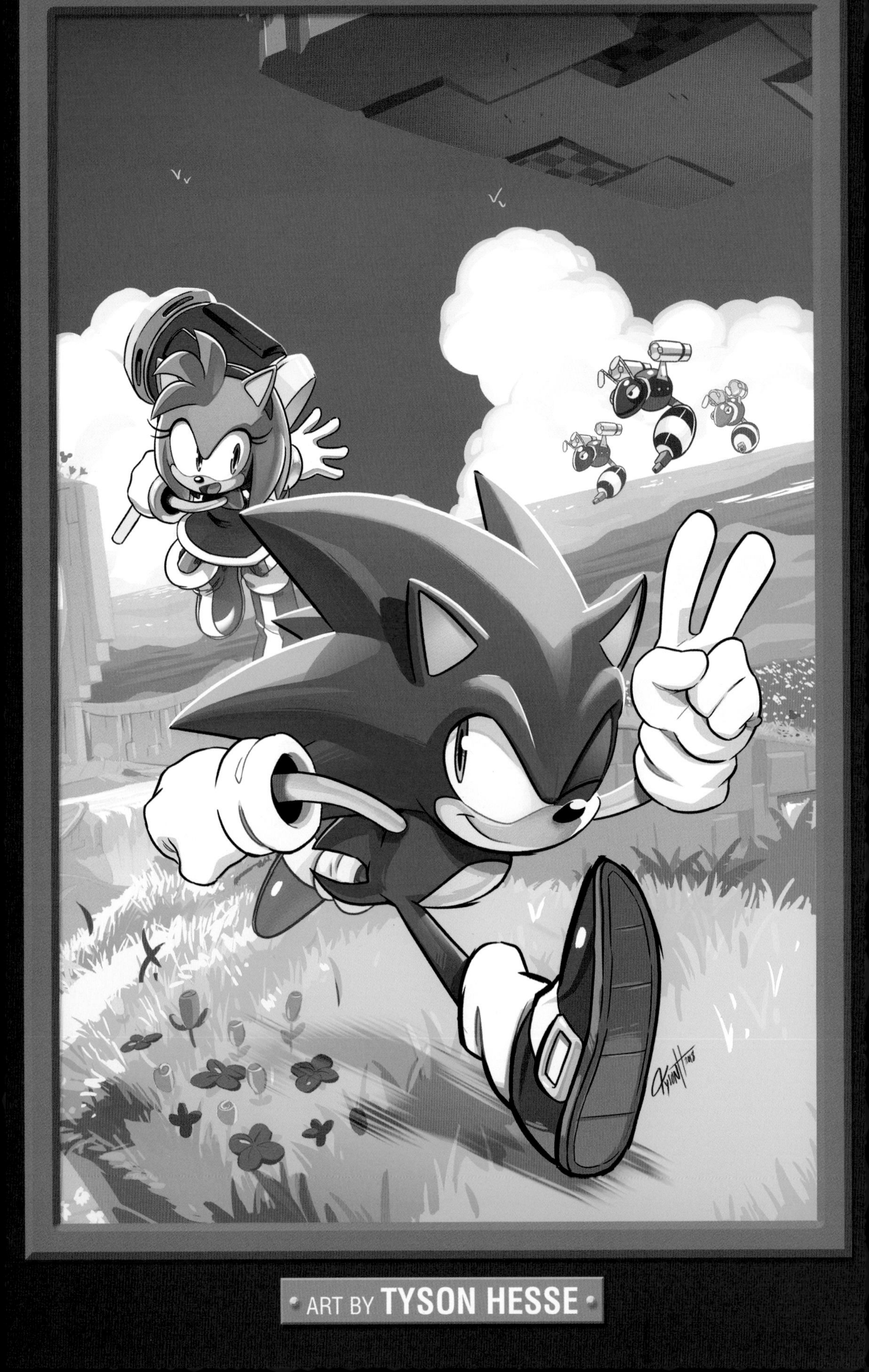

ART BY TYSON HESSE

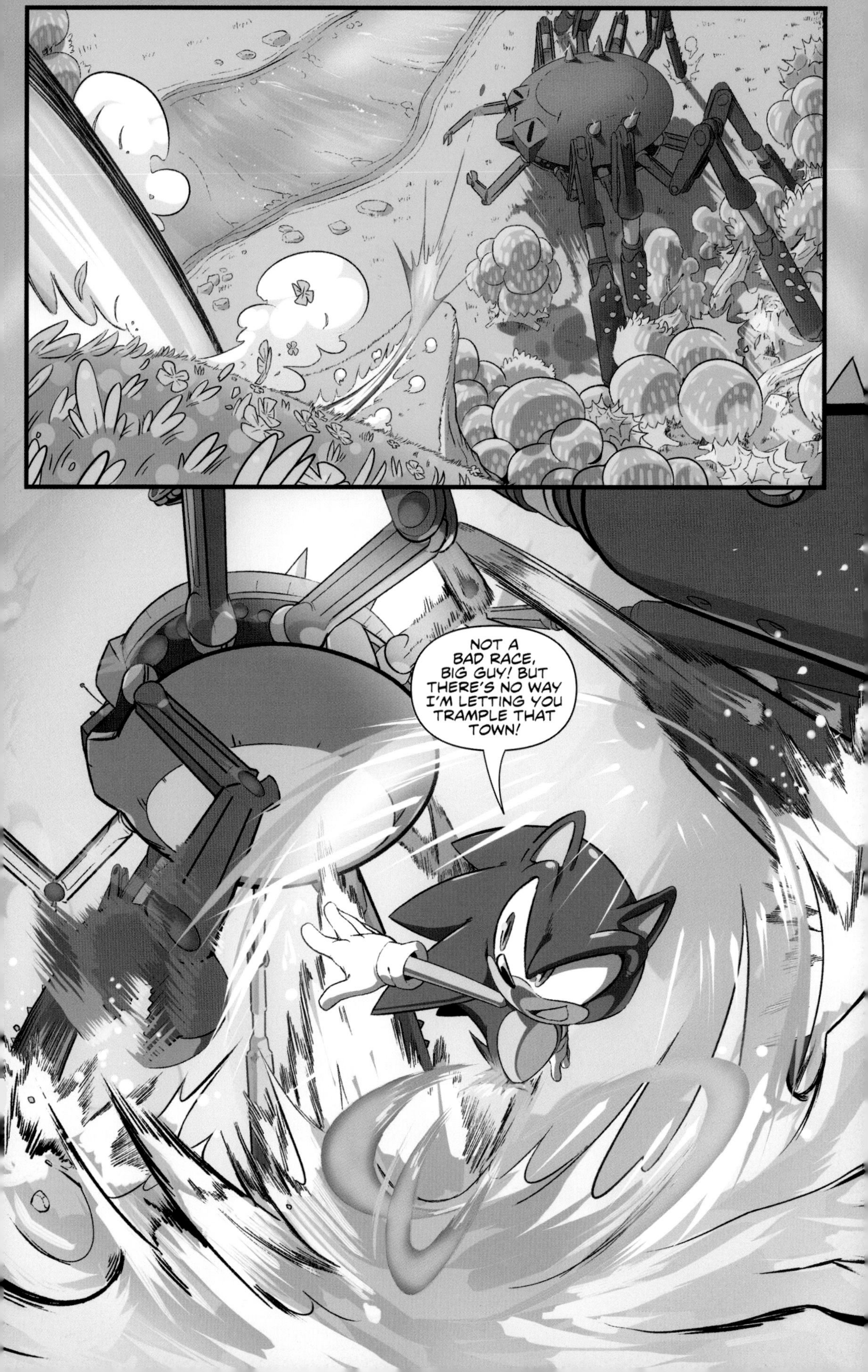
NOT A BAD RACE, BIG GUY! BUT THERE'S NO WAY I'M LETTING YOU TRAMPLE THAT TOWN!

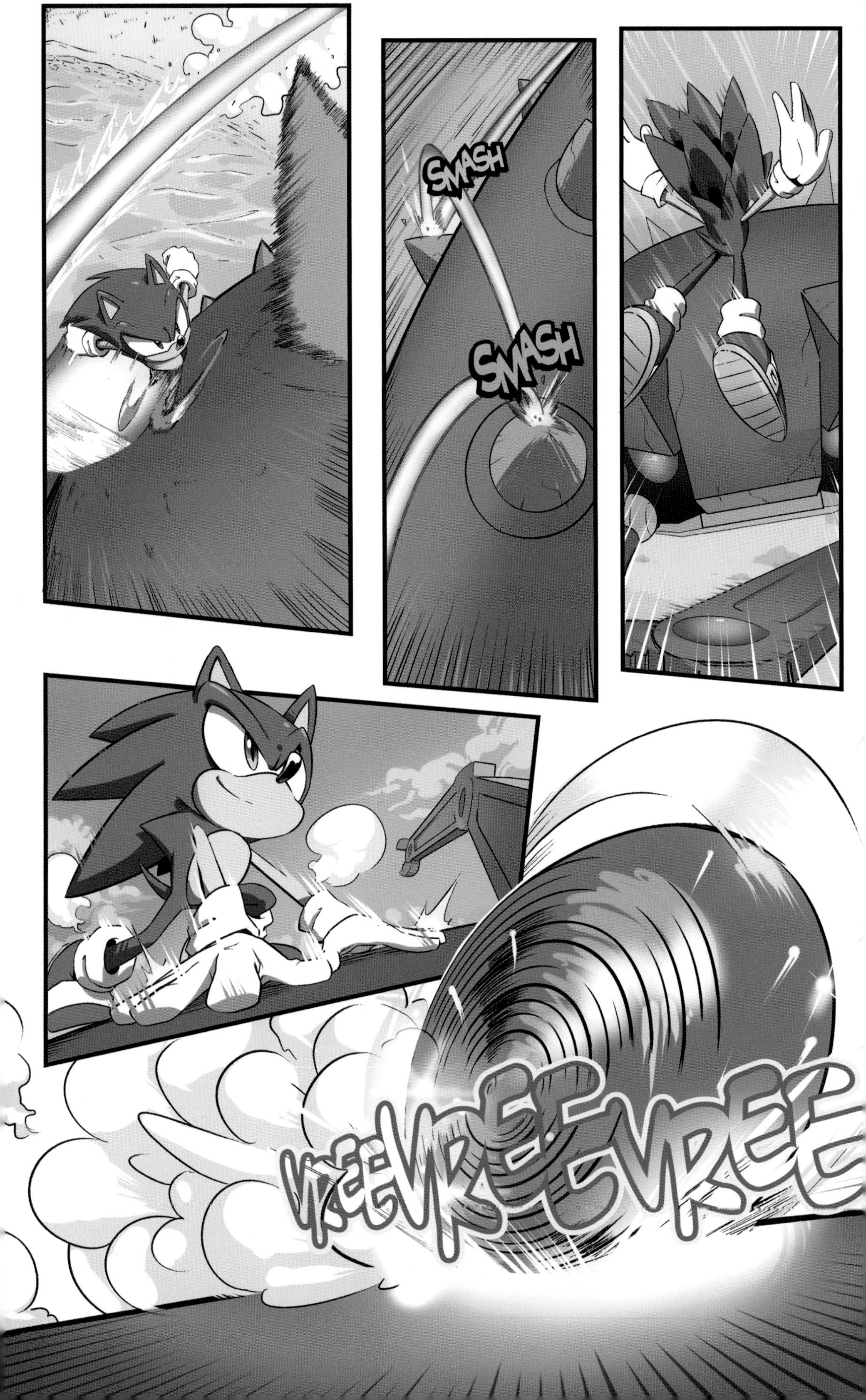
SMASH
SMASH
VREEVREEVREE

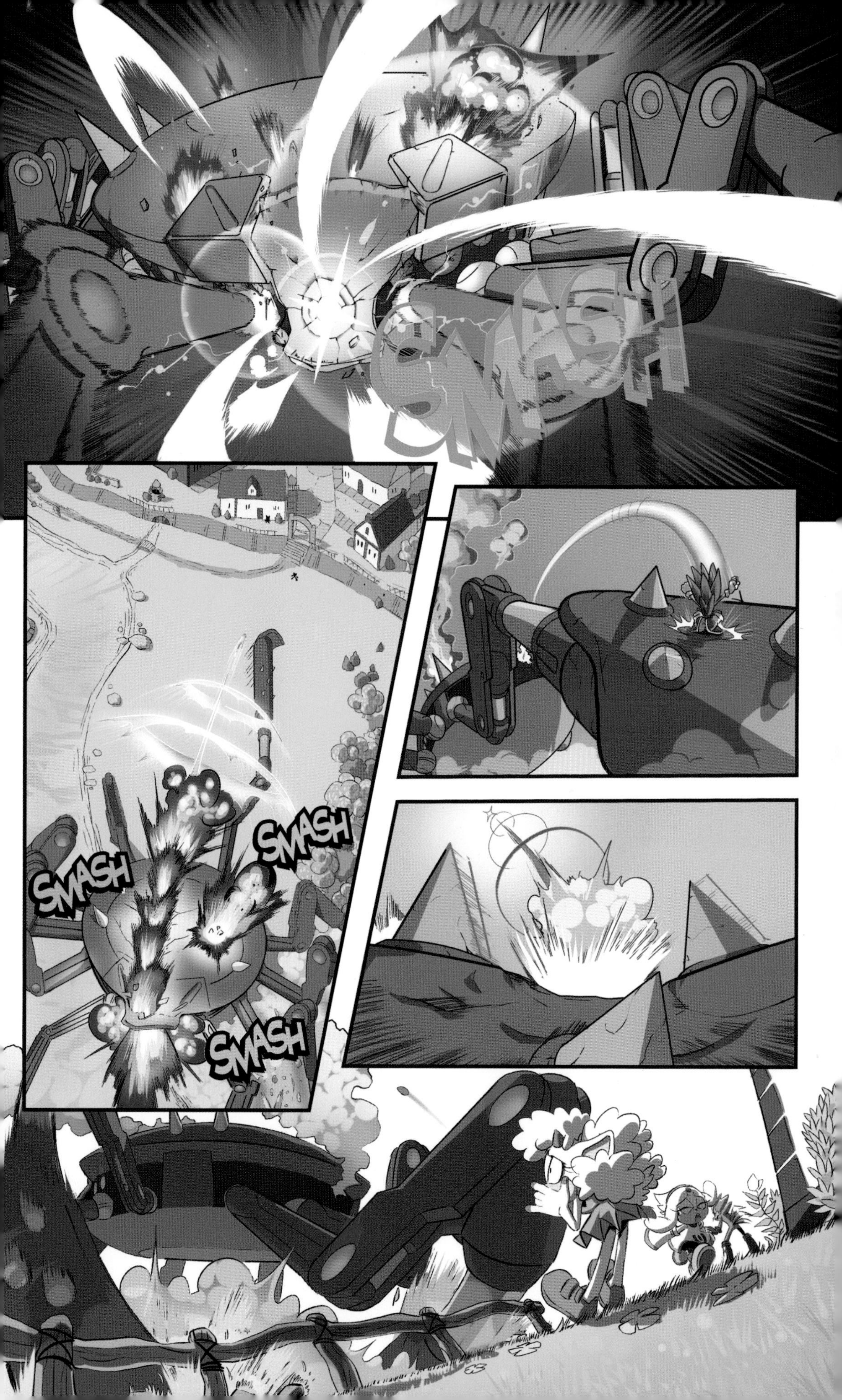
SMASH
SMASH
SMASH
SMASH

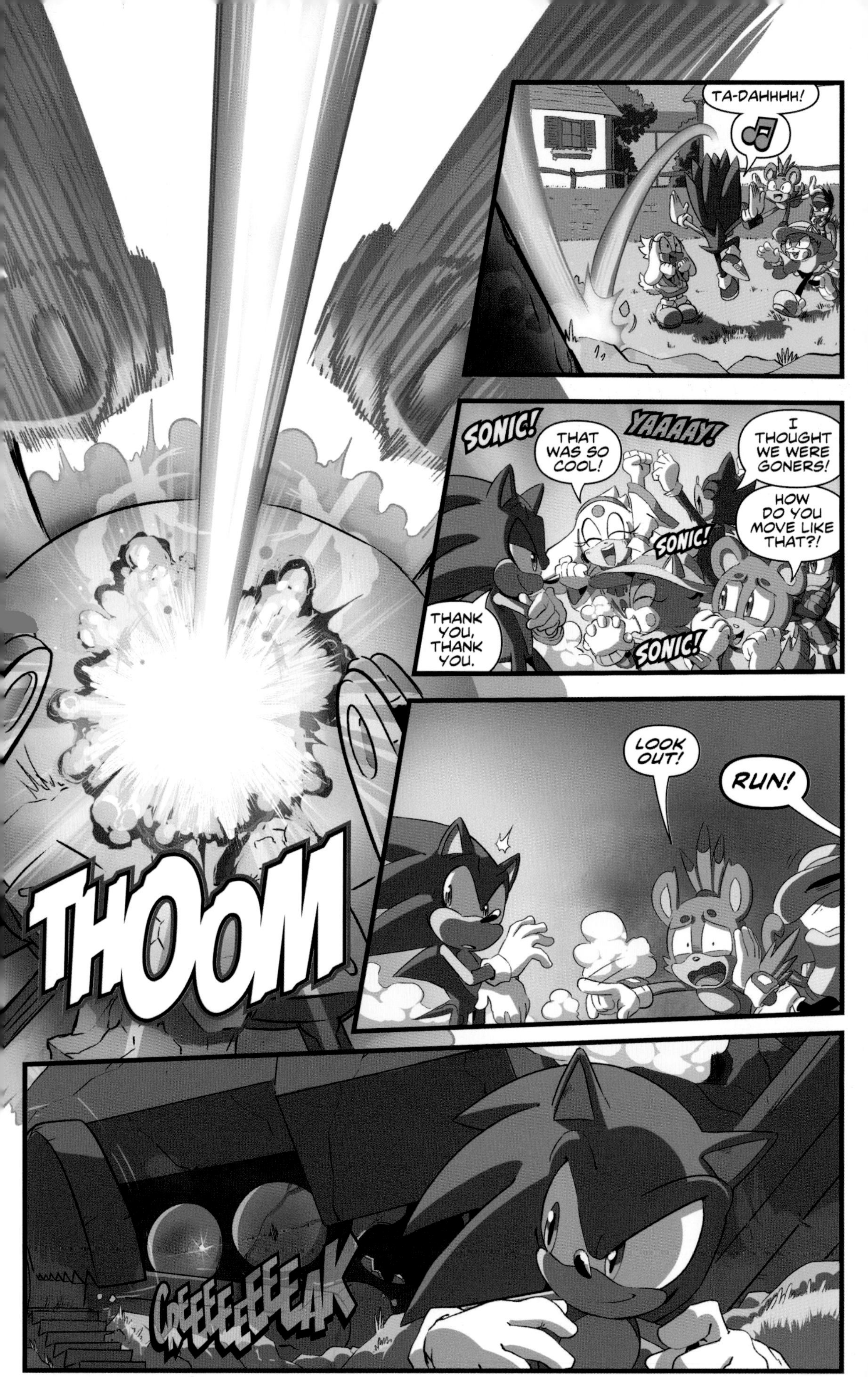
TA-DAHHHH!
SONIC!
THAT WAS SO COOL!
YAAAAY!
I THOUGHT WE WERE GONERS!
SONIC!
HOW DO YOU MOVE LIKE THAT?!
THANK YOU, THANK YOU.
SONIC!
THOOM
LOOK OUT!
RUN!
CREEEEEEEEAK

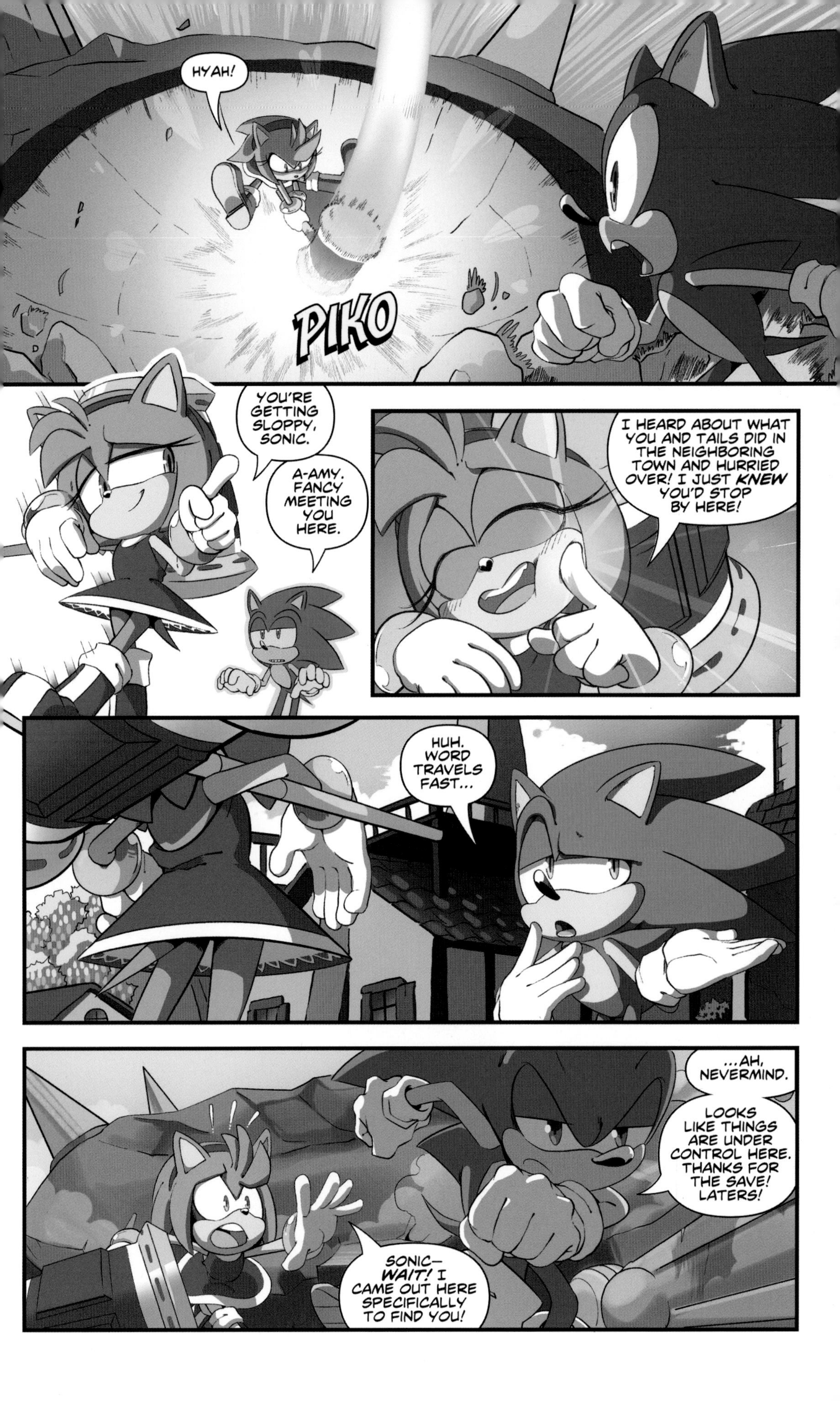

HYAH!
PIKO
YOU'RE GETTING SLOPPY, SONIC.
A-AMY. FANCY MEETING YOU HERE.
I HEARD ABOUT WHAT YOU AND TAILS DID IN THE NEIGHBORING TOWN AND HURRIED OVER! I JUST **KNEW** YOU'D STOP BY HERE!
HUH. WORD TRAVELS FAST...
...AH, NEVERMIND.
LOOKS LIKE THINGS ARE UNDER CONTROL HERE. THANKS FOR THE SAVE! LATERS!
SONIC— **WAIT!** I CAME OUT HERE SPECIFICALLY TO FIND YOU!

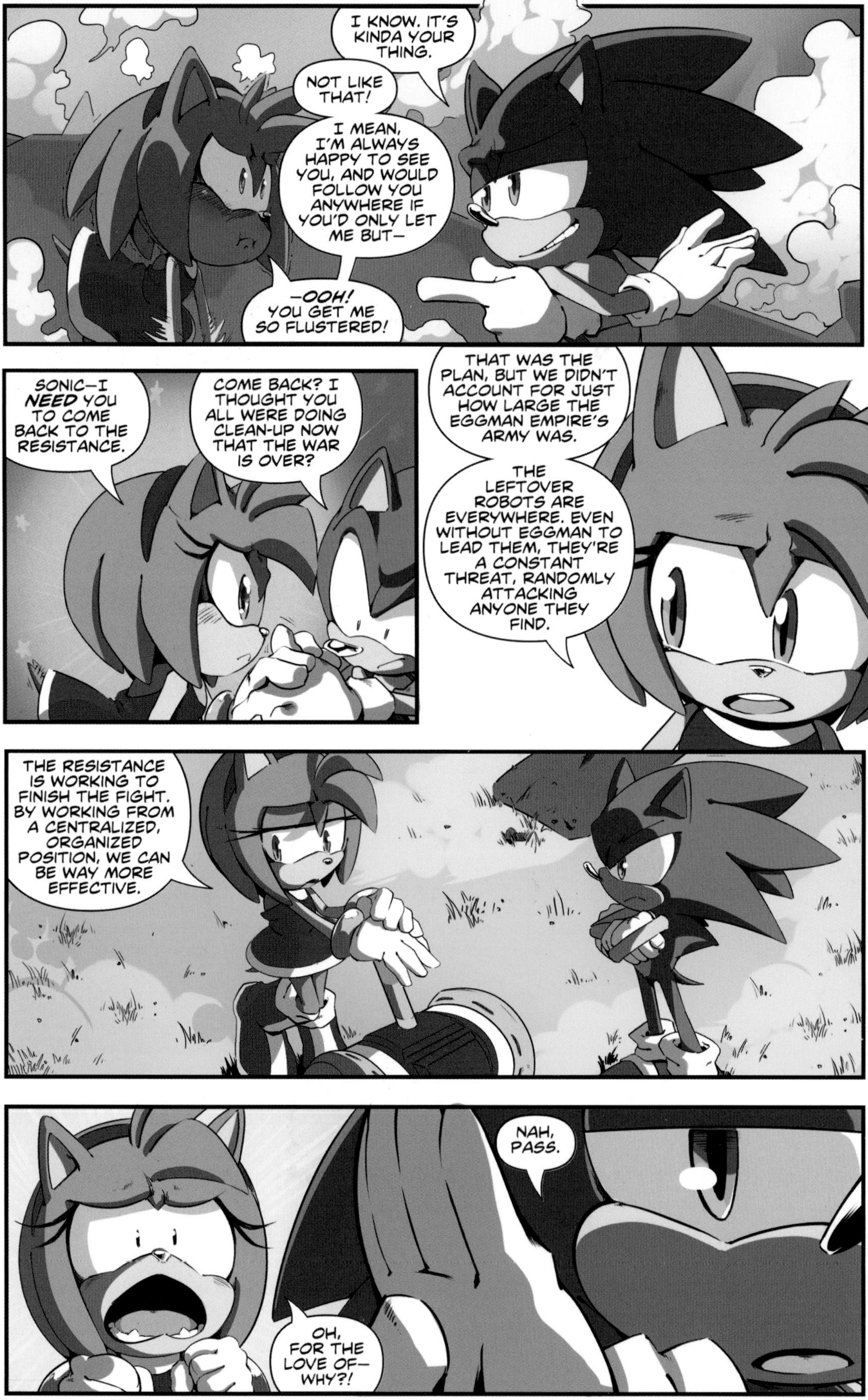
I KNOW. IT'S KINDA YOUR THING.
NOT LIKE THAT!
I MEAN, I'M ALWAYS HAPPY TO SEE YOU, AND WOULD FOLLOW YOU ANYWHERE IF YOU'D ONLY LET ME BUT—
—OOH! YOU GET ME SO FLUSTERED!
SONIC—I NEED YOU TO COME BACK TO THE RESISTANCE.
COME BACK? I THOUGHT YOU ALL WERE DOING CLEAN-UP NOW THAT THE WAR IS OVER?
THAT WAS THE PLAN, BUT WE DIDN'T ACCOUNT FOR JUST HOW LARGE THE EGGMAN EMPIRE'S ARMY WAS.
THE LEFTOVER ROBOTS ARE EVERYWHERE. EVEN WITHOUT EGGMAN TO LEAD THEM, THEY'RE A CONSTANT THREAT, RANDOMLY ATTACKING ANYONE THEY FIND.
THE RESISTANCE IS WORKING TO FINISH THE FIGHT. BY WORKING FROM A CENTRALIZED, ORGANIZED POSITION, WE CAN BE WAY MORE EFFECTIVE.
NAH, PASS.
OH, FOR THE LOVE OF— WHY?!

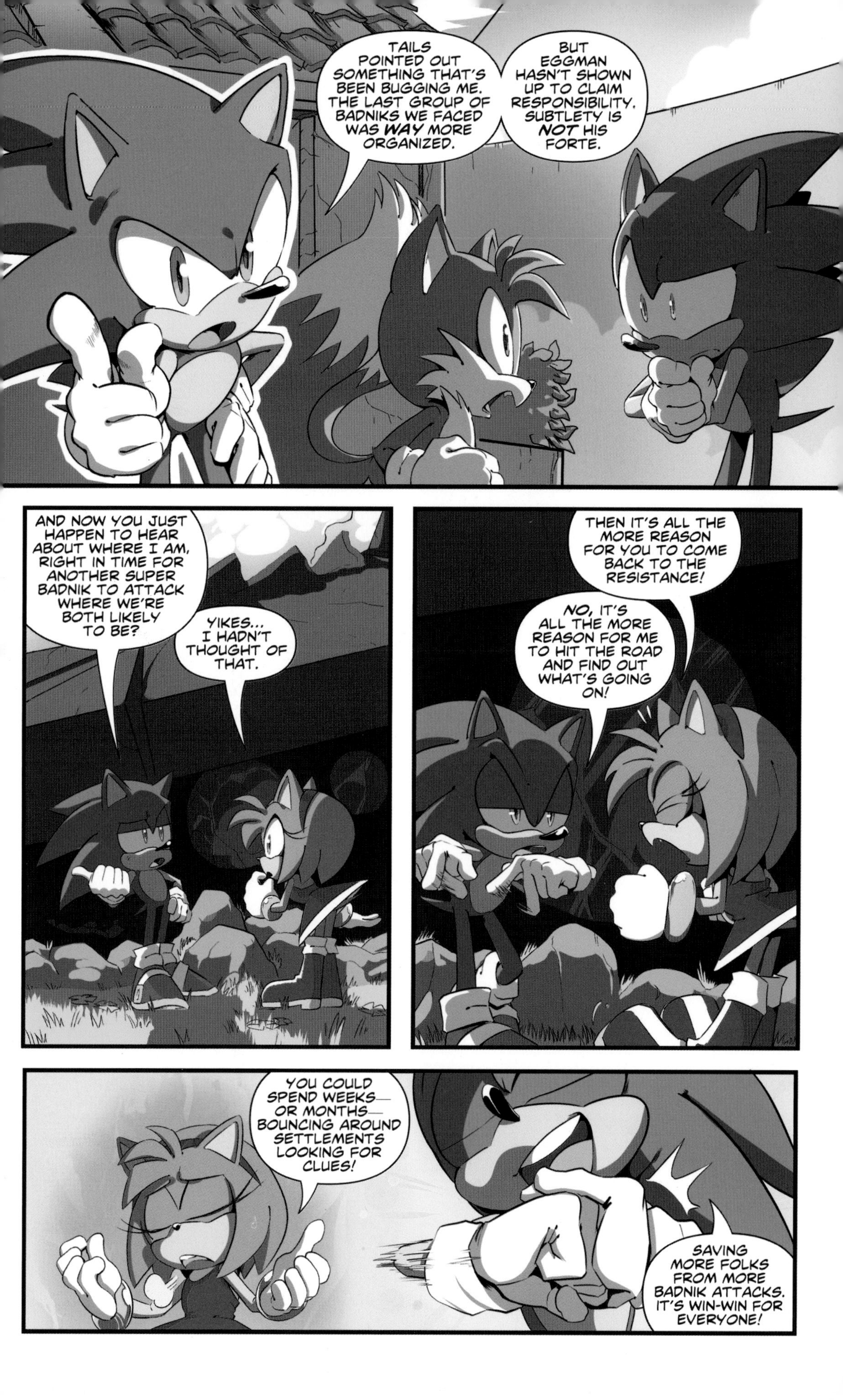
TAILS POINTED OUT SOMETHING THAT'S BEEN BUGGING ME. THE LAST GROUP OF BADNIKS WE FACED WAS **WAY** MORE ORGANIZED.
BUT EGGMAN HASN'T SHOWN UP TO CLAIM RESPONSIBILITY. SUBTLETY IS **NOT** HIS FORTE.
AND NOW YOU JUST HAPPEN TO HEAR ABOUT WHERE I AM, RIGHT IN TIME FOR ANOTHER SUPER BADNIK TO ATTACK WHERE WE'RE BOTH LIKELY TO BE?
YIKES... I HADN'T THOUGHT OF THAT.
THEN IT'S ALL THE MORE REASON FOR YOU TO COME BACK TO THE RESISTANCE!
NO, IT'S ALL THE MORE REASON FOR ME TO HIT THE ROAD AND FIND OUT WHAT'S GOING ON!
YOU COULD SPEND WEEKS— OR MONTHS— BOUNCING AROUND SETTLEMENTS LOOKING FOR CLUES!
SAVING MORE FOLKS FROM MORE BADNIK ATTACKS. IT'S WIN-WIN FOR EVERYONE!

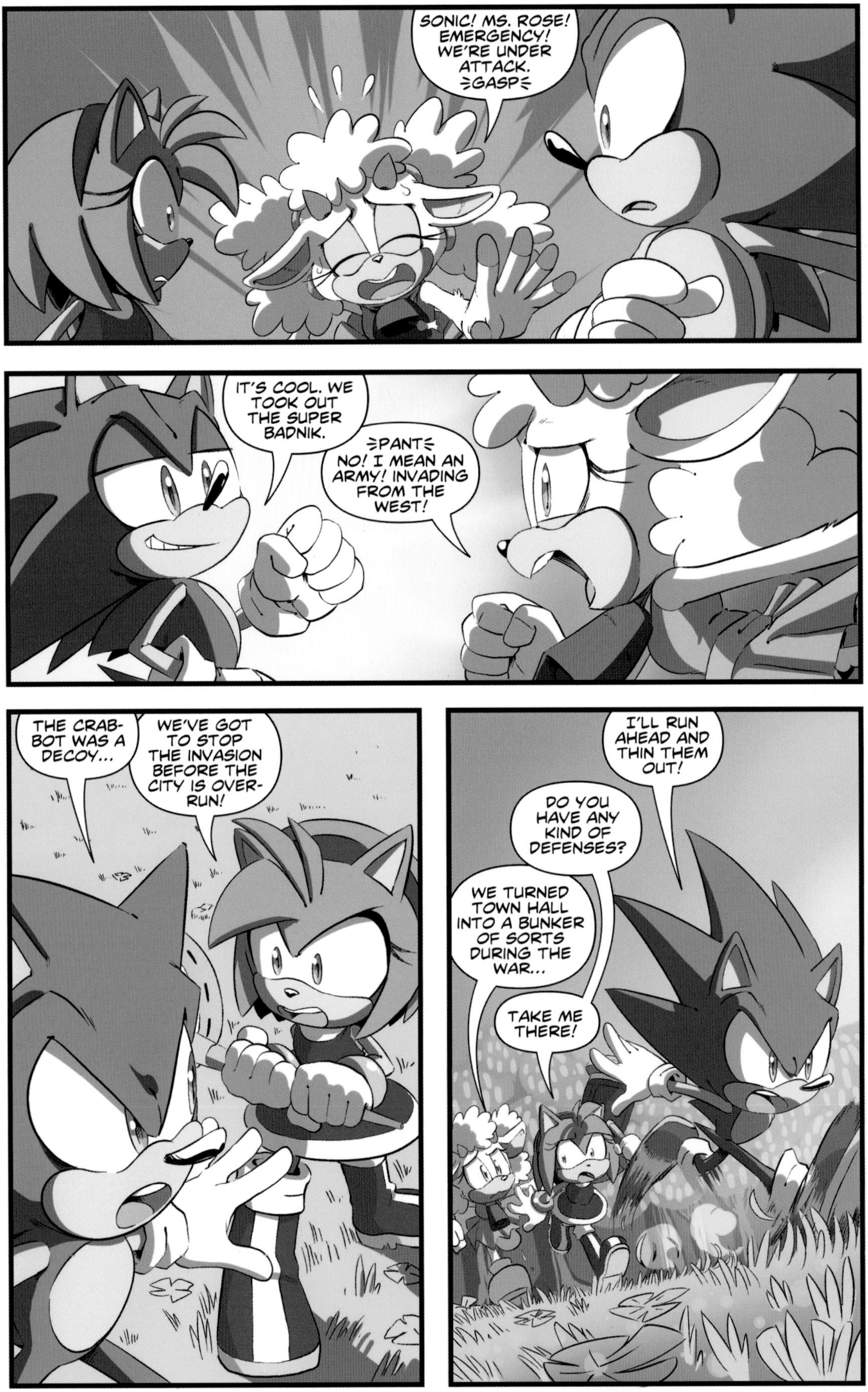
SONIC! MS. ROSE! EMERGENCY! WE'RE UNDER ATTACK.
≶GASP≶
IT'S COOL. WE TOOK OUT THE SUPER BADNIK.
≶PANT≶
NO! I MEAN AN ARMY! INVADING FROM THE WEST!
THE CRAB-BOT WAS A DECOY...
WE'VE GOT TO STOP THE INVASION BEFORE THE CITY IS OVER-RUN!
I'LL RUN AHEAD AND THIN THEM OUT!
DO YOU HAVE ANY KIND OF DEFENSES?
WE TURNED TOWN HALL INTO A BUNKER OF SORTS DURING THE WAR...
TAKE ME THERE!

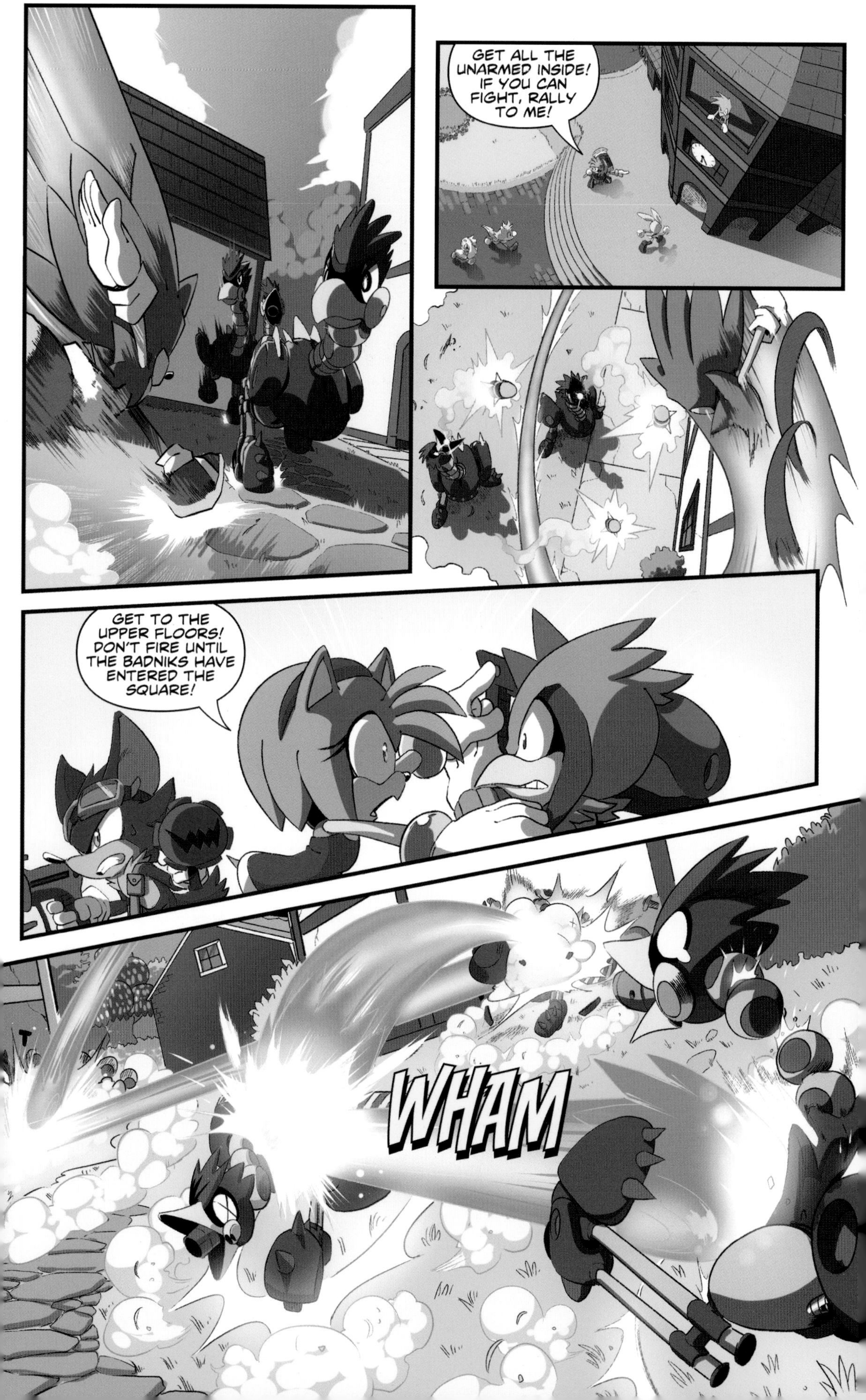
GET ALL THE UNARMED INSIDE! IF YOU CAN FIGHT, RALLY TO ME!
GET TO THE UPPER FLOORS! DON'T FIRE UNTIL THE BADNIKS HAVE ENTERED THE SQUARE!
WHAM

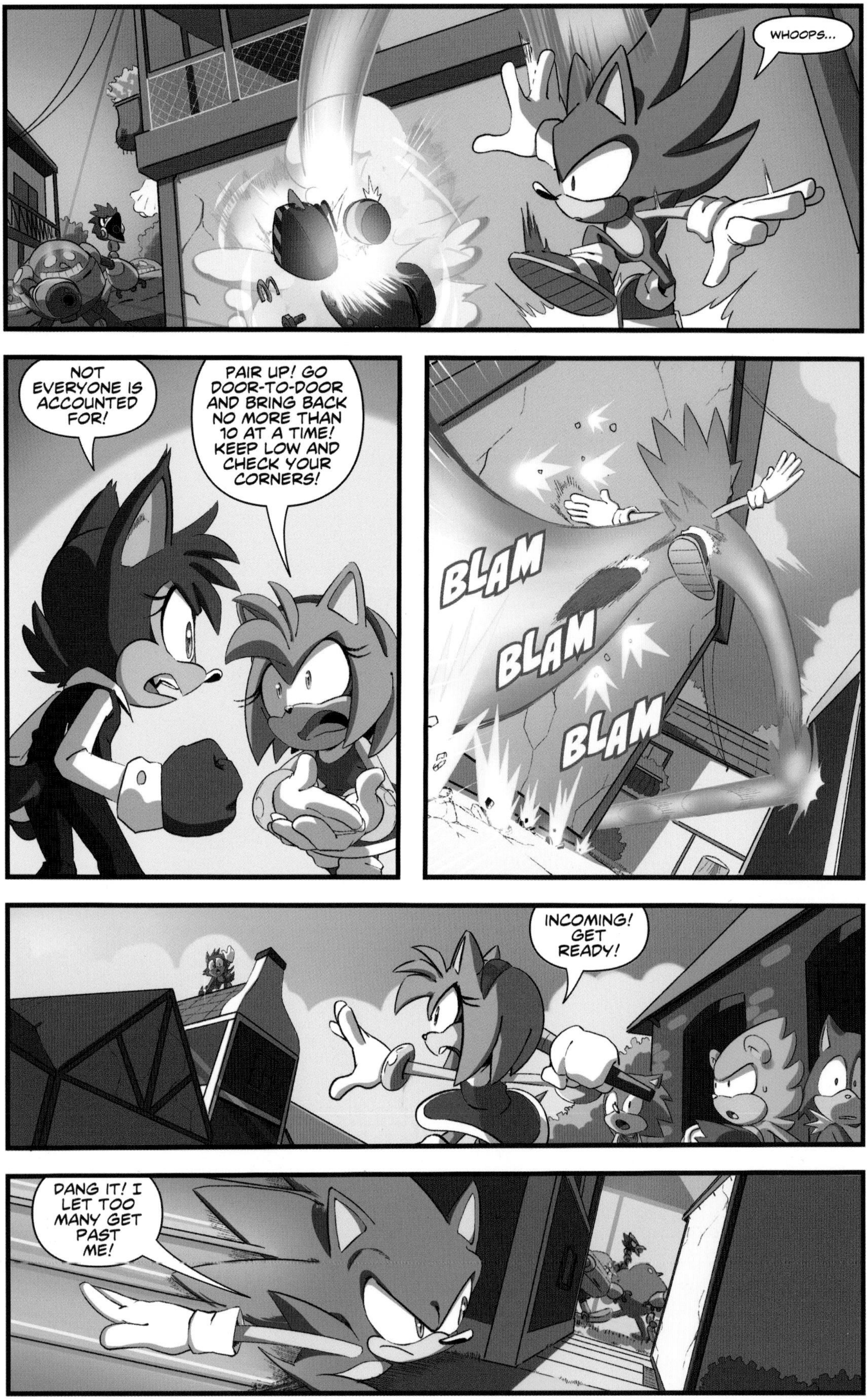
WHOOPS...
NOT EVERYONE IS ACCOUNTED FOR!
PAIR UP! GO DOOR-TO-DOOR AND BRING BACK NO MORE THAN 10 AT A TIME! KEEP LOW AND CHECK YOUR CORNERS!
BLAM
BLAM
BLAM
INCOMING! GET READY!
DANG IT! I LET TOO MANY GET PAST ME!

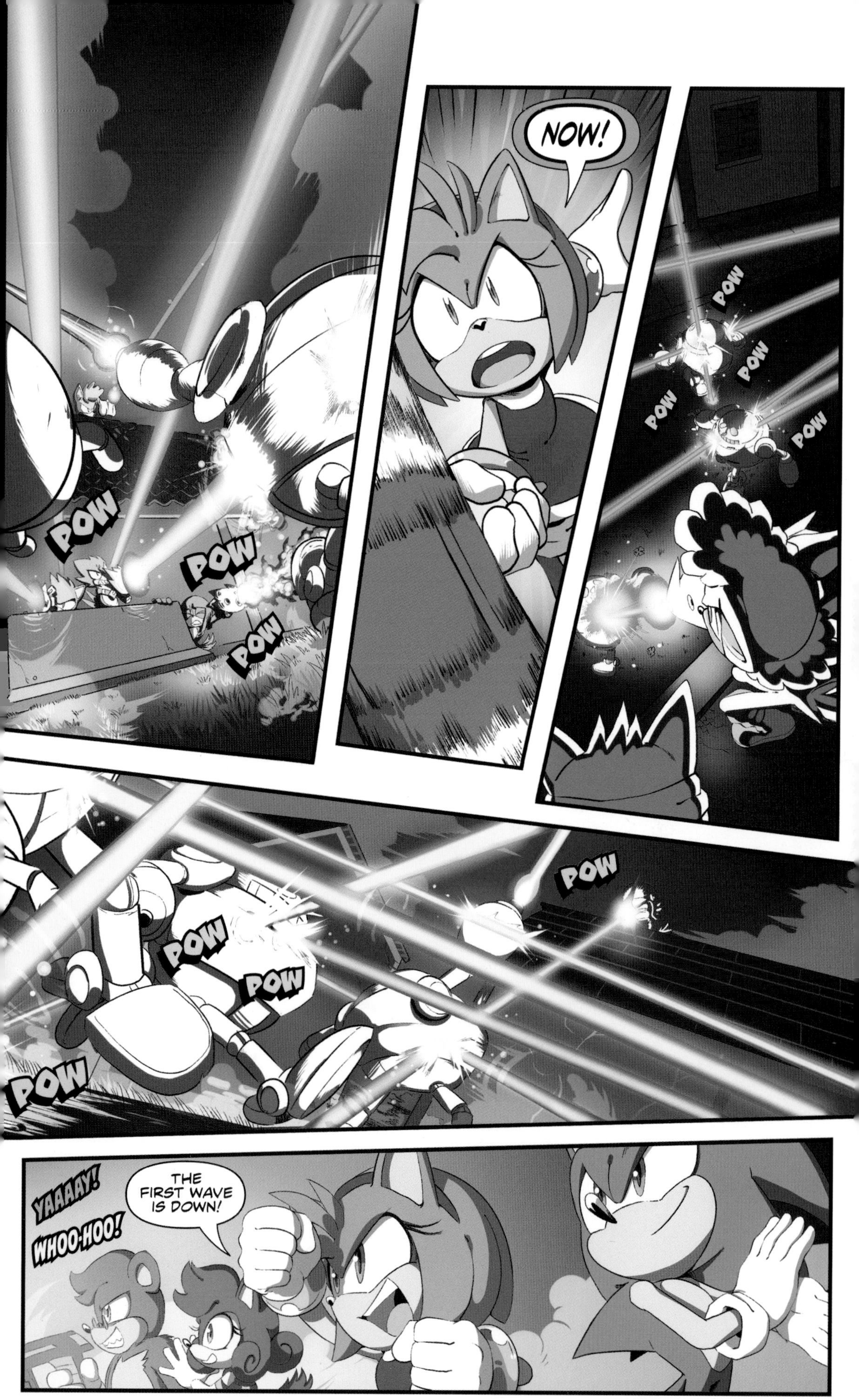

POW
POW
POW
NOW!
POW
POW
POW
POW
POW
POW
POW
POW
YAAAAY!
WHOO-HOO!
THE FIRST WAVE IS DOWN!

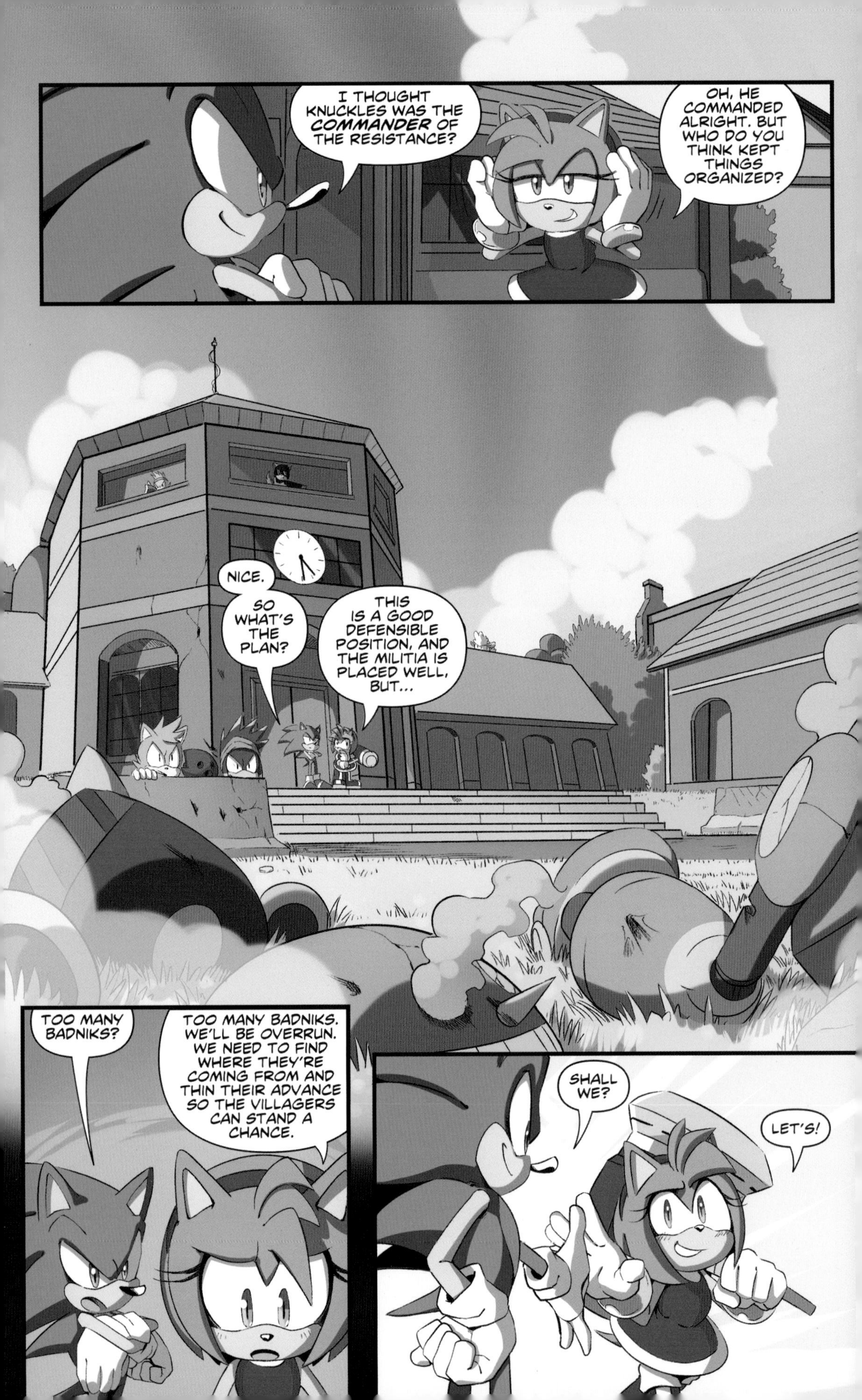

I THOUGHT KNUCKLES WAS THE COMMANDER OF THE RESISTANCE?
OH, HE COMMANDED ALRIGHT. BUT WHO DO YOU THINK KEPT THINGS ORGANIZED?
NICE.
SO WHAT'S THE PLAN?
THIS IS A GOOD DEFENSIBLE POSITION, AND THE MILITIA IS PLACED WELL, BUT...
TOO MANY BADNIKS?
TOO MANY BADNIKS. WE'LL BE OVERRUN. WE NEED TO FIND WHERE THEY'RE COMING FROM AND THIN THEIR ADVANCE SO THE VILLAGERS CAN STAND A CHANCE.
SHALL WE?
LET'S!

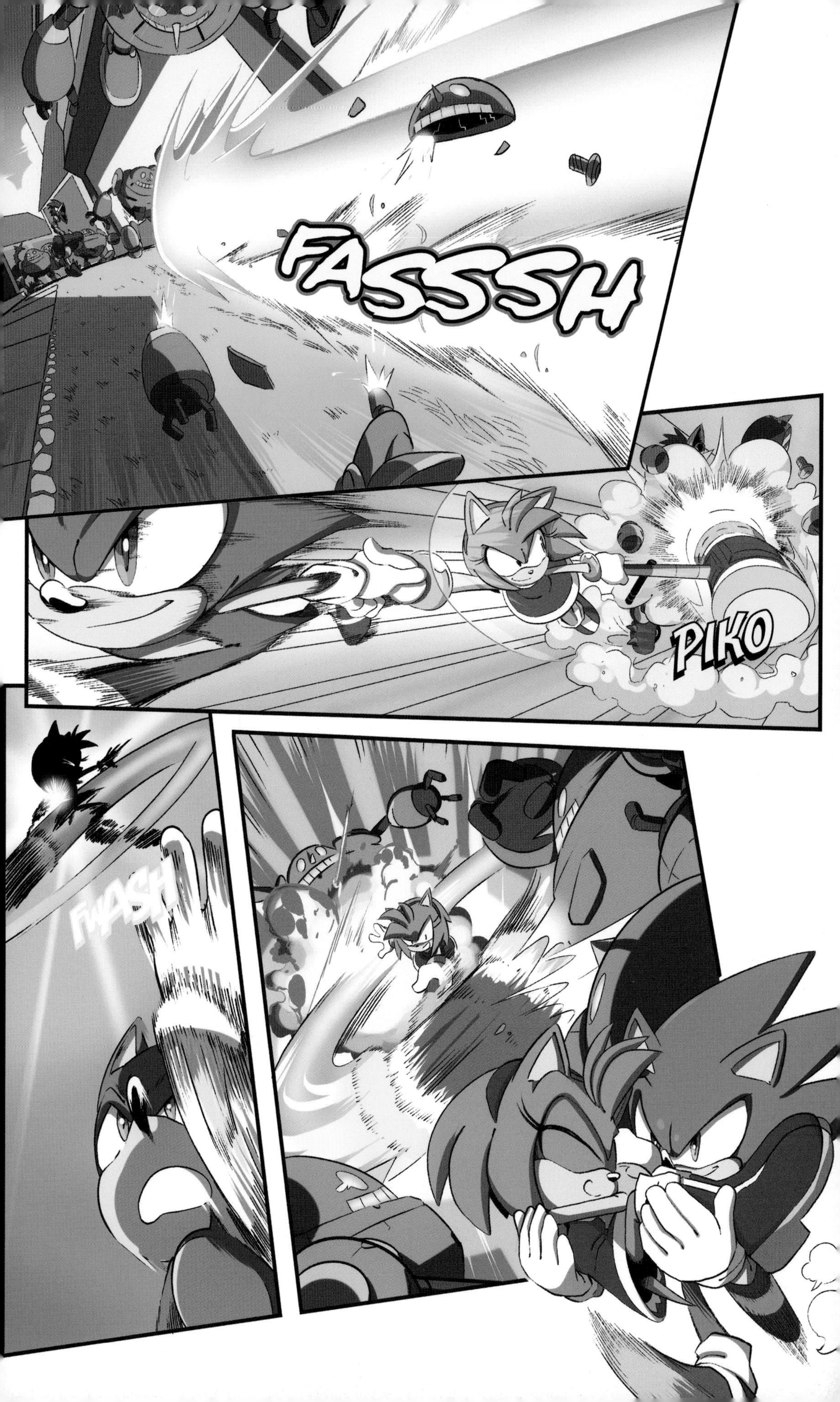
FASSSH
PIKO
FWASH

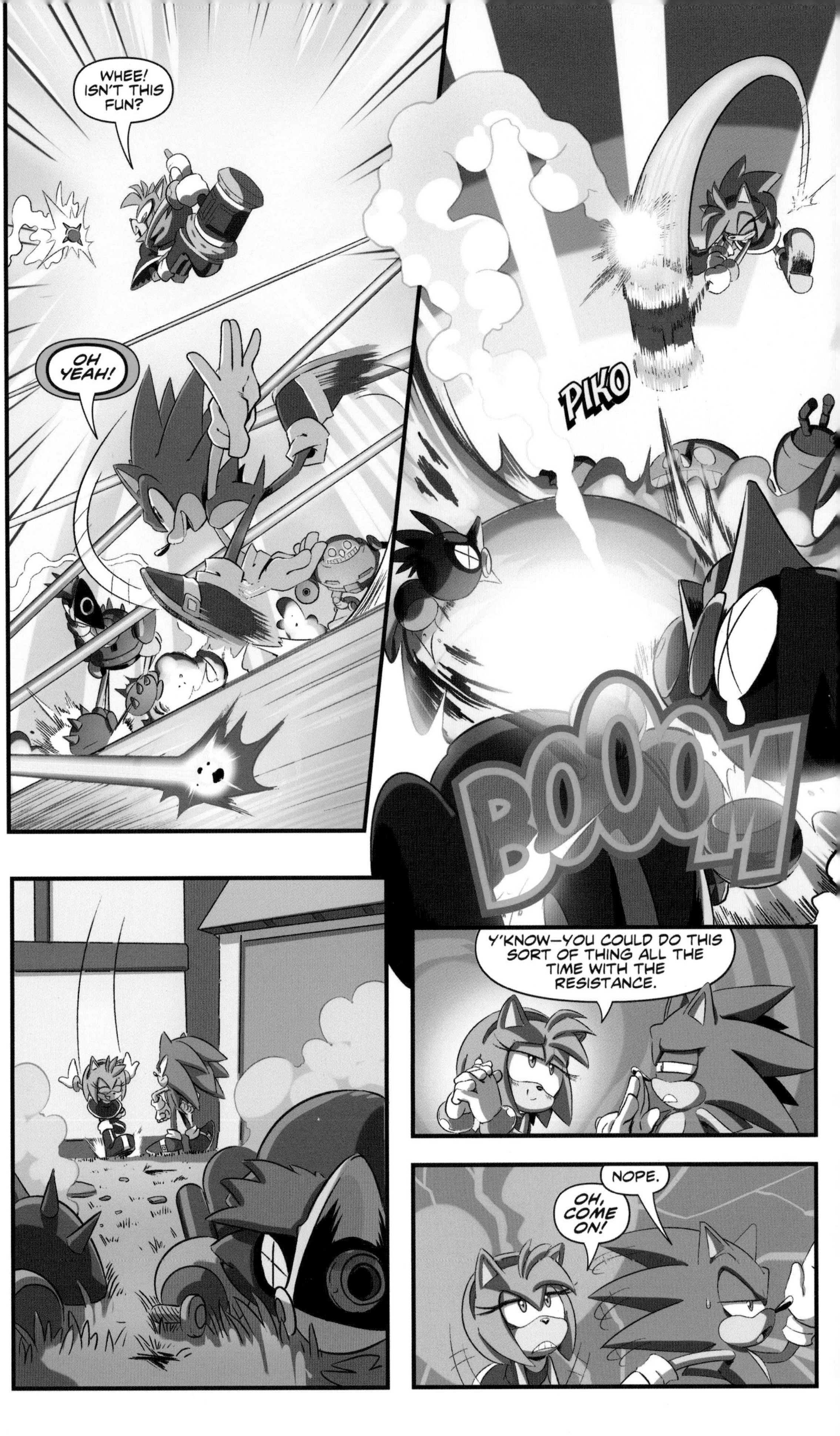
WHEE! ISN'T THIS FUN?
OH YEAH!
PIKO
BOOOOM
Y'KNOW—YOU COULD DO THIS SORT OF THING ALL THE TIME WITH THE RESISTANCE.
NOPE.
OH, COME ON!

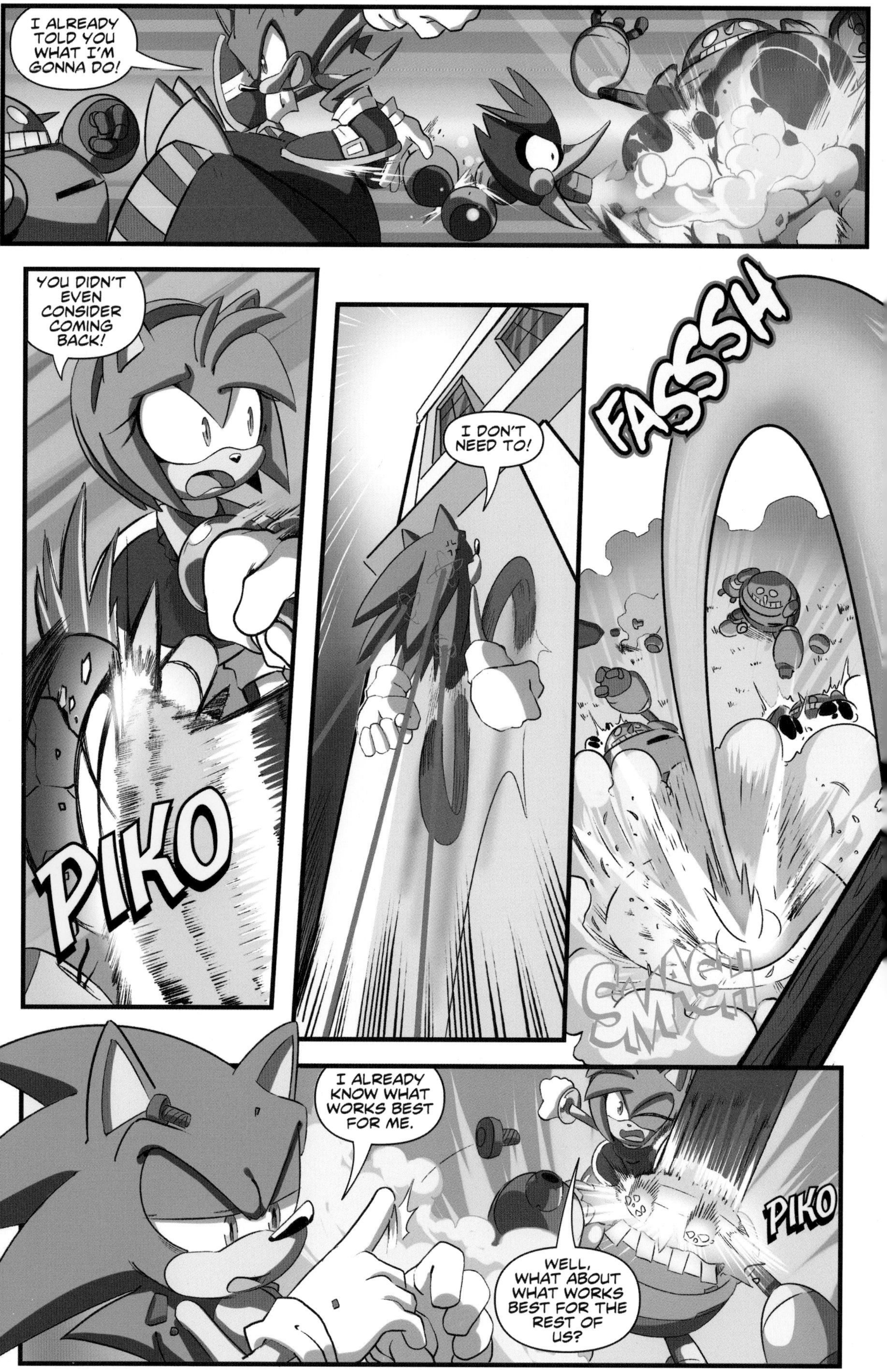
I ALREADY TOLD YOU WHAT I'M GONNA DO!
YOU DIDN'T EVEN CONSIDER COMING BACK!
PIKO
I DON'T NEED TO!
FASSSH
SMASH
I ALREADY KNOW WHAT WORKS BEST FOR ME.
PIKO
WELL, WHAT ABOUT WHAT WORKS BEST FOR THE REST OF US?

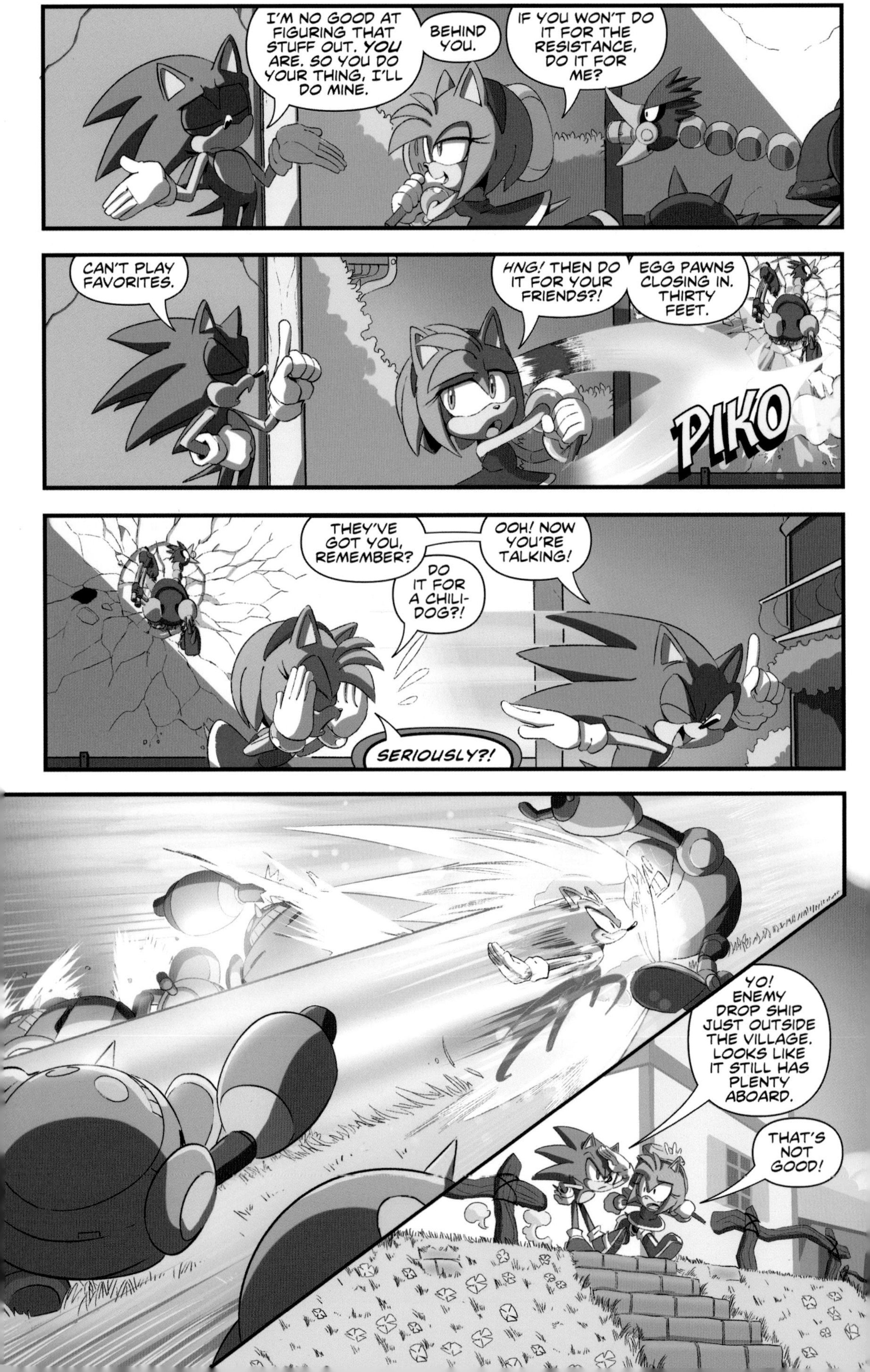
I'M NO GOOD AT FIGURING THAT STUFF OUT. YOU ARE. SO YOU DO YOUR THING, I'LL DO MINE.
BEHIND YOU.
IF YOU WON'T DO IT FOR THE RESISTANCE, DO IT FOR ME?
CAN'T PLAY FAVORITES.
HNG! THEN DO IT FOR YOUR FRIENDS?!
EGG PAWNS CLOSING IN. THIRTY FEET.
PIKO
THEY'VE GOT YOU, REMEMBER?
DO IT FOR A CHILI-DOG?!
OOH! NOW YOU'RE TALKING!
SERIOUSLY?!
YO! ENEMY DROP SHIP JUST OUTSIDE THE VILLAGE. LOOKS LIKE IT STILL HAS PLENTY ABOARD.
THAT'S NOT GOOD!

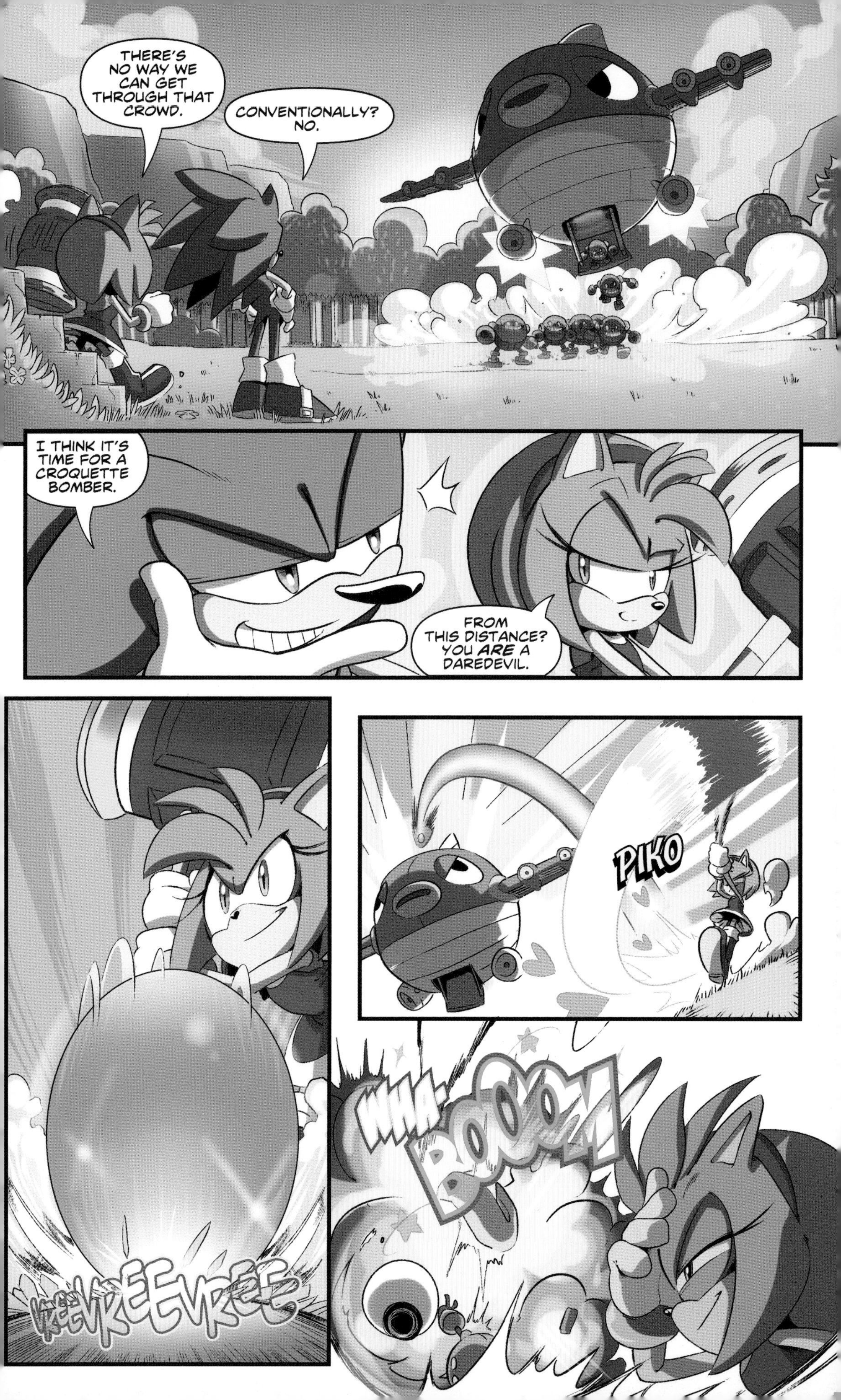
THERE'S NO WAY WE CAN GET THROUGH THAT CROWD.
CONVENTIONALLY? NO.
I THINK IT'S TIME FOR A CROQUETTE BOMBER.
FROM THIS DISTANCE? YOU *ARE* A DAREDEVIL.
VREEVREEVREE
PIKO
WHA-BOOOOM

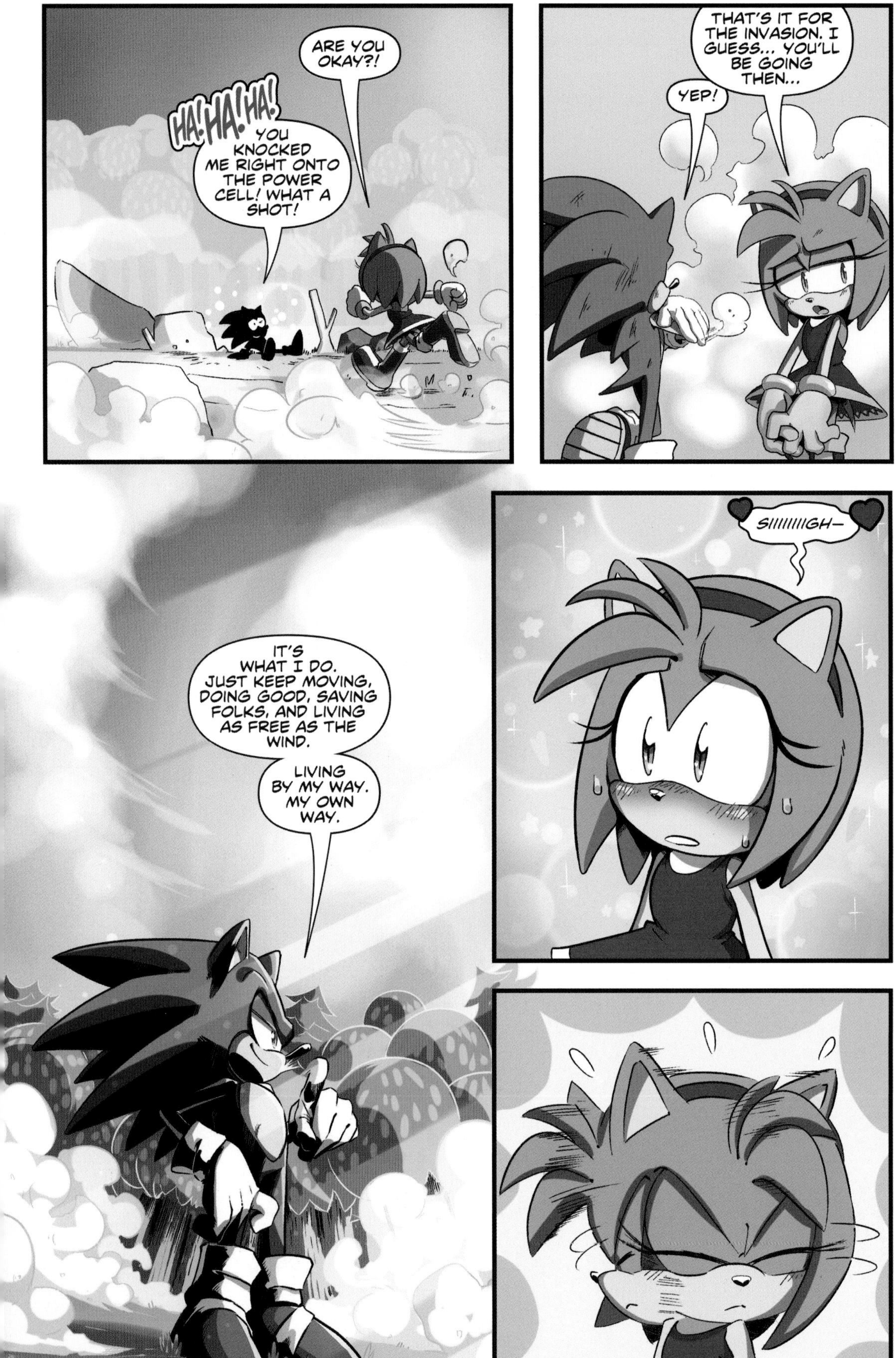
ARE YOU OKAY?!
HA! HA! HA!
YOU KNOCKED ME RIGHT ONTO THE POWER CELL! WHAT A SHOT!
THAT'S IT FOR THE INVASION. I GUESS... YOU'LL BE GOING THEN...
YEP!
IT'S WHAT I DO. JUST KEEP MOVING, DOING GOOD, SAVING FOLKS, AND LIVING AS FREE AS THE WIND.
LIVING BY MY WAY. MY OWN WAY.
SIIIIIIIGH—

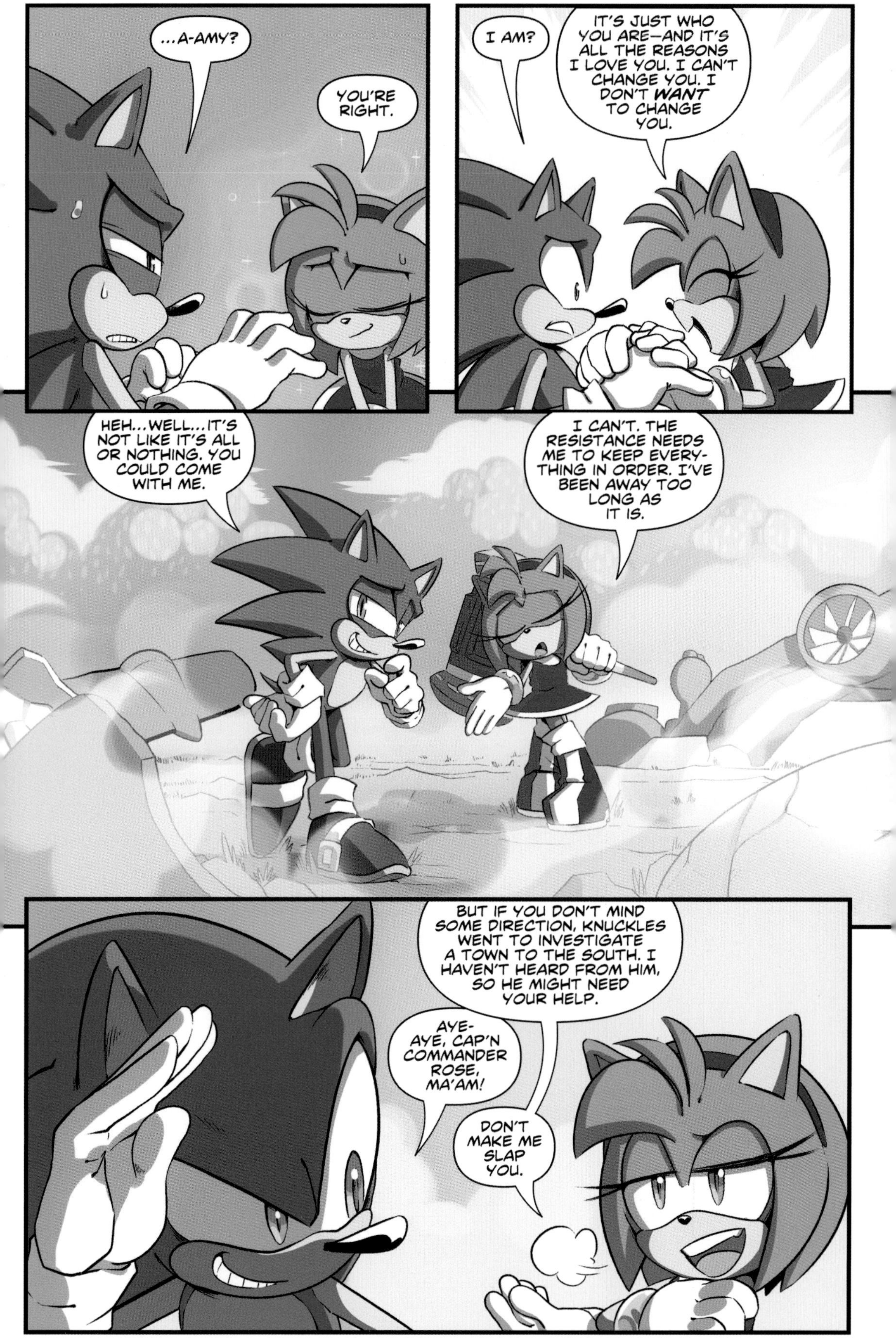
...A-AMY?
YOU'RE RIGHT.
I AM?
IT'S JUST WHO YOU ARE—AND IT'S ALL THE REASONS I LOVE YOU. I CAN'T CHANGE YOU. I DON'T ***WANT*** TO CHANGE YOU.
HEH...WELL...IT'S NOT LIKE IT'S ALL OR NOTHING. YOU COULD COME WITH ME.
I CAN'T. THE RESISTANCE NEEDS ME TO KEEP EVERY-THING IN ORDER. I'VE BEEN AWAY TOO LONG AS IT IS.
BUT IF YOU DON'T MIND SOME DIRECTION, KNUCKLES WENT TO INVESTIGATE A TOWN TO THE SOUTH. I HAVEN'T HEARD FROM HIM, SO HE MIGHT NEED YOUR HELP.
AYE-AYE, CAP'N COMMANDER ROSE, MA'AM!
DON'T MAKE ME SLAP YOU.

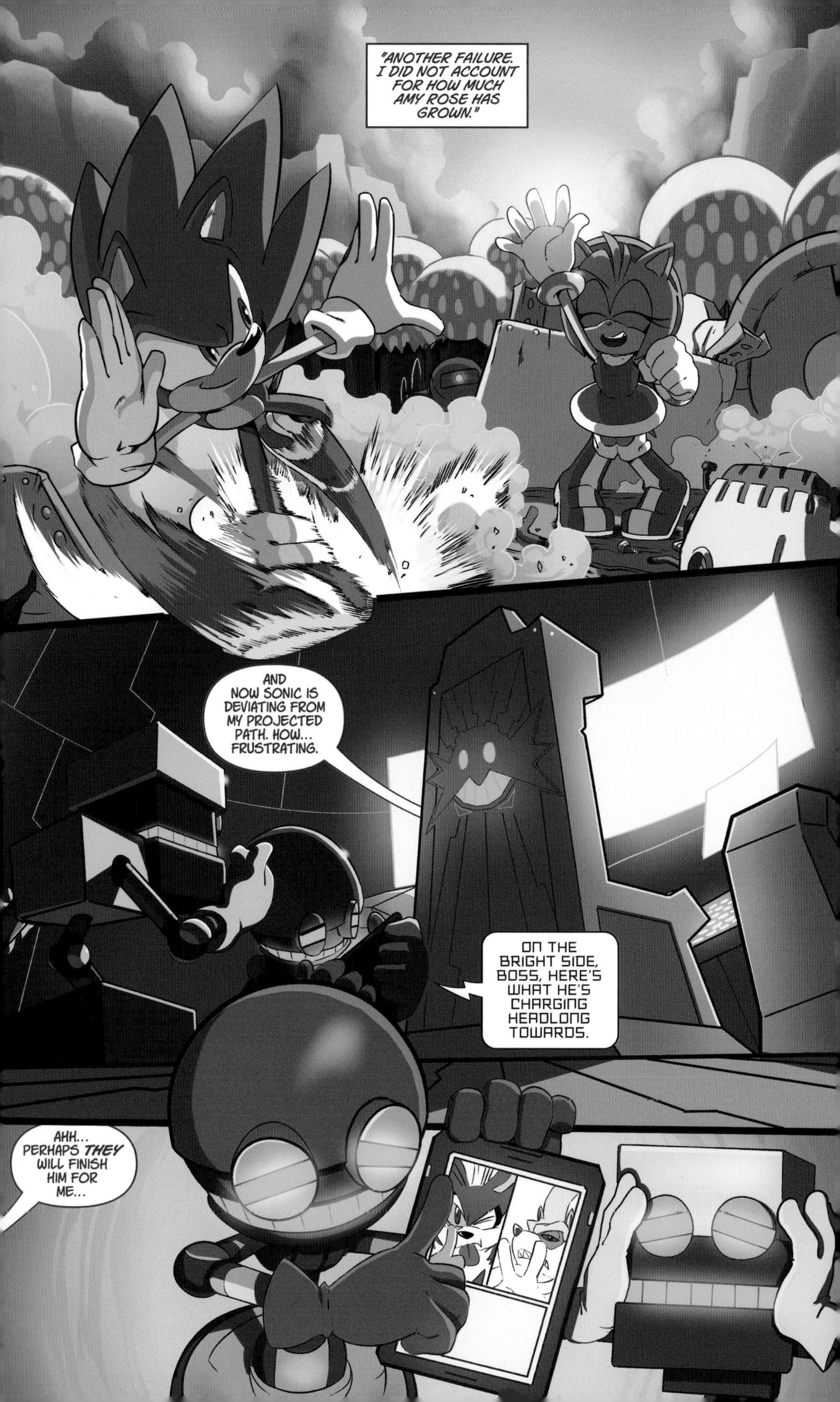
"ANOTHER FAILURE. I DID NOT ACCOUNT FOR HOW MUCH AMY ROSE HAS GROWN."
AND NOW SONIC IS DEVIATING FROM MY PROJECTED PATH. HOW... FRUSTRATING.
ON THE BRIGHT SIDE, BOSS, HERE'S WHAT HE'S CHARGING HEADLONG TOWARDS.
AHH... PERHAPS *THEY* WILL FINISH HIM FOR ME...

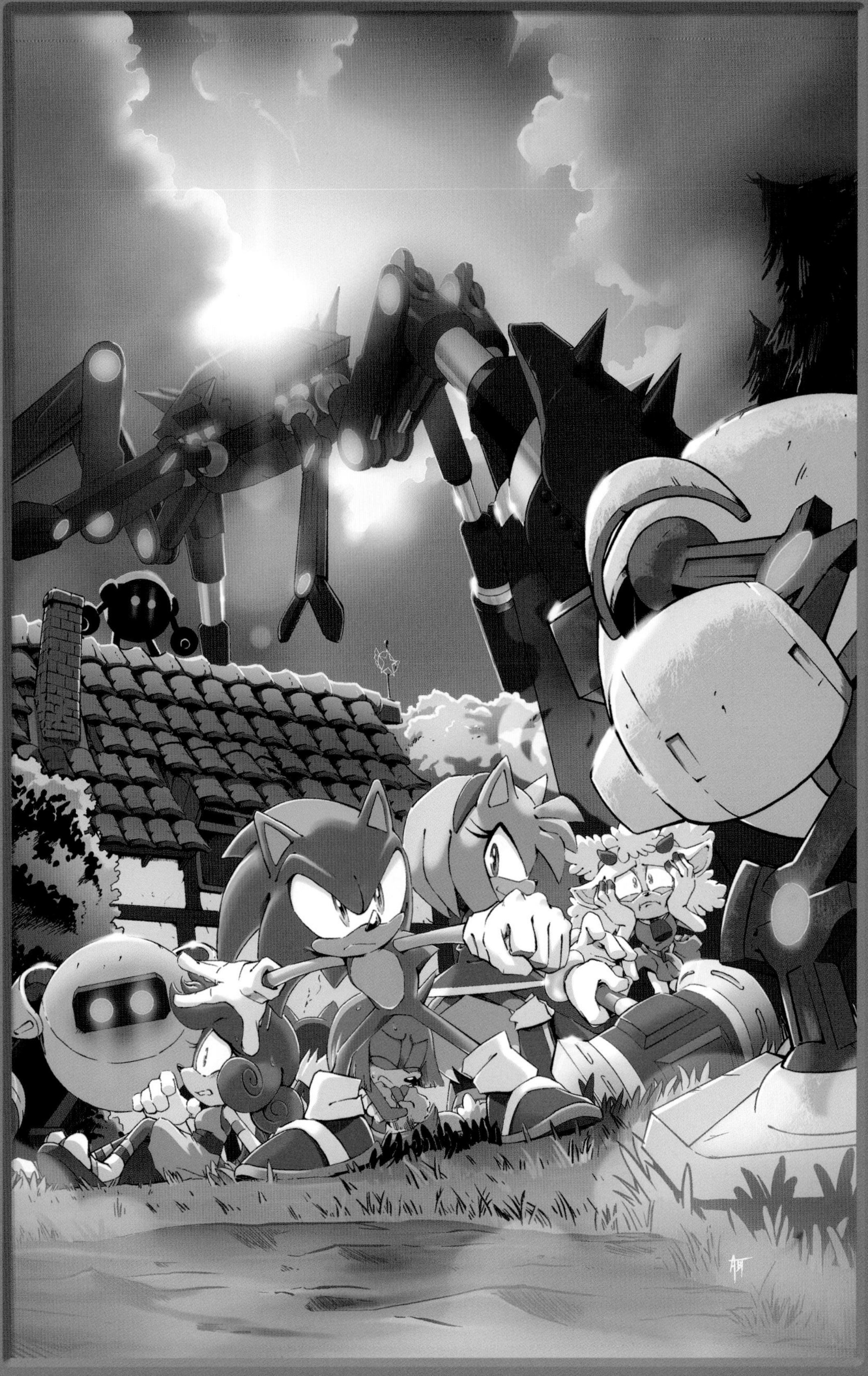

ART BY **ADAM BRYCE THOMAS**

TYSON
2018

ART BY **TYSON HESSE**

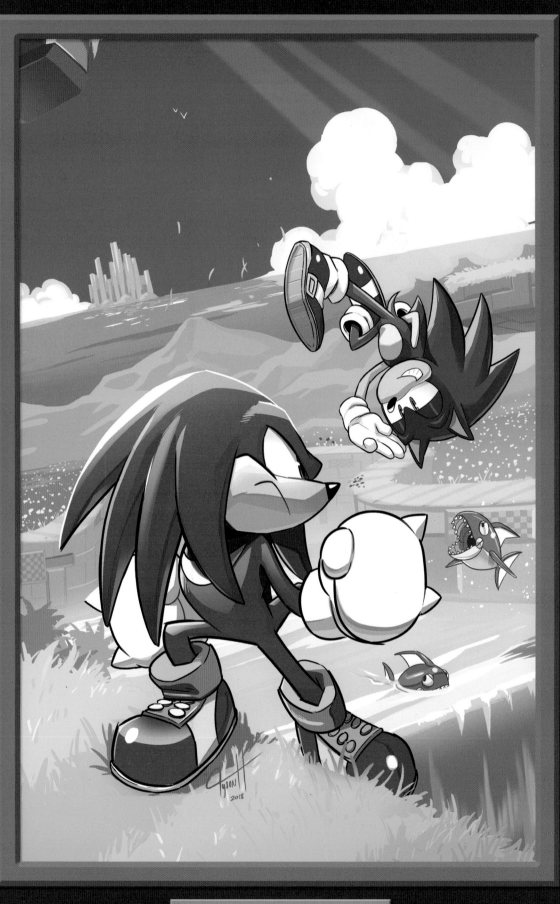

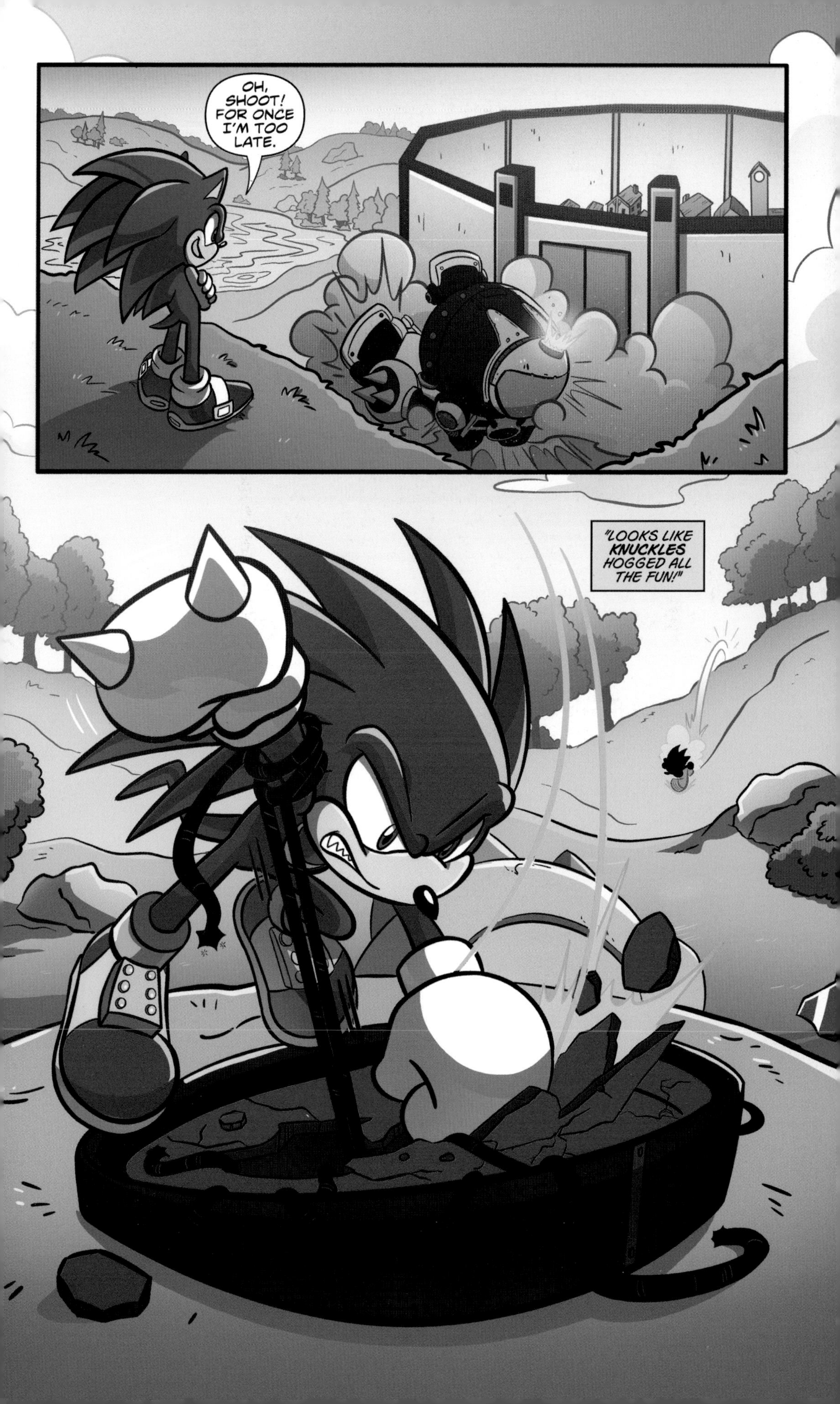
OH, SHOOT! FOR ONCE I'M TOO LATE.
"LOOKS LIKE KNUCKLES HOGGED ALL THE FUN!"

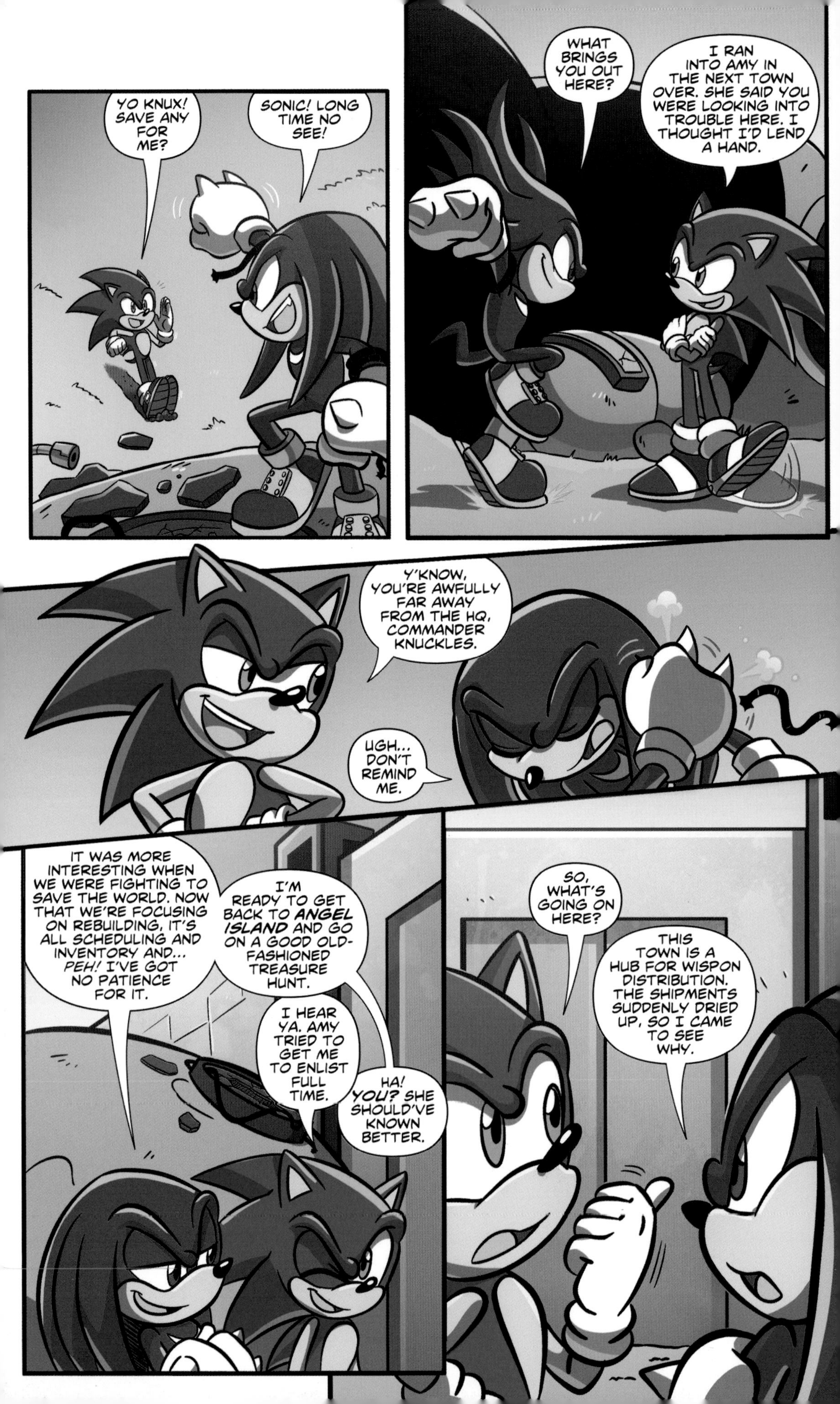

YO KNUX! SAVE ANY FOR ME?
SONIC! LONG TIME NO SEE!
WHAT BRINGS YOU OUT HERE?
I RAN INTO AMY IN THE NEXT TOWN OVER. SHE SAID YOU WERE LOOKING INTO TROUBLE HERE. I THOUGHT I'D LEND A HAND.
Y'KNOW, YOU'RE AWFULLY FAR AWAY FROM THE HQ, COMMANDER KNUCKLES.
UGH... DON'T REMIND ME.
IT WAS MORE INTERESTING WHEN WE WERE FIGHTING TO SAVE THE WORLD. NOW THAT WE'RE FOCUSING ON REBUILDING, IT'S ALL SCHEDULING AND INVENTORY AND... *PEH!* I'VE GOT NO PATIENCE FOR IT.
I'M READY TO GET BACK TO ***ANGEL ISLAND*** AND GO ON A GOOD OLD-FASHIONED TREASURE HUNT.
I HEAR YA. AMY TRIED TO GET ME TO ENLIST FULL TIME.
HA! ***YOU?*** SHE SHOULD'VE KNOWN BETTER.
SO, WHAT'S GOING ON HERE?
THIS TOWN IS A HUB FOR WISPON DISTRIBUTION. THE SHIPMENTS SUDDENLY DRIED UP, SO I CAME TO SEE WHY.

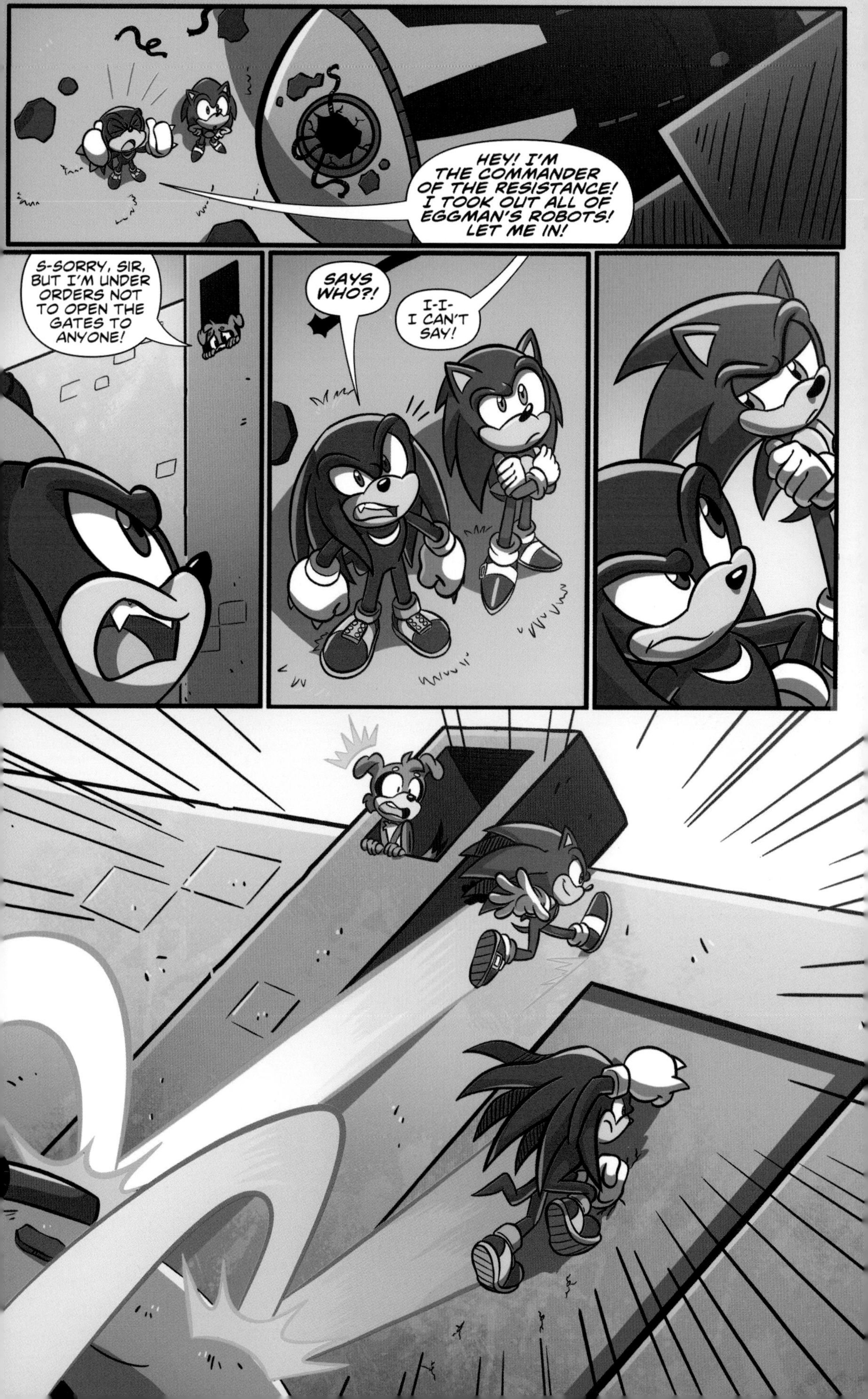
HEY! I'M THE COMMANDER OF THE RESISTANCE! I TOOK OUT ALL OF EGGMAN'S ROBOTS! LET ME IN!
S-SORRY, SIR, BUT I'M UNDER ORDERS NOT TO OPEN THE GATES TO ANYONE!
SAYS WHO?!
I-I- I CAN'T SAY!

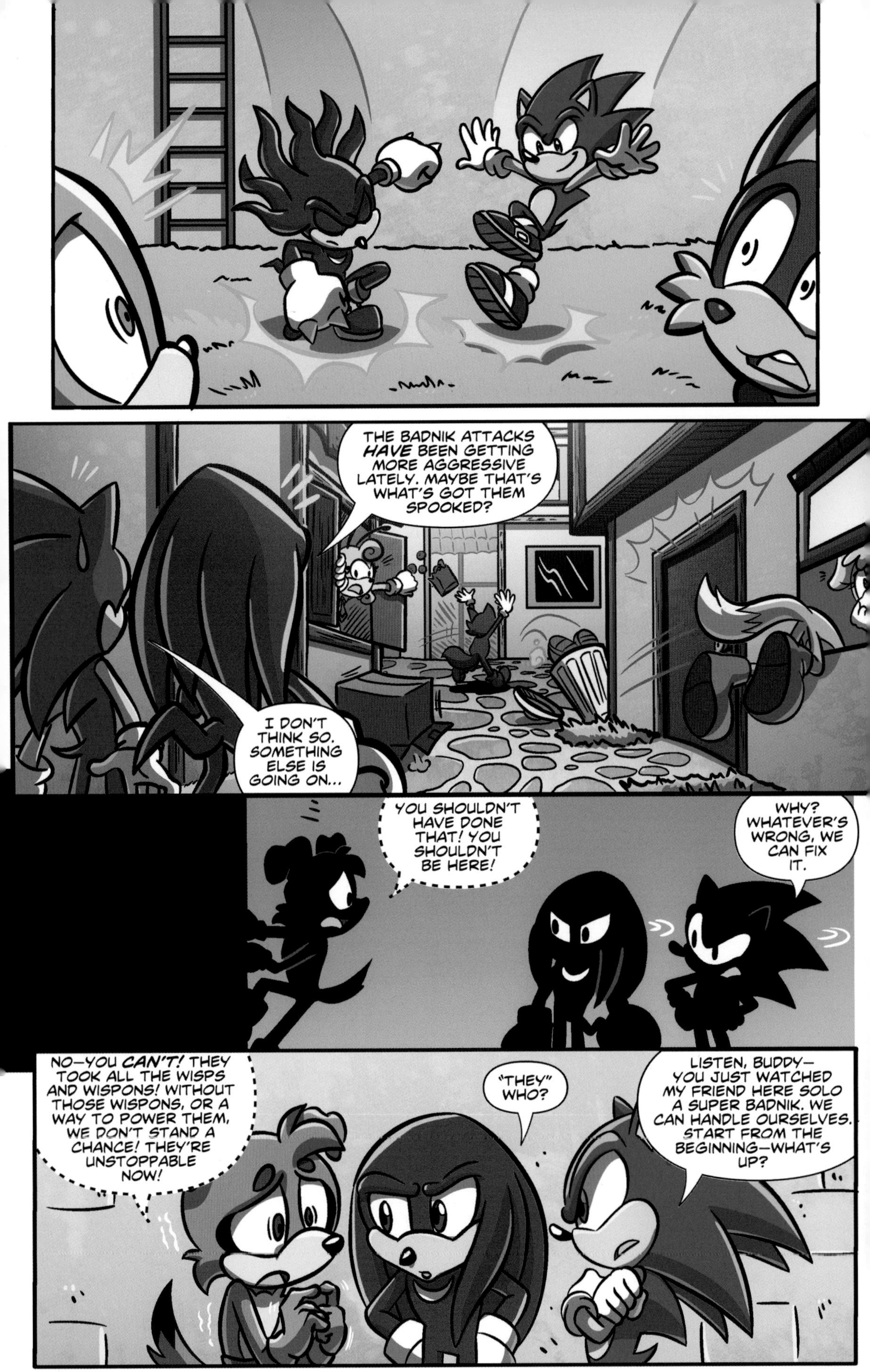

THE BADNIK ATTACKS HAVE BEEN GETTING MORE AGGRESSIVE LATELY. MAYBE THAT'S WHAT'S GOT THEM SPOOKED?
I DON'T THINK SO. SOMETHING ELSE IS GOING ON...
YOU SHOULDN'T HAVE DONE THAT! YOU SHOULDN'T BE HERE!
WHY? WHATEVER'S WRONG, WE CAN FIX IT.
NO—YOU CAN'T! THEY TOOK ALL THE WISPS AND WISPONS! WITHOUT THOSE WISPONS, OR A WAY TO POWER THEM, WE DON'T STAND A CHANCE! THEY'RE UNSTOPPABLE NOW!
"THEY" WHO?
LISTEN, BUDDY—YOU JUST WATCHED MY FRIEND HERE SOLO A SUPER BADNIK. WE CAN HANDLE OURSELVES. START FROM THE BEGINNING—WHAT'S UP?

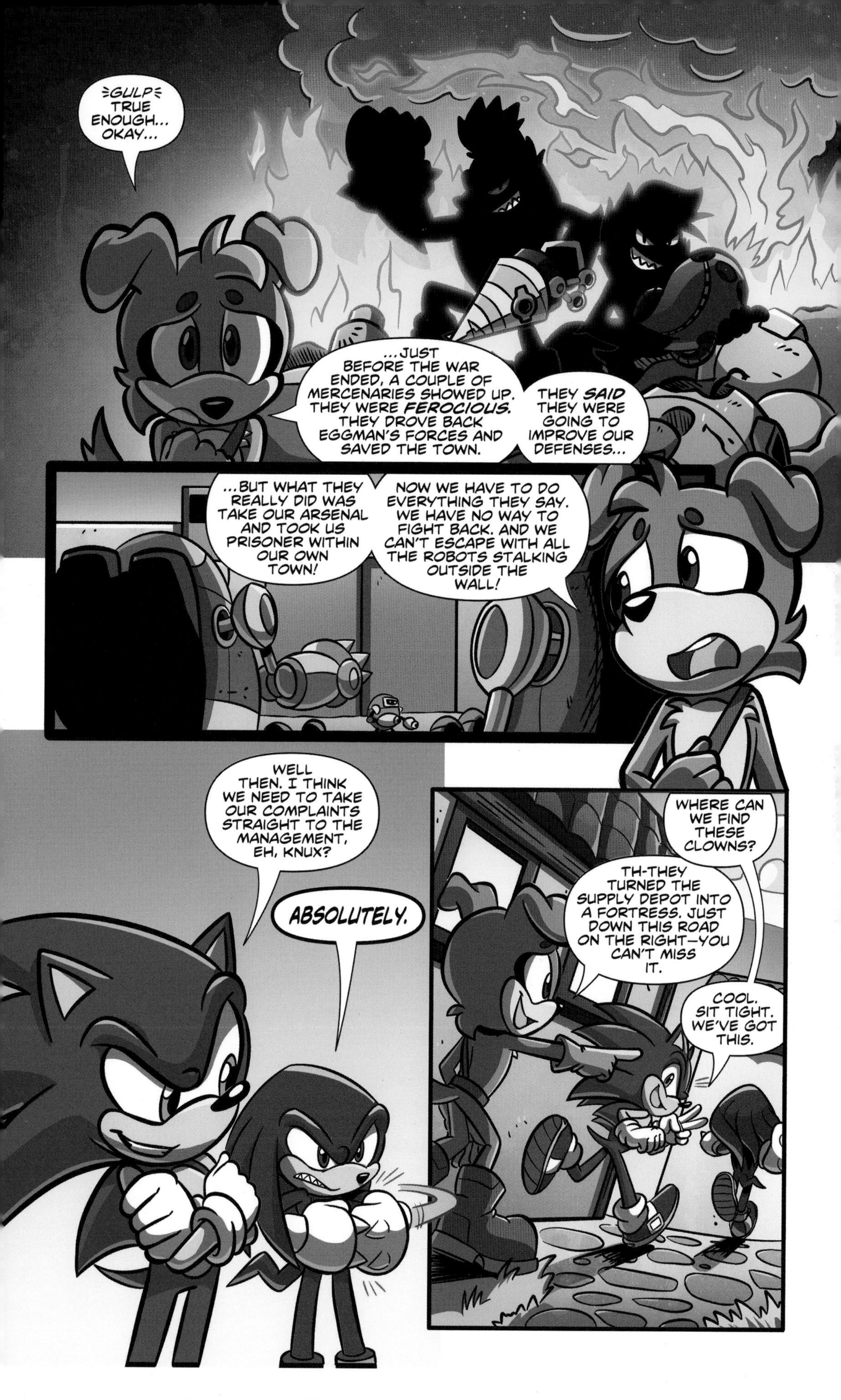

≶GULP≶ TRUE ENOUGH... OKAY...
...JUST BEFORE THE WAR ENDED, A COUPLE OF MERCENARIES SHOWED UP. THEY WERE FEROCIOUS. THEY DROVE BACK EGGMAN'S FORCES AND SAVED THE TOWN.
THEY SAID THEY WERE GOING TO IMPROVE OUR DEFENSES...
...BUT WHAT THEY REALLY DID WAS TAKE OUR ARSENAL AND TOOK US PRISONER WITHIN OUR OWN TOWN!
NOW WE HAVE TO DO EVERYTHING THEY SAY. WE HAVE NO WAY TO FIGHT BACK. AND WE CAN'T ESCAPE WITH ALL THE ROBOTS STALKING OUTSIDE THE WALL!
WELL THEN. I THINK WE NEED TO TAKE OUR COMPLAINTS STRAIGHT TO THE MANAGEMENT, EH, KNUX?
ABSOLUTELY.
WHERE CAN WE FIND THESE CLOWNS?
TH-THEY TURNED THE SUPPLY DEPOT INTO A FORTRESS. JUST DOWN THIS ROAD ON THE RIGHT—YOU CAN'T MISS IT.
COOL. SIT TIGHT. WE'VE GOT THIS.

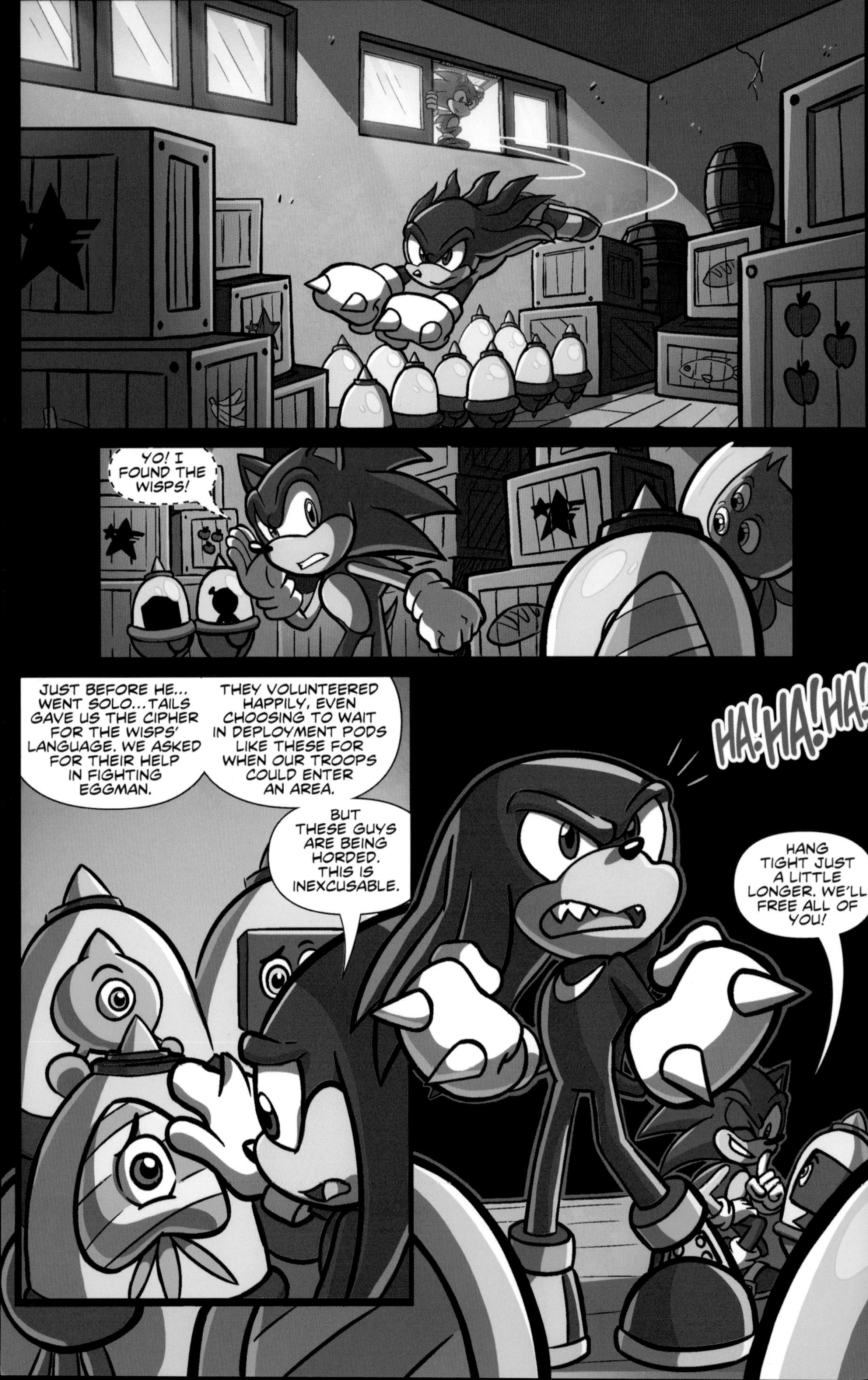
YO! I FOUND THE WISPS!
JUST BEFORE HE... WENT SOLO...TAILS GAVE US THE CIPHER FOR THE WISPS' LANGUAGE. WE ASKED FOR THEIR HELP IN FIGHTING EGGMAN.
THEY VOLUNTEERED HAPPILY, EVEN CHOOSING TO WAIT IN DEPLOYMENT PODS LIKE THESE FOR WHEN OUR TROOPS COULD ENTER AN AREA.
BUT THESE GUYS ARE BEING HORDED. THIS IS INEXCUSABLE.
HA! HA! HA!
HANG TIGHT JUST A LITTLE LONGER. WE'LL FREE ALL OF YOU!

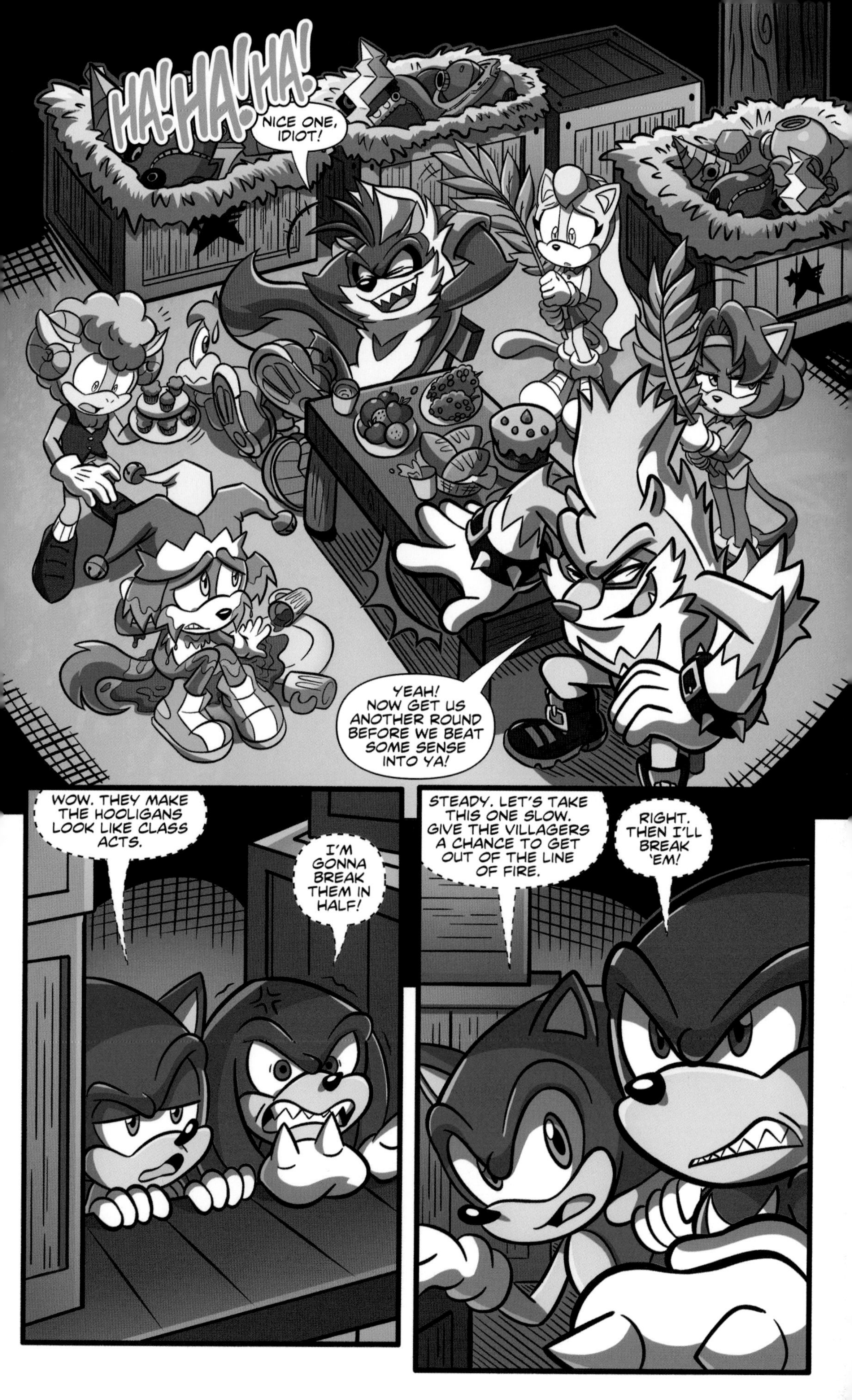
HA! HA! HA!
NICE ONE, IDIOT!
YEAH! NOW GET US ANOTHER ROUND BEFORE WE BEAT SOME SENSE INTO YA!
WOW. THEY MAKE THE HOOLIGANS LOOK LIKE CLASS ACTS.
I'M GONNA BREAK THEM IN HALF!
STEADY. LET'S TAKE THIS ONE SLOW. GIVE THE VILLAGERS A CHANCE TO GET OUT OF THE LINE OF FIRE.
RIGHT. THEN I'LL BREAK 'EM!

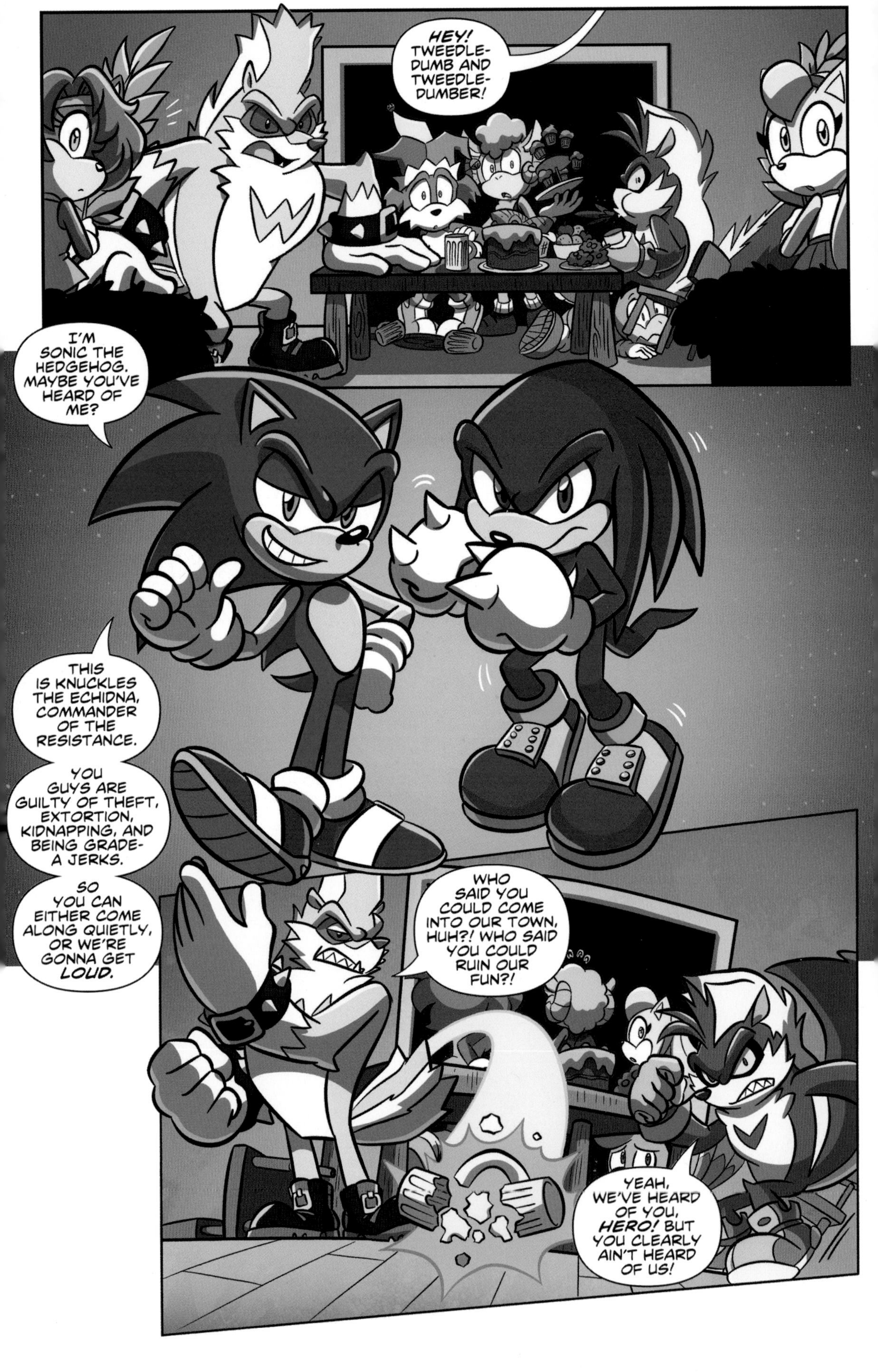
HEY! TWEEDLE-DUMB AND TWEEDLE-DUMBER!
I'M SONIC THE HEDGEHOG. MAYBE YOU'VE HEARD OF ME?
THIS IS KNUCKLES THE ECHIDNA, COMMANDER OF THE RESISTANCE.
YOU GUYS ARE GUILTY OF THEFT, EXTORTION, KIDNAPPING, AND BEING GRADE-A JERKS.
SO YOU CAN EITHER COME ALONG QUIETLY, OR WE'RE GONNA GET LOUD.
WHO SAID YOU COULD COME INTO OUR TOWN, HUH?! WHO SAID YOU COULD RUIN OUR FUN?!
YEAH, WE'VE HEARD OF YOU, HERO! BUT YOU CLEARLY AIN'T HEARD OF US!

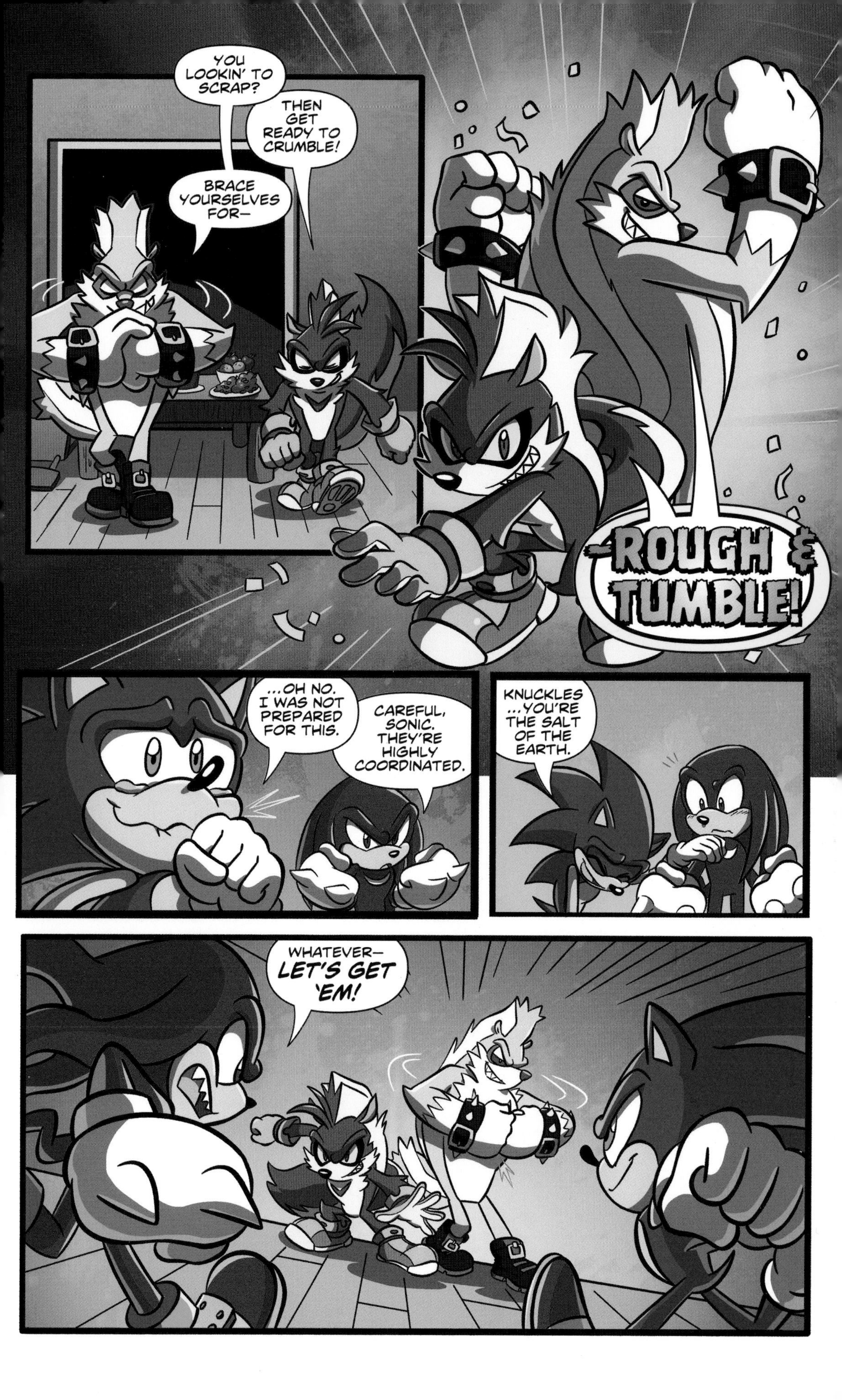

YOU LOOKIN' TO SCRAP?
THEN GET READY TO CRUMBLE!
BRACE YOURSELVES FOR—
—ROUGH & TUMBLE!
...OH NO. I WAS NOT PREPARED FOR THIS.
CAREFUL, SONIC. THEY'RE HIGHLY COORDINATED.
KNUCKLES ...YOU'RE THE SALT OF THE EARTH.
WHATEVER— LET'S GET 'EM!

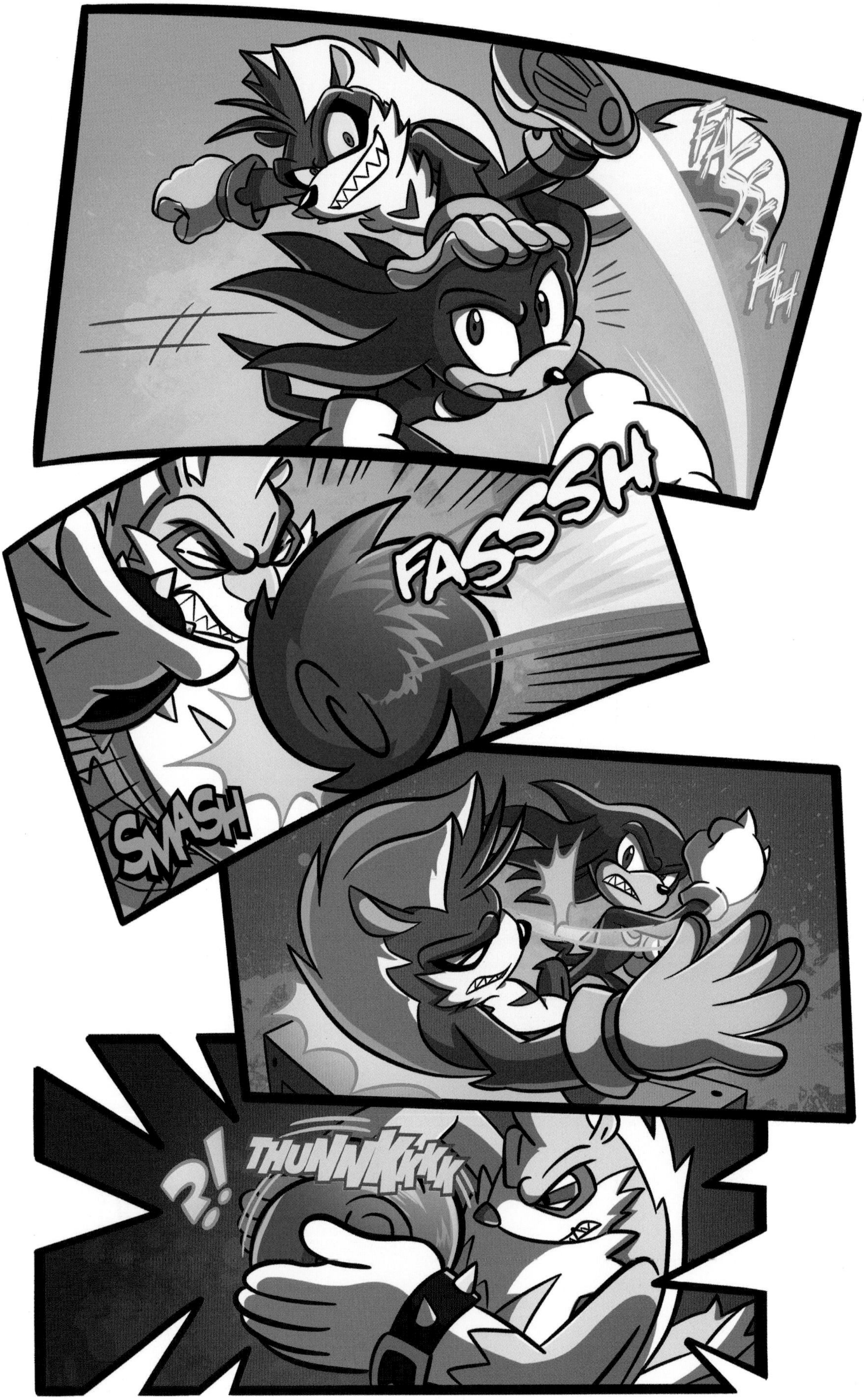
FASSSHH
FASSSH
SMASH
?!
THUNNKKKK

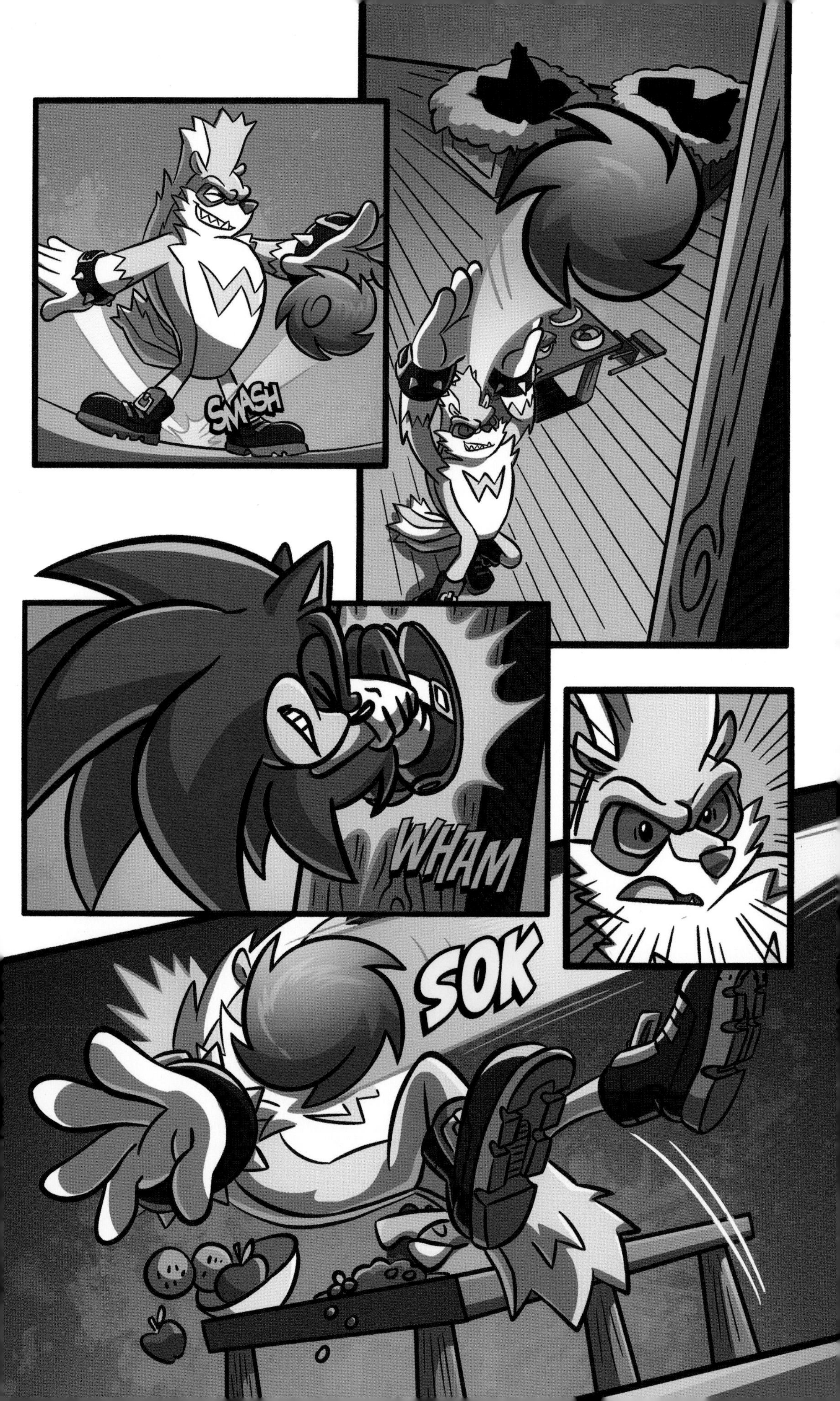
SMASH
WHAM
SOK

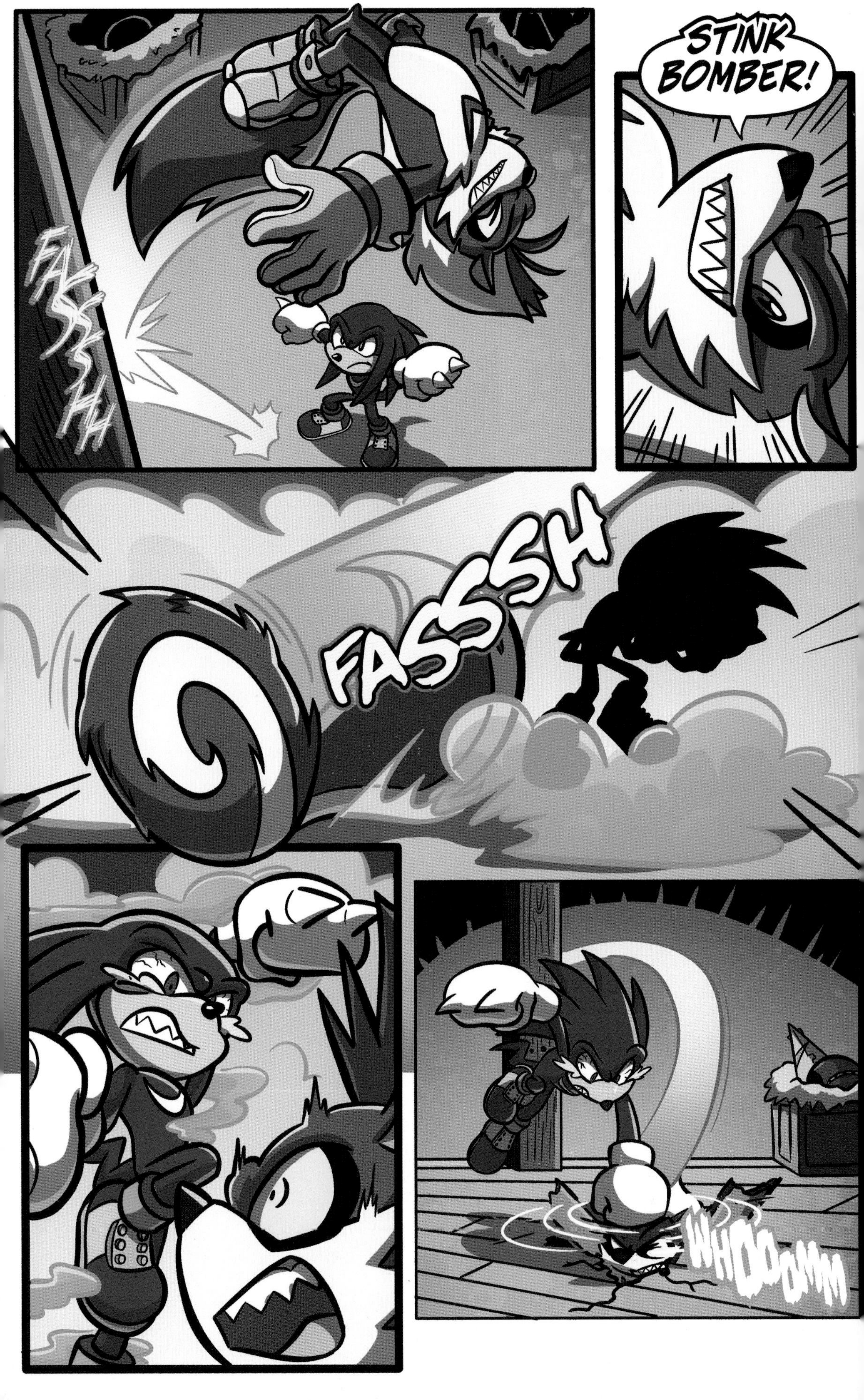
FASSSHH
STINK BOMBER!
FASSSH
WHOOOMM

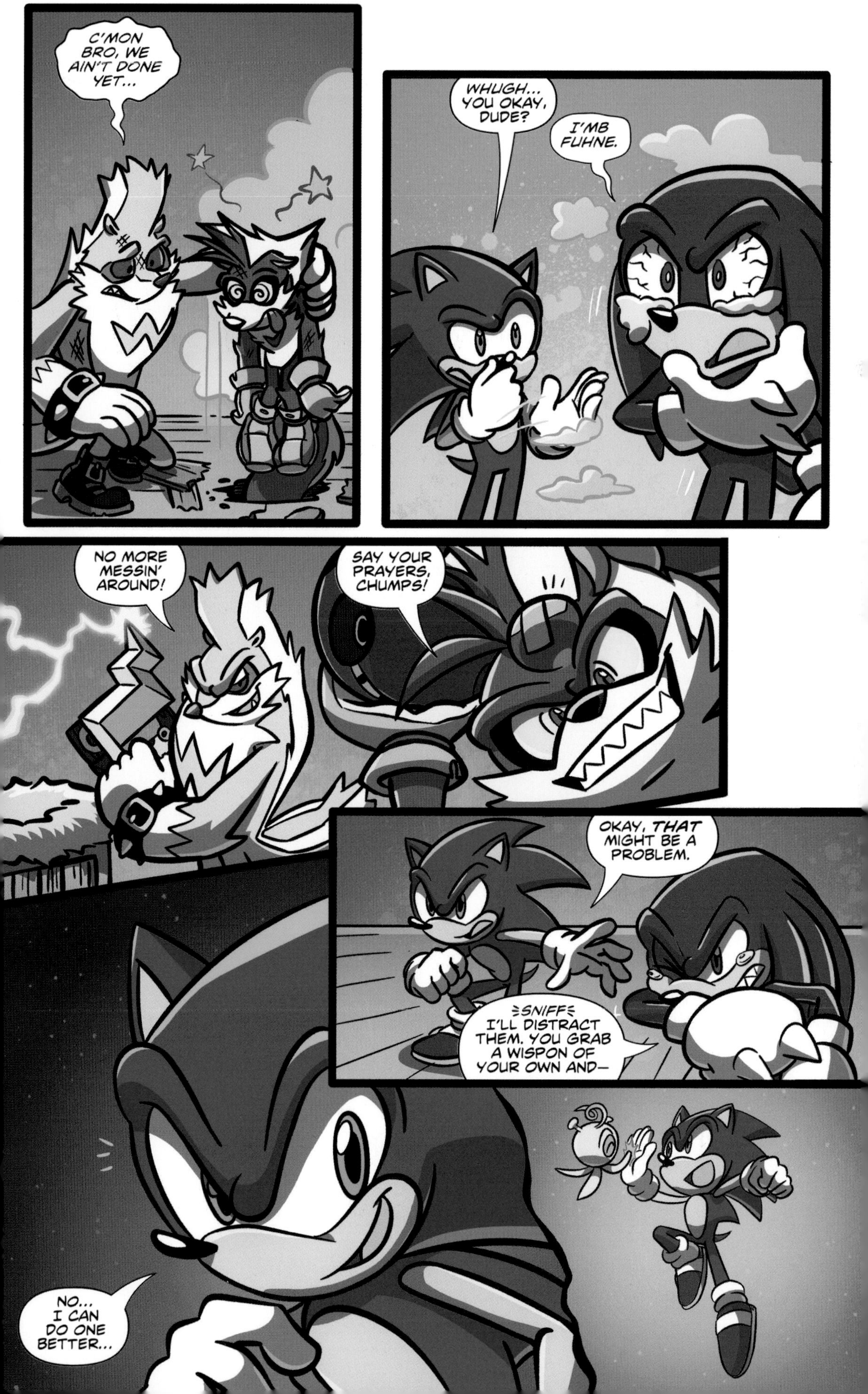
C'MON BRO, WE AIN'T DONE YET...
WHUGH... YOU OKAY, DUDE?
I'MB FUHNE.
NO MORE MESSIN' AROUND!
SAY YOUR PRAYERS, CHUMPS!
OKAY, THAT MIGHT BE A PROBLEM.
SNIFF I'LL DISTRACT THEM. YOU GRAB A WISPON OF YOUR OWN AND—
NO... I CAN DO ONE BETTER...

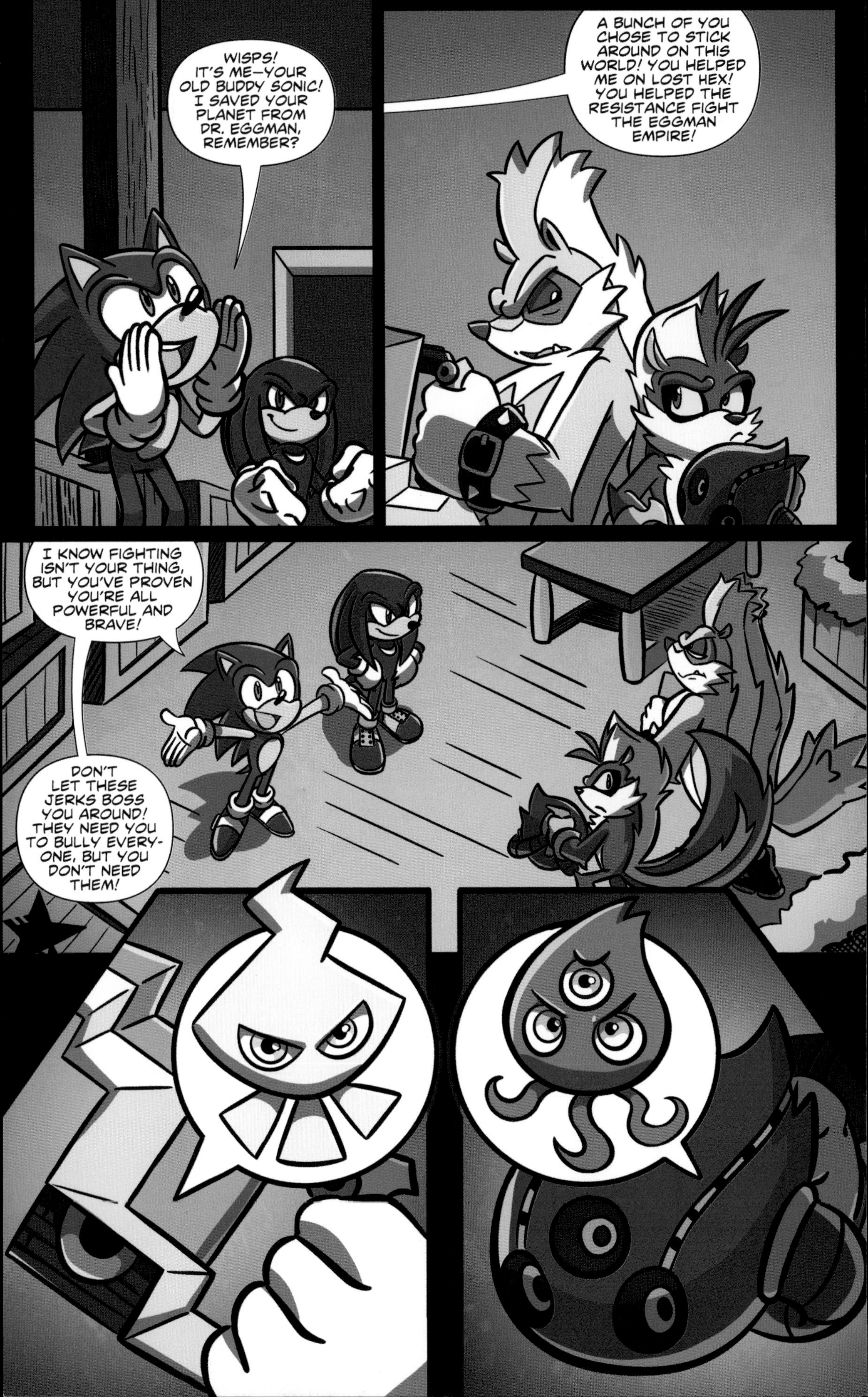
WISPS! IT'S ME—YOUR OLD BUDDY SONIC! I SAVED YOUR PLANET FROM DR. EGGMAN, REMEMBER?
A BUNCH OF YOU CHOSE TO STICK AROUND ON THIS WORLD! YOU HELPED ME ON LOST HEX! YOU HELPED THE RESISTANCE FIGHT THE EGGMAN EMPIRE!
I KNOW FIGHTING ISN'T YOUR THING, BUT YOU'VE PROVEN YOU'RE ALL POWERFUL AND BRAVE!
DON'T LET THESE JERKS BOSS YOU AROUND! THEY NEED YOU TO BULLY EVERY-ONE, BUT YOU DON'T NEED THEM!

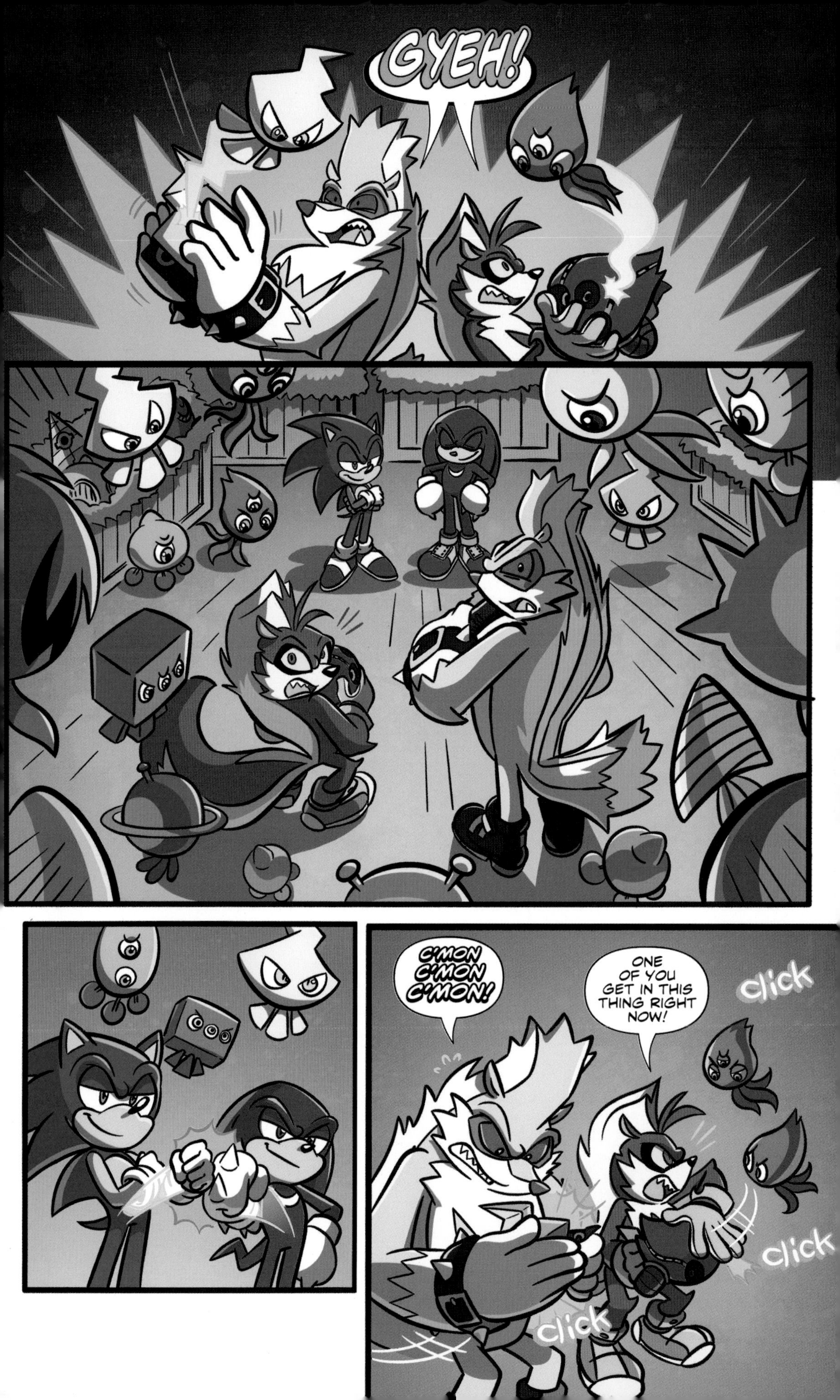
GYEH!
C'MON C'MON C'MON!
ONE OF YOU GET IN THIS THING RIGHT NOW!
click
click
click

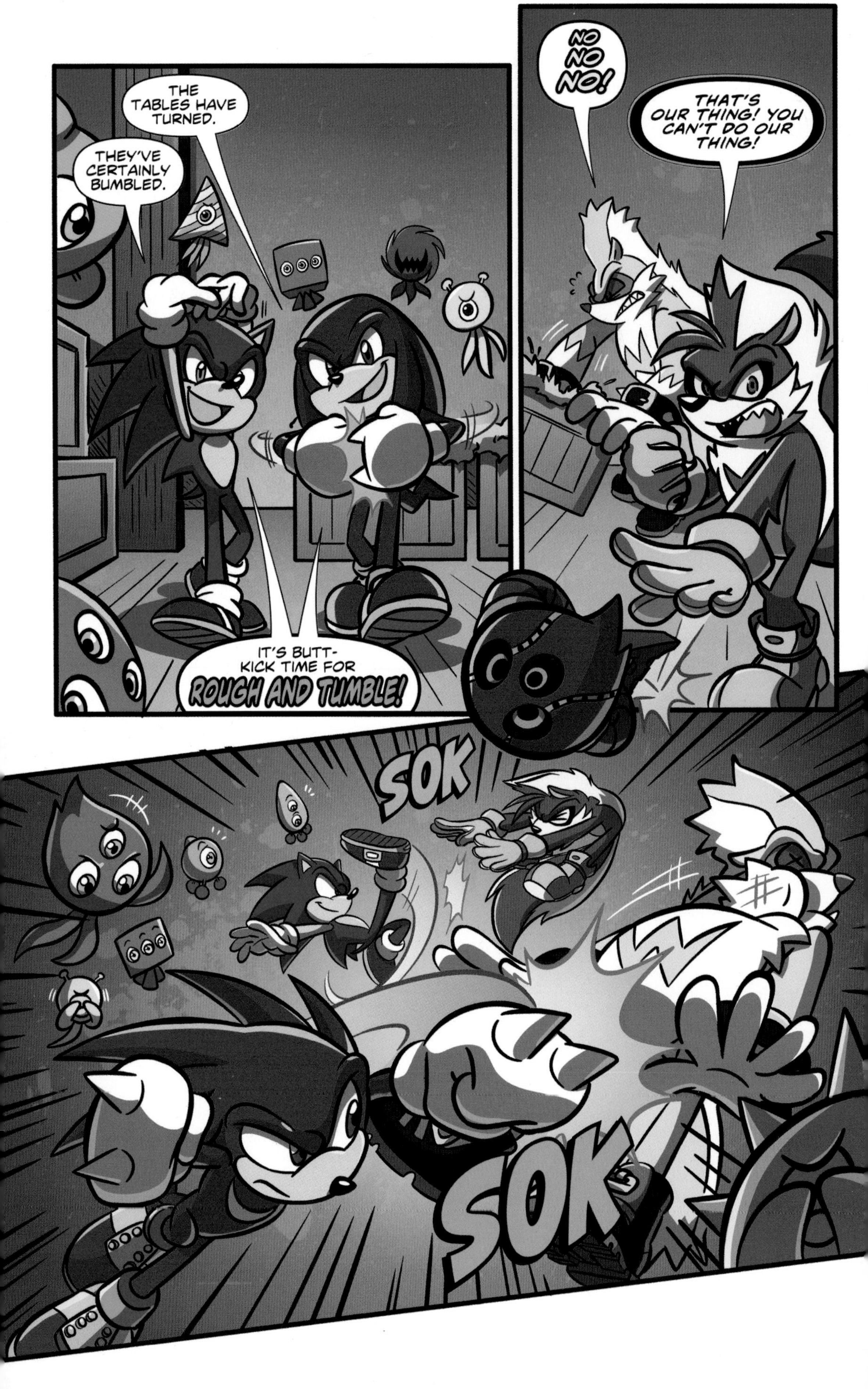
THE TABLES HAVE TURNED.
THEY'VE CERTAINLY BUMBLED.
IT'S BUTT-KICK TIME FOR ROUGH AND TUMBLE!
NO NO NO!
THAT'S OUR THING! YOU CAN'T DO OUR THING!
SOK
SOK

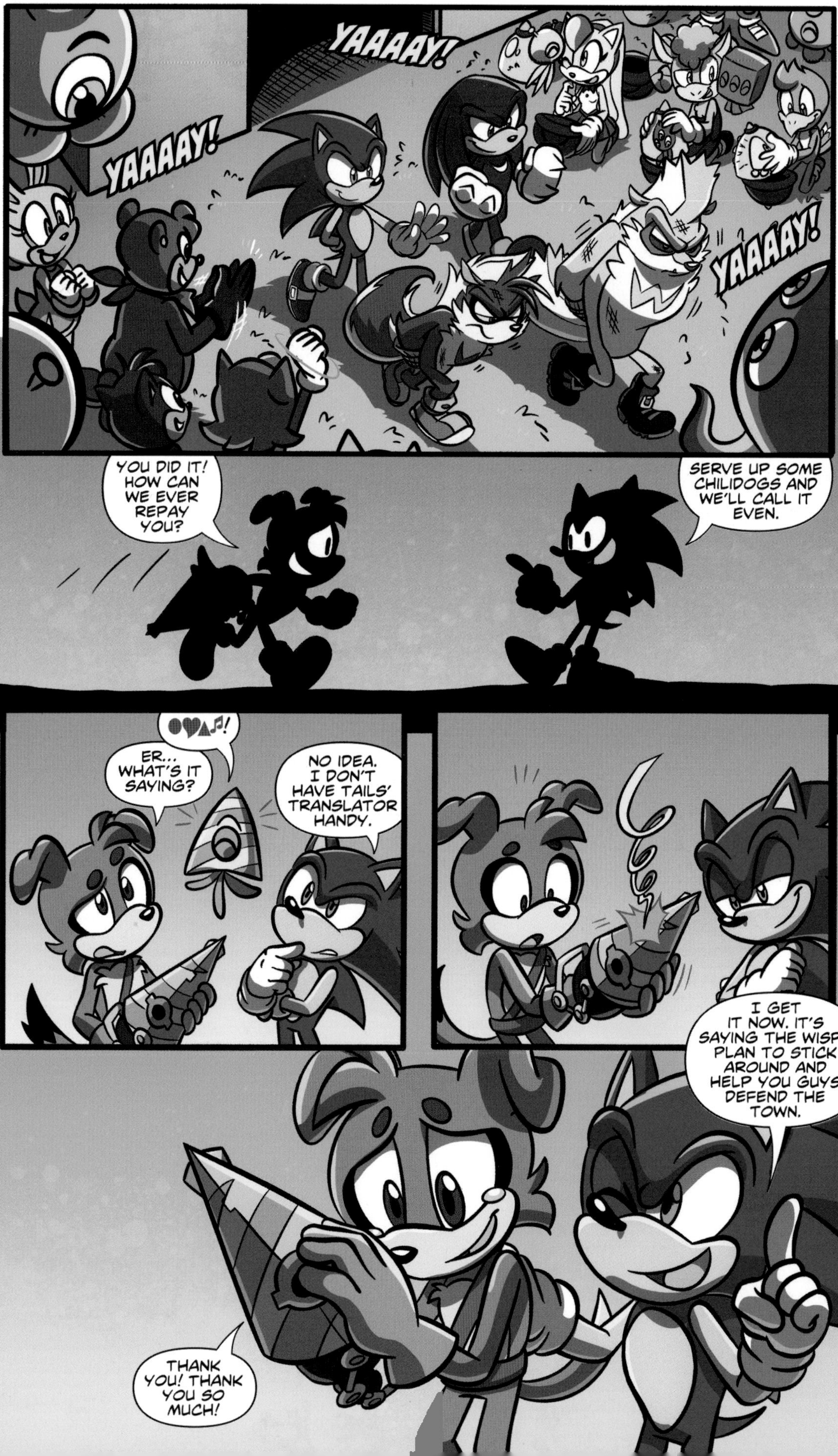
YAAAAY!
YAAAAY!
YAAAAY!
YOU DID IT! HOW CAN WE EVER REPAY YOU?
SERVE UP SOME CHILIDOGS AND WE'LL CALL IT EVEN.
ER... WHAT'S IT SAYING?
NO IDEA. I DON'T HAVE TAILS' TRANSLATOR HANDY.
I GET IT NOW. IT'S SAYING THE WISPS PLAN TO STICK AROUND AND HELP YOU GUYS DEFEND THE TOWN.
THANK YOU! THANK YOU SO MUCH!

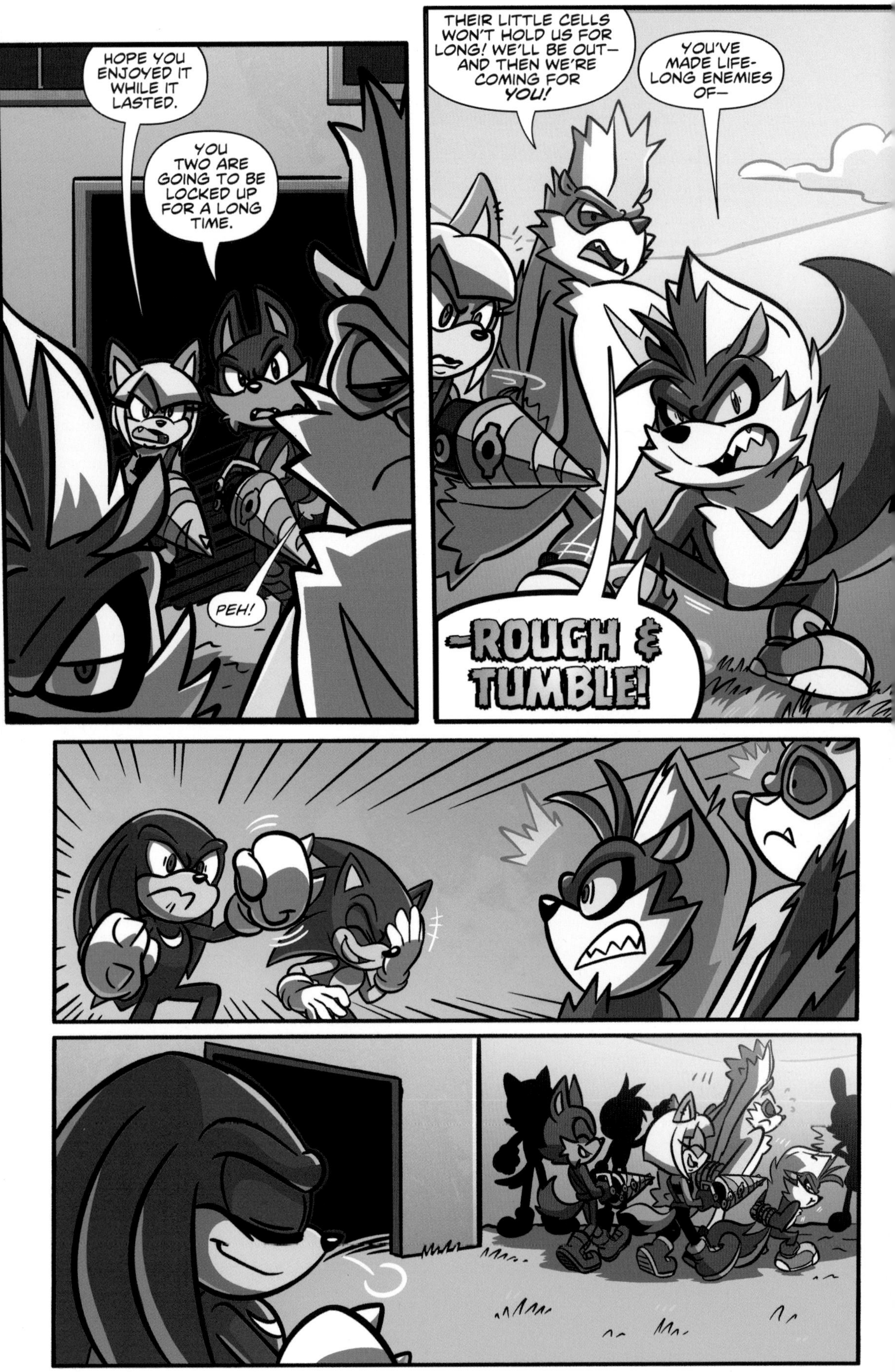
HOPE YOU ENJOYED IT WHILE IT LASTED.
YOU TWO ARE GOING TO BE LOCKED UP FOR A LONG TIME.
PEH!
THEIR LITTLE CELLS WON'T HOLD US FOR LONG! WE'LL BE OUT— AND THEN WE'RE COMING FOR YOU!
YOU'VE MADE LIFE-LONG ENEMIES OF—
-ROUGH & TUMBLE!

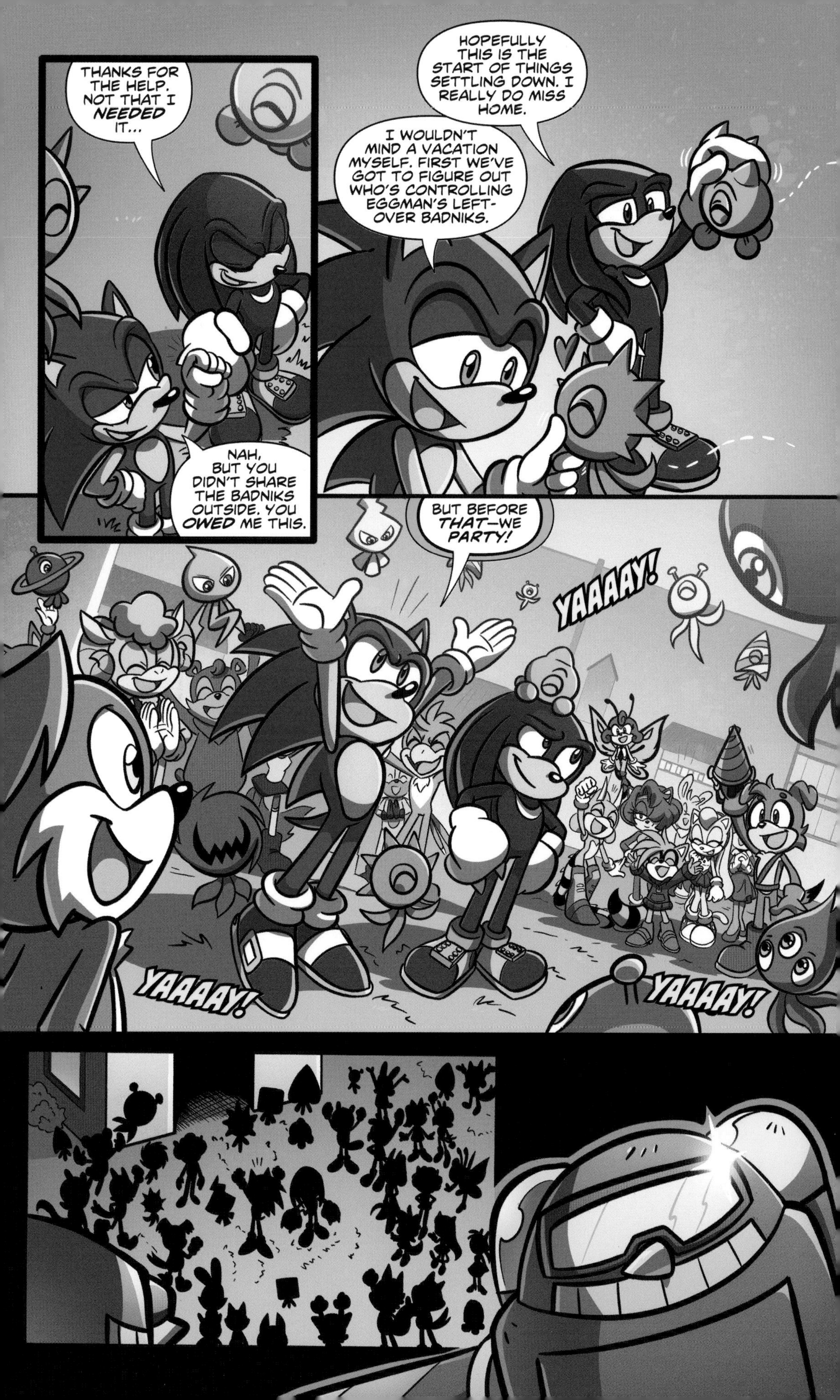
THANKS FOR THE HELP. NOT THAT I NEEDED IT...
NAH, BUT YOU DIDN'T SHARE THE BADNIKS OUTSIDE. YOU OWED ME THIS.
HOPEFULLY THIS IS THE START OF THINGS SETTLING DOWN. I REALLY DO MISS HOME.
I WOULDN'T MIND A VACATION MYSELF. FIRST WE'VE GOT TO FIGURE OUT WHO'S CONTROLLING EGGMAN'S LEFT-OVER BADNIKS.
BUT BEFORE THAT—WE PARTY!
YAAAAY!
YAAAAY!
YAAAAY!

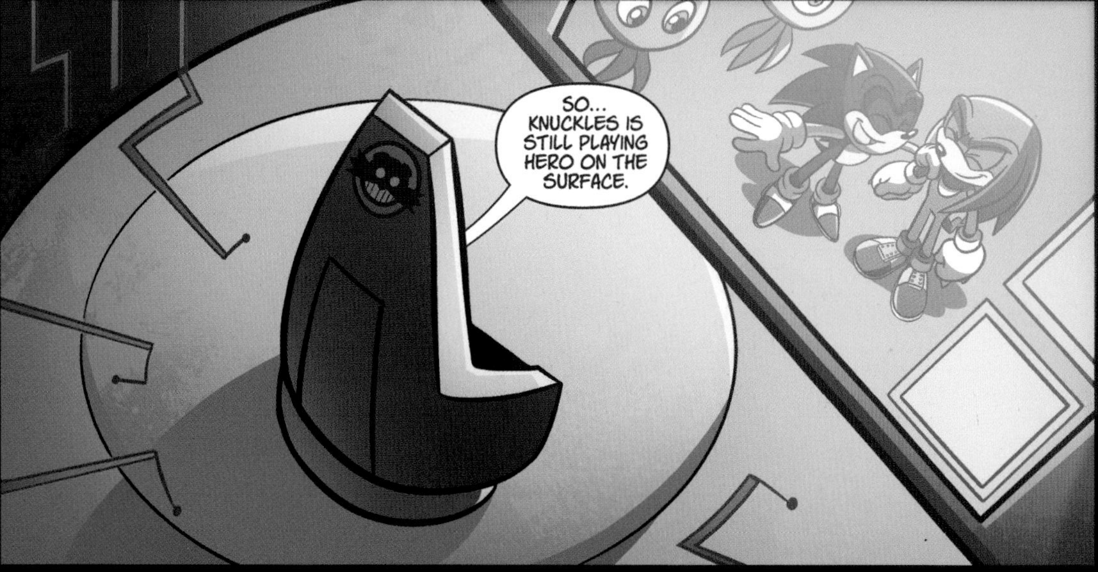
SO... KNUCKLES IS STILL PLAYING HERO ON THE SURFACE.

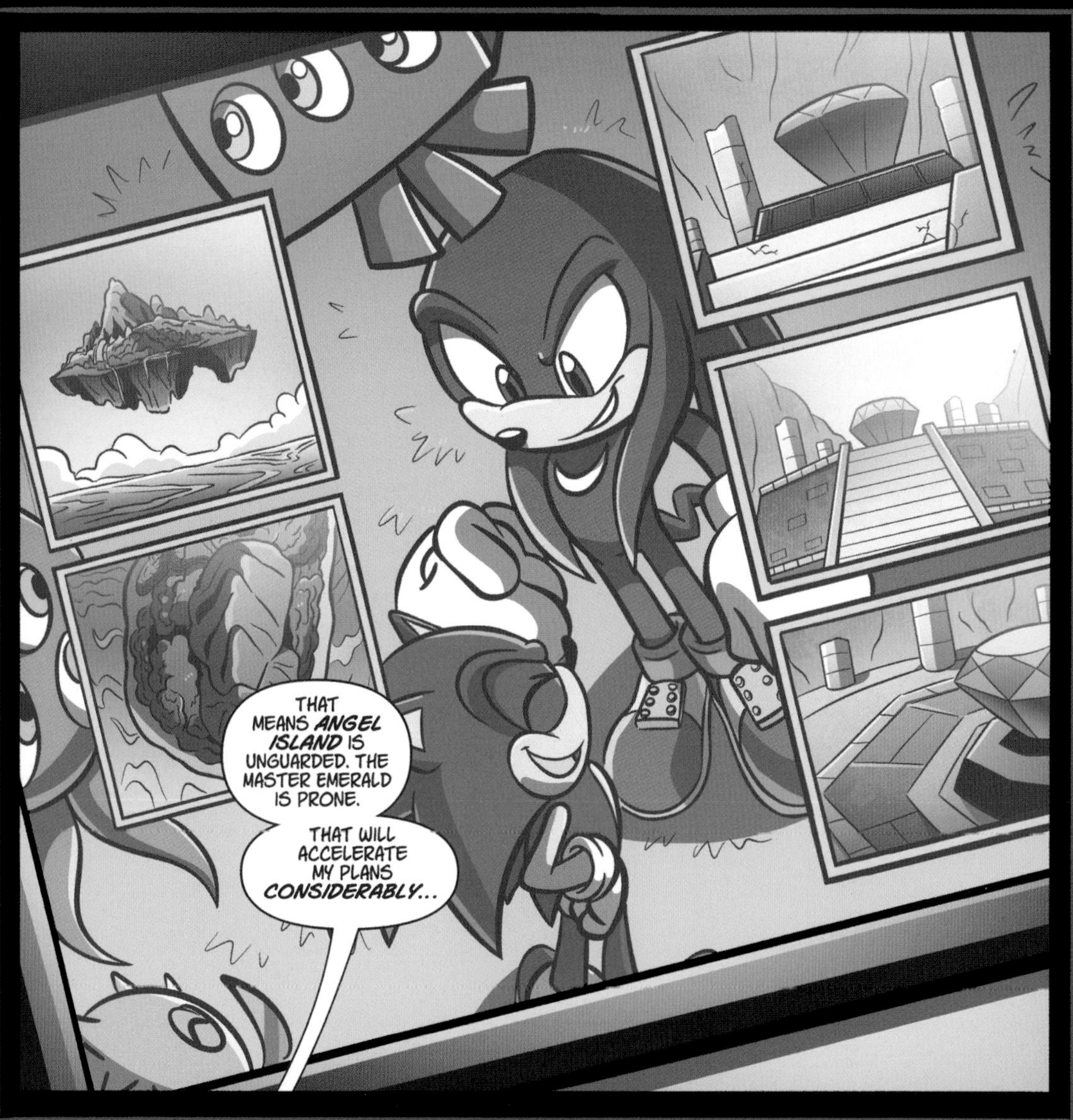
THAT MEANS *ANGEL ISLAND* IS UNGUARDED. THE MASTER EMERALD IS PRONE.
THAT WILL ACCELERATE MY PLANS *CONSIDERABLY*...

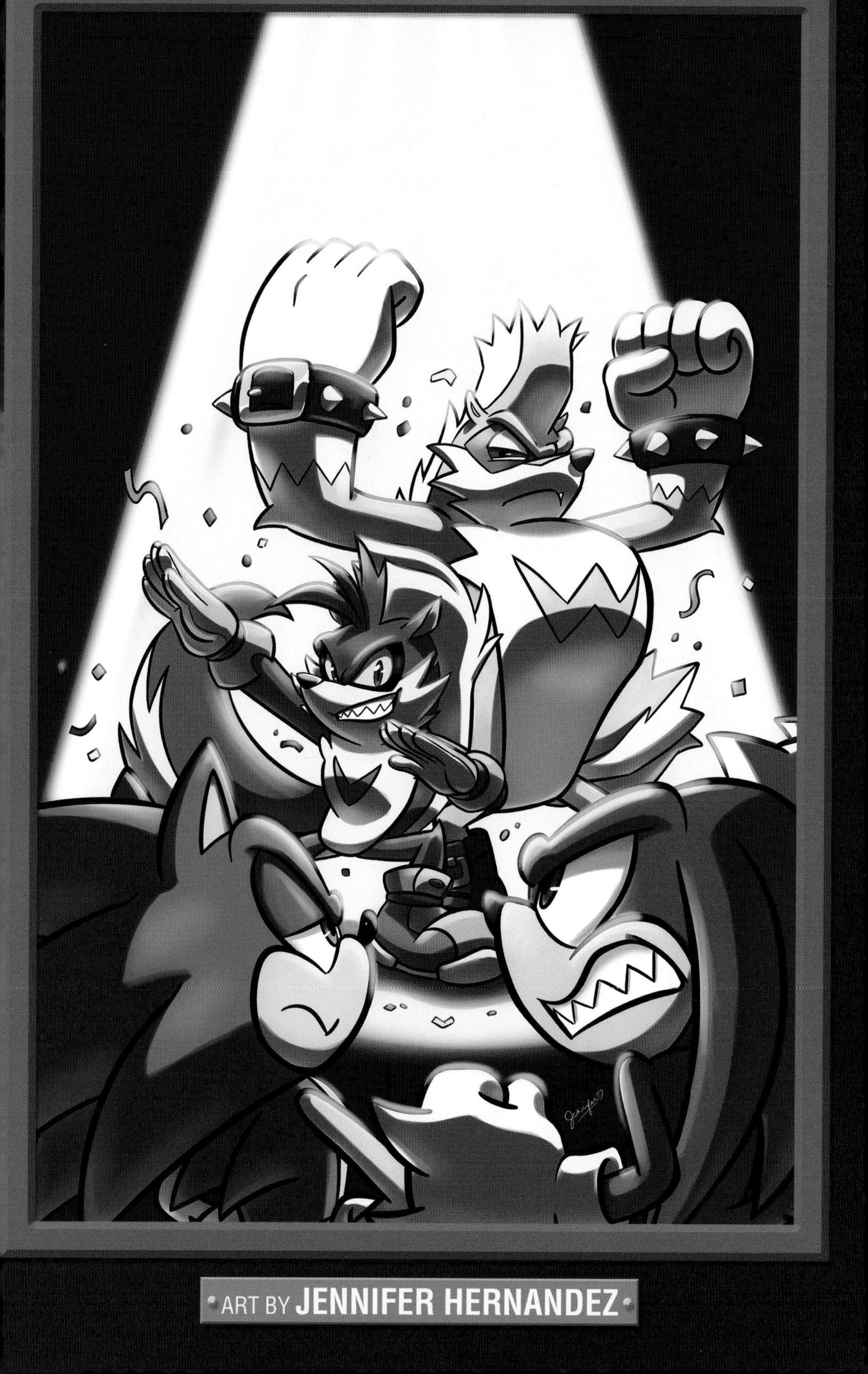

ART BY **JENNIFER HERNANDEZ**

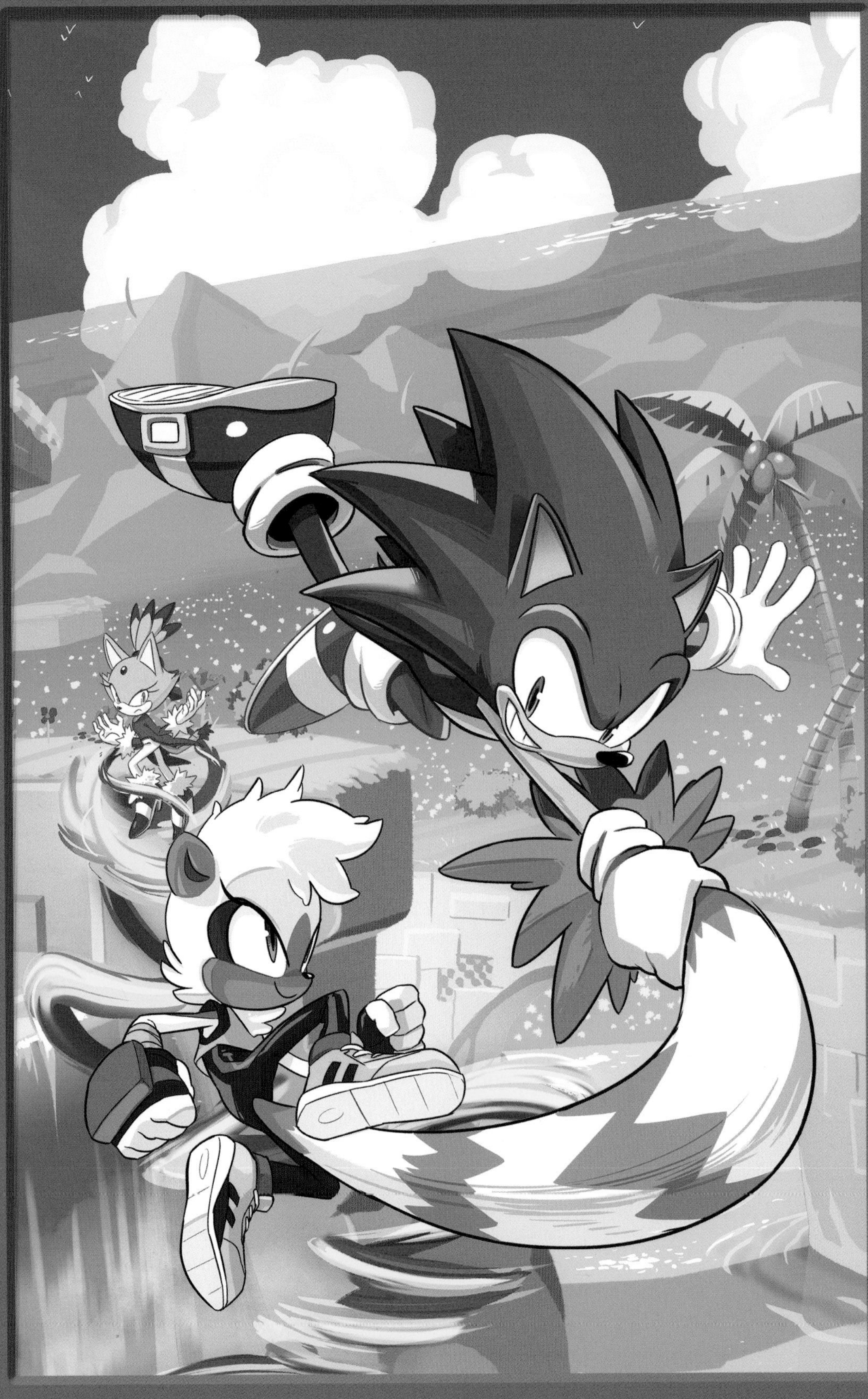

ART BY TYSON HESSE

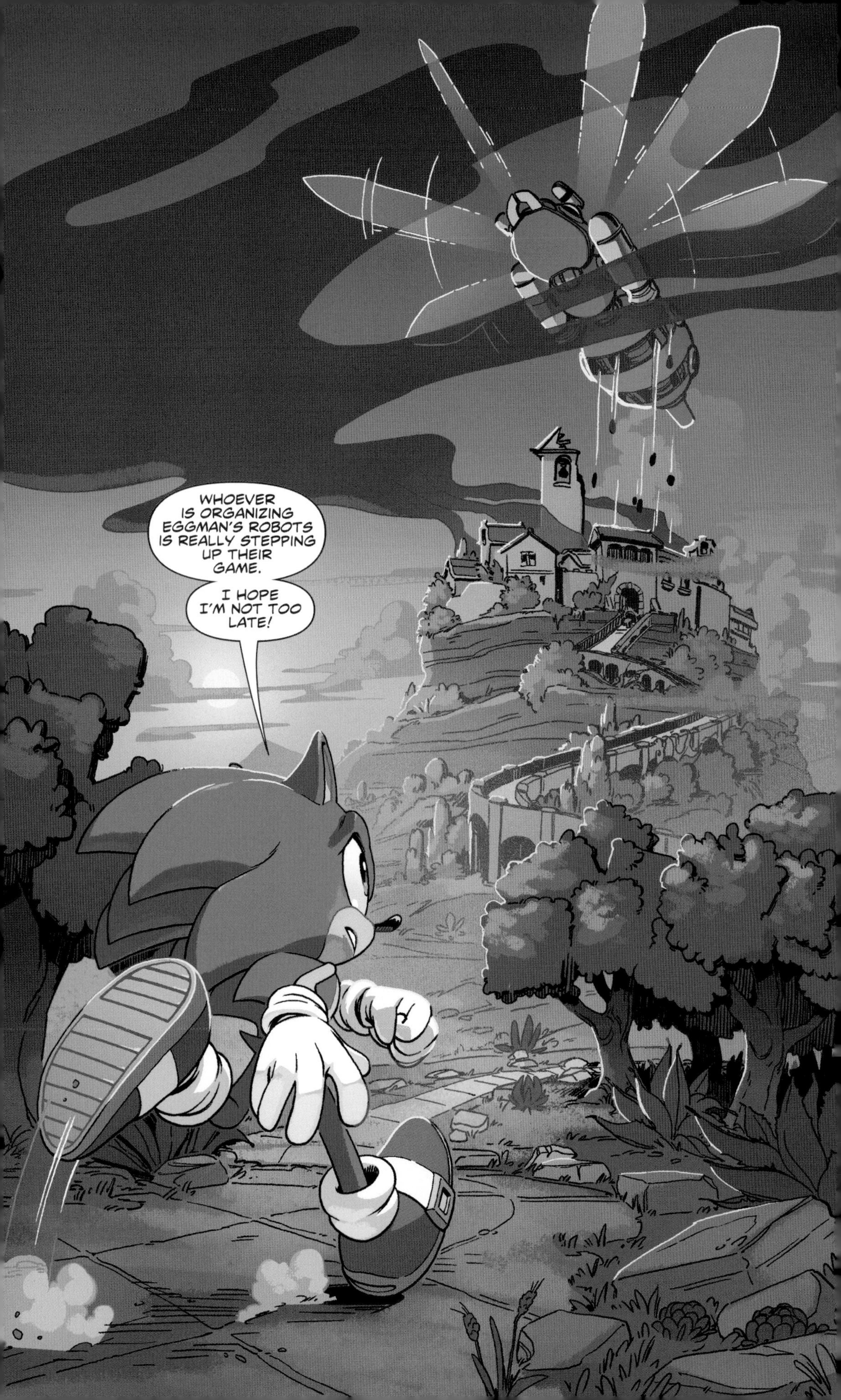
WHOEVER IS ORGANIZING EGGMAN'S ROBOTS IS REALLY STEPPING UP THEIR GAME.
I HOPE I'M NOT TOO LATE!

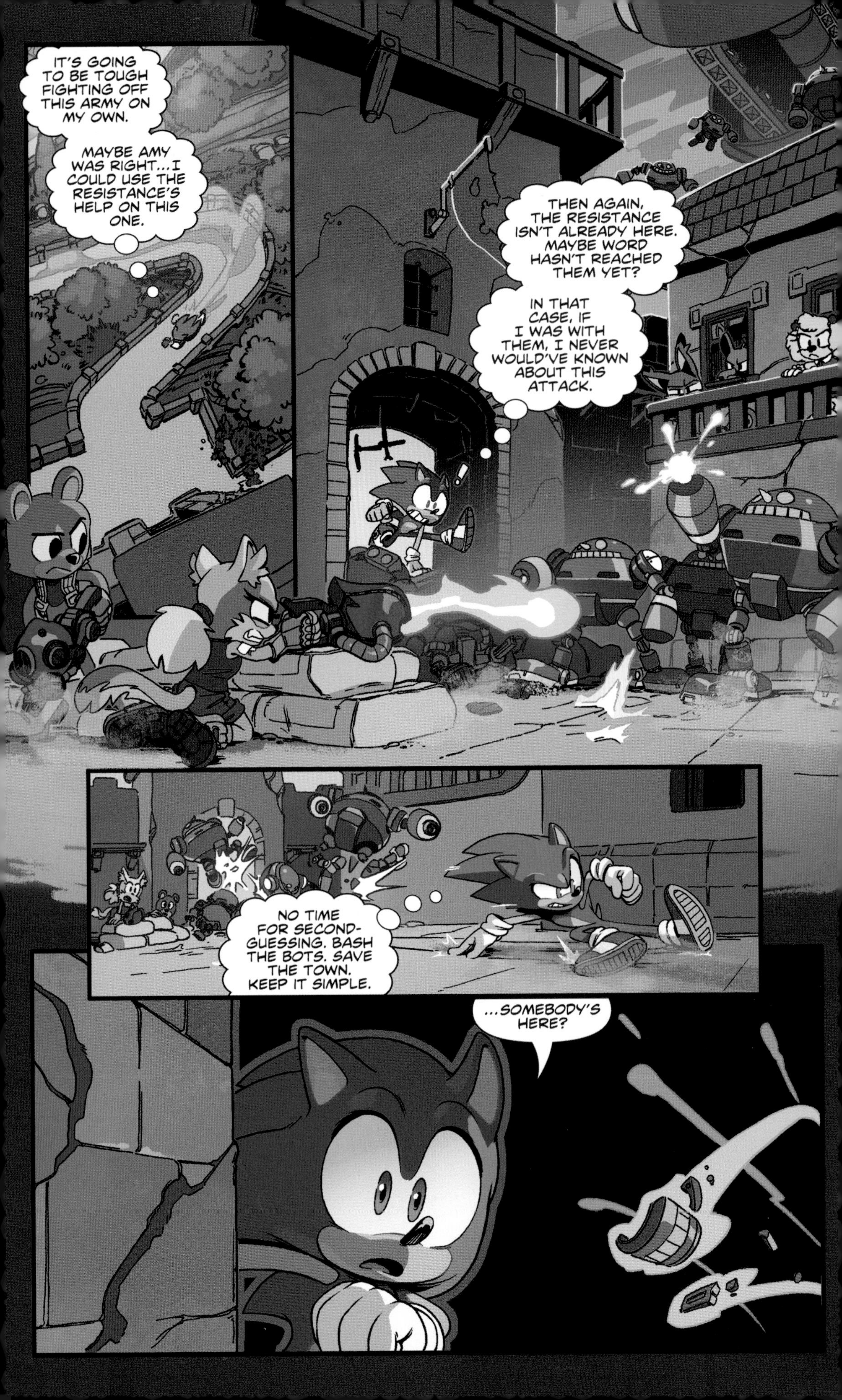

IT'S GOING TO BE TOUGH FIGHTING OFF THIS ARMY ON MY OWN.
MAYBE AMY WAS RIGHT... I COULD USE THE RESISTANCE'S HELP ON THIS ONE.
THEN AGAIN, THE RESISTANCE ISN'T ALREADY HERE. MAYBE WORD HASN'T REACHED THEM YET?
IN THAT CASE, IF I WAS WITH THEM, I NEVER WOULD'VE KNOWN ABOUT THIS ATTACK.
NO TIME FOR SECOND-GUESSING. BASH THE BOTS. SAVE THE TOWN. KEEP IT SIMPLE.
...SOMEBODY'S HERE?

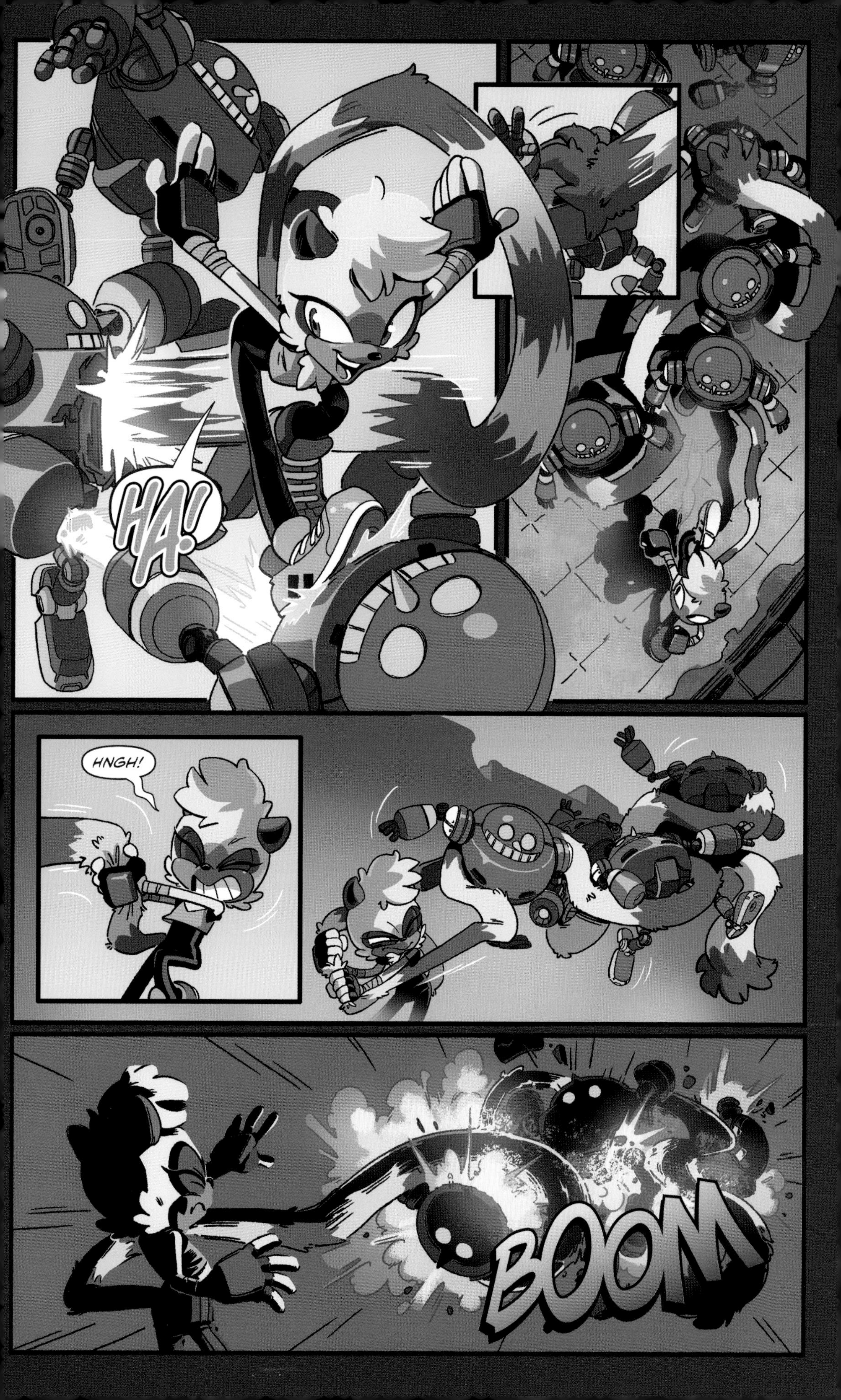
HA!
HNGH!
BOOM

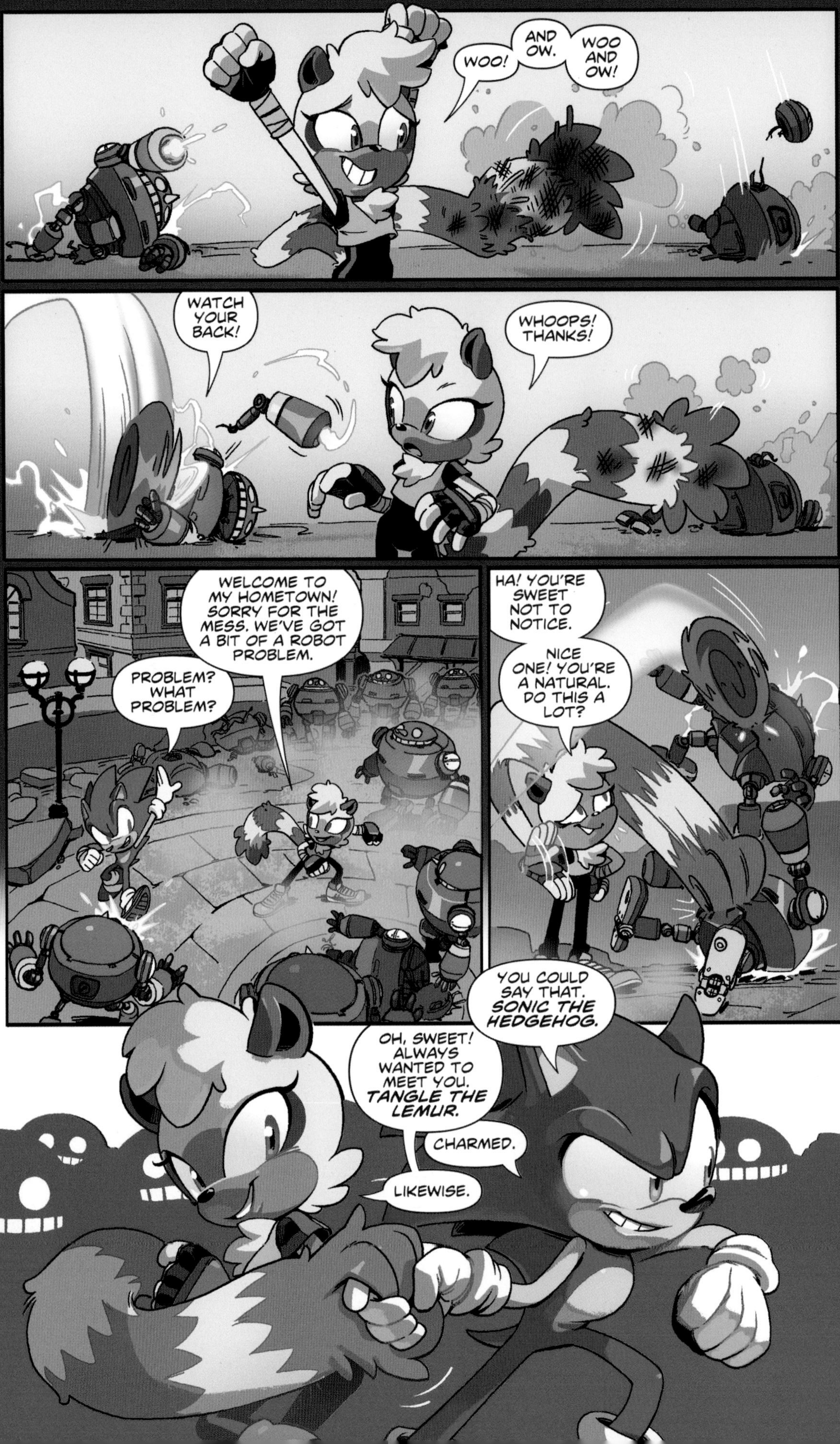
WOO!
AND OW.
WOO AND OW!
WATCH YOUR BACK!
WHOOPS! THANKS!
WELCOME TO MY HOMETOWN! SORRY FOR THE MESS. WE'VE GOT A BIT OF A ROBOT PROBLEM.
PROBLEM? WHAT PROBLEM?
HA! YOU'RE SWEET NOT TO NOTICE.
NICE ONE! YOU'RE A NATURAL. DO THIS A LOT?
YOU COULD SAY THAT. SONIC THE HEDGEHOG.
OH, SWEET! ALWAYS WANTED TO MEET YOU. TANGLE THE LEMUR.
CHARMED.
LIKEWISE.

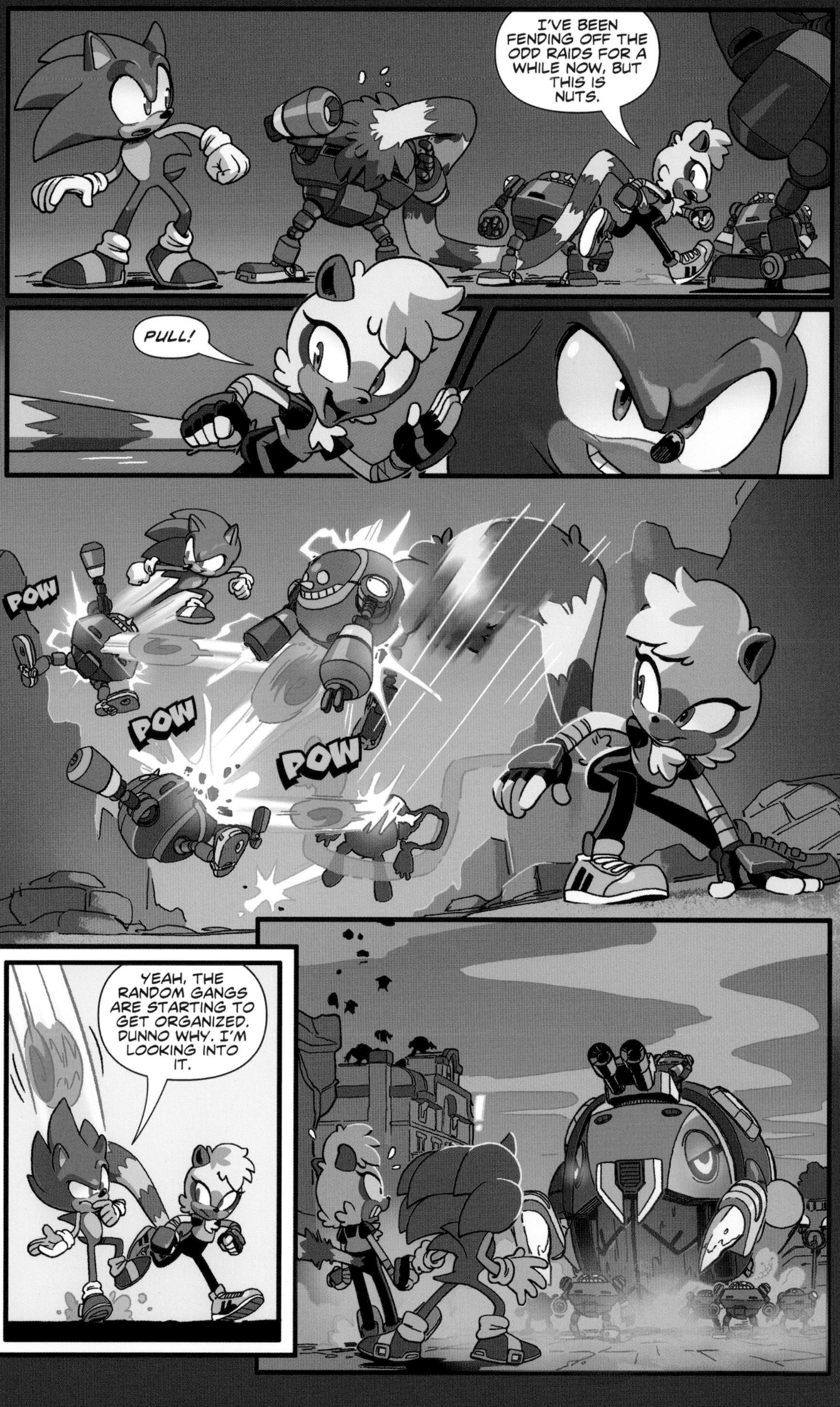
I'VE BEEN FENDING OFF THE ODD RAIDS FOR A WHILE NOW, BUT THIS IS NUTS.
PULL!
POW
POW
POW
YEAH, THE RANDOM GANGS ARE STARTING TO GET ORGANIZED. DUNNO WHY. I'M LOOKING INTO IT.
!

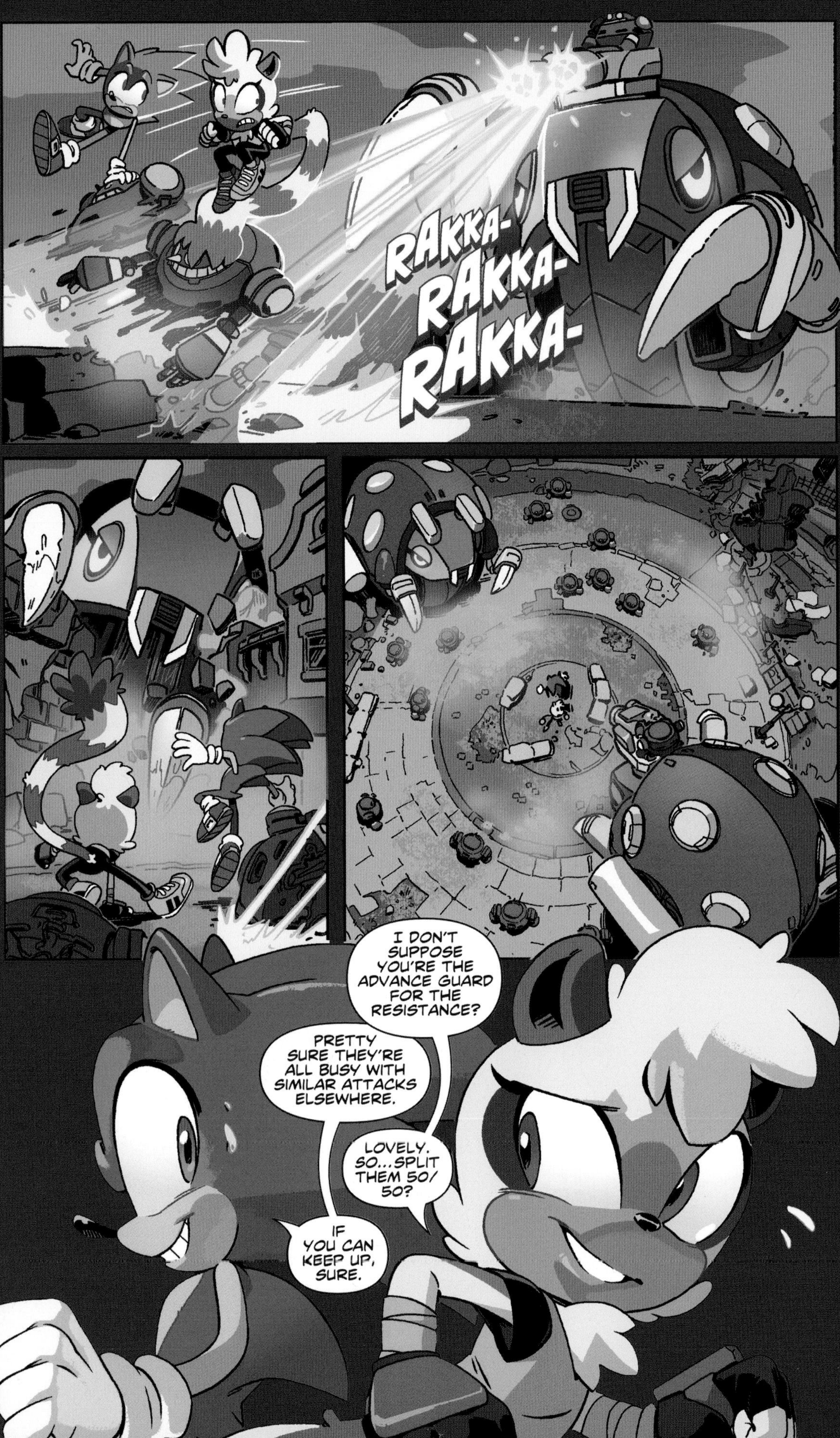
RAKKA-
RAKKA-
RAKKA-
I DON'T SUPPOSE YOU'RE THE ADVANCE GUARD FOR THE RESISTANCE?
PRETTY SURE THEY'RE ALL BUSY WITH SIMILAR ATTACKS ELSEWHERE.
LOVELY. SO...SPLIT THEM 50/50?
IF YOU CAN KEEP UP, SURE.

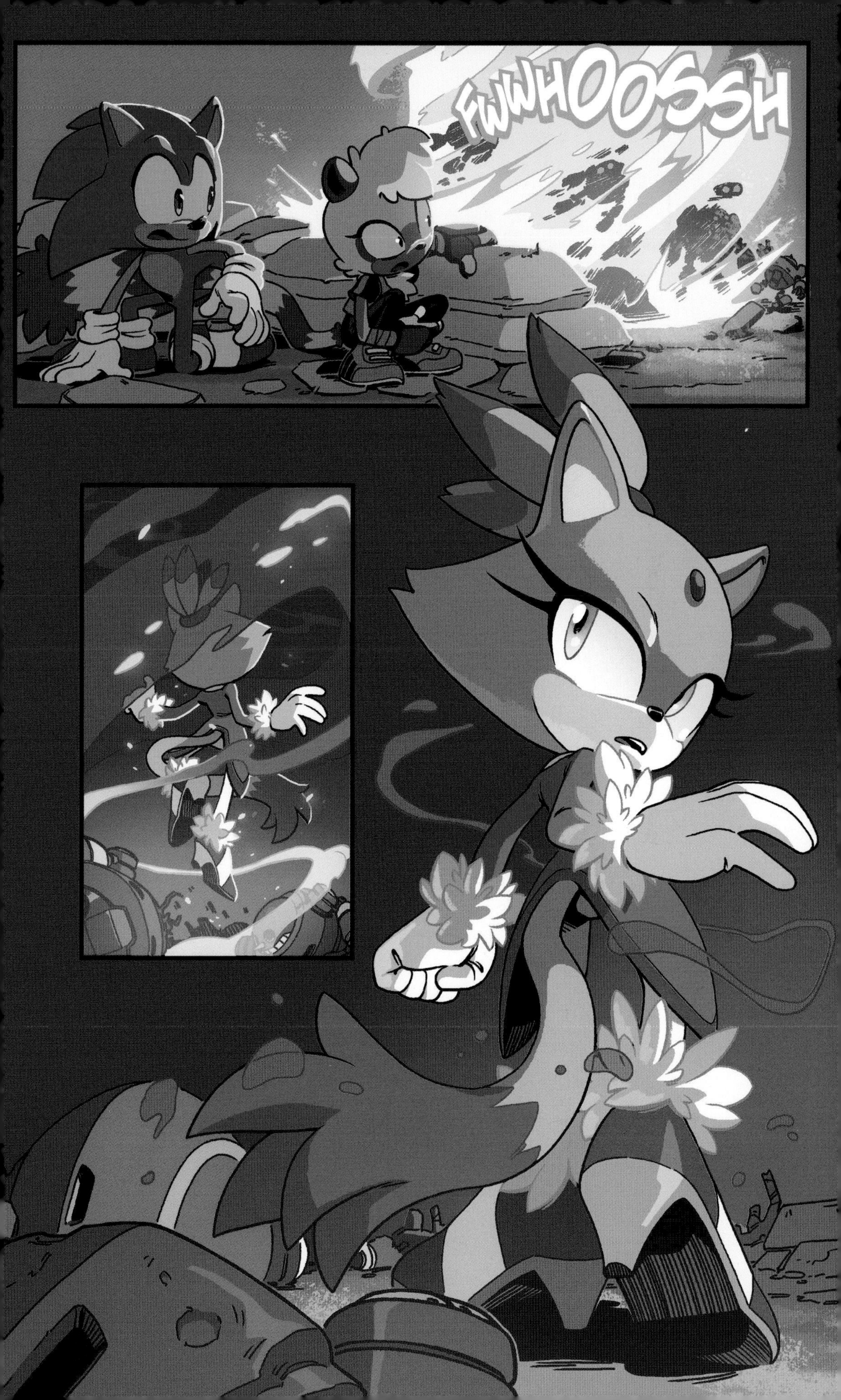
FWWHOOSSH

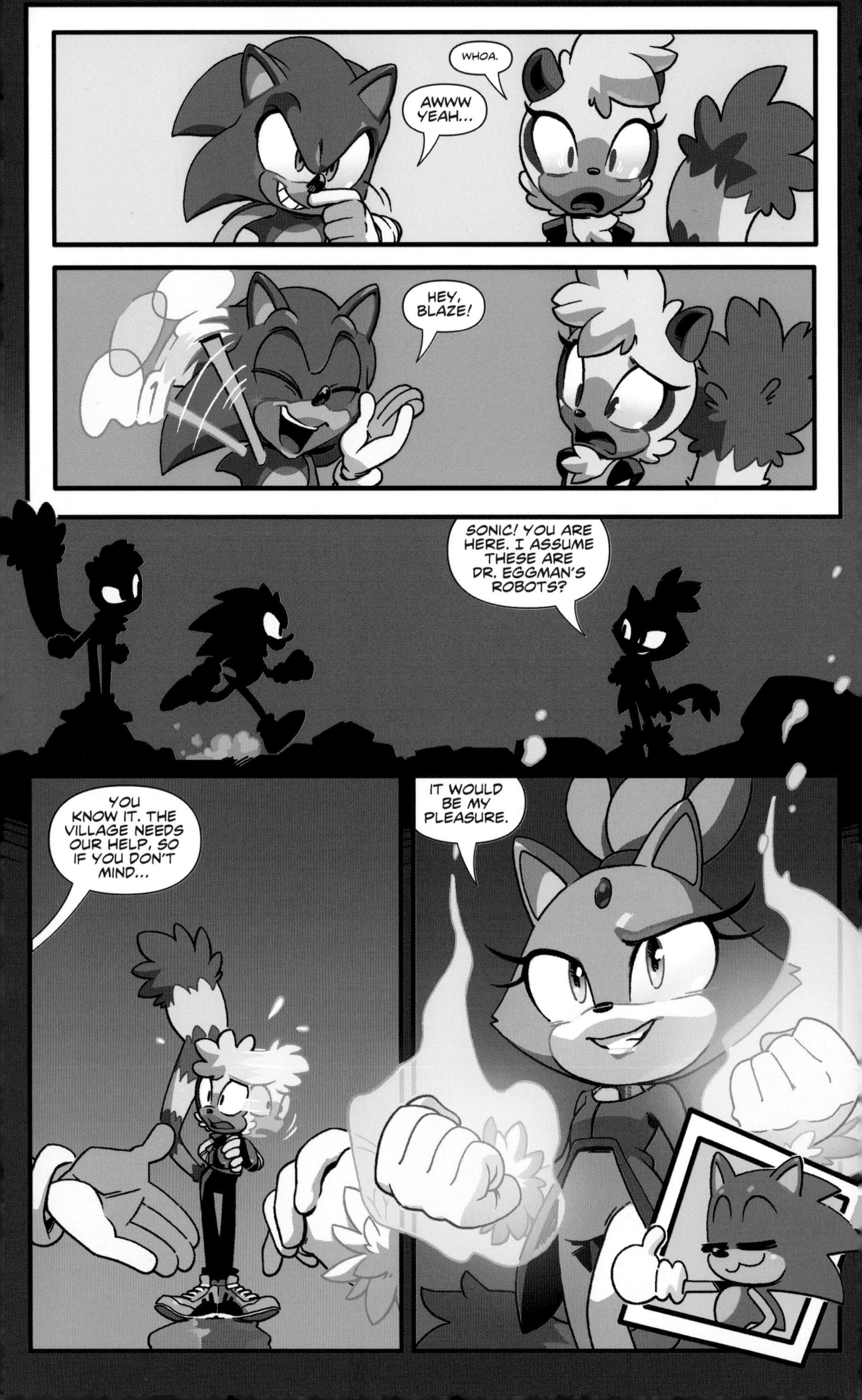
WHOA.
AWWW YEAH...
HEY, BLAZE!
SONIC! YOU ARE HERE. I ASSUME THESE ARE DR. EGGMAN'S ROBOTS?
YOU KNOW IT. THE VILLAGE NEEDS OUR HELP, SO IF YOU DON'T MIND...
IT WOULD BE MY PLEASURE.

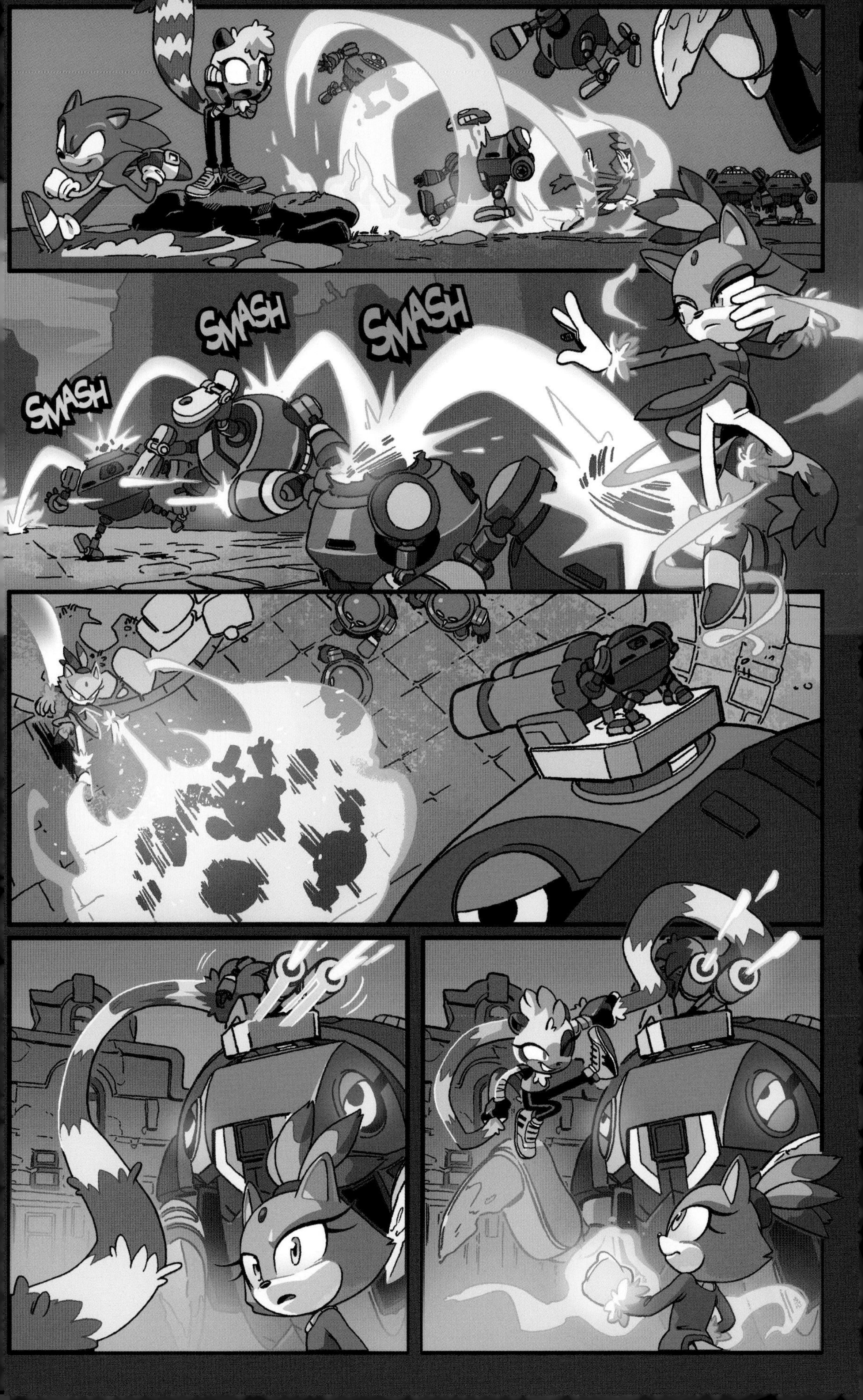
SMASH
SMASH
SMASH

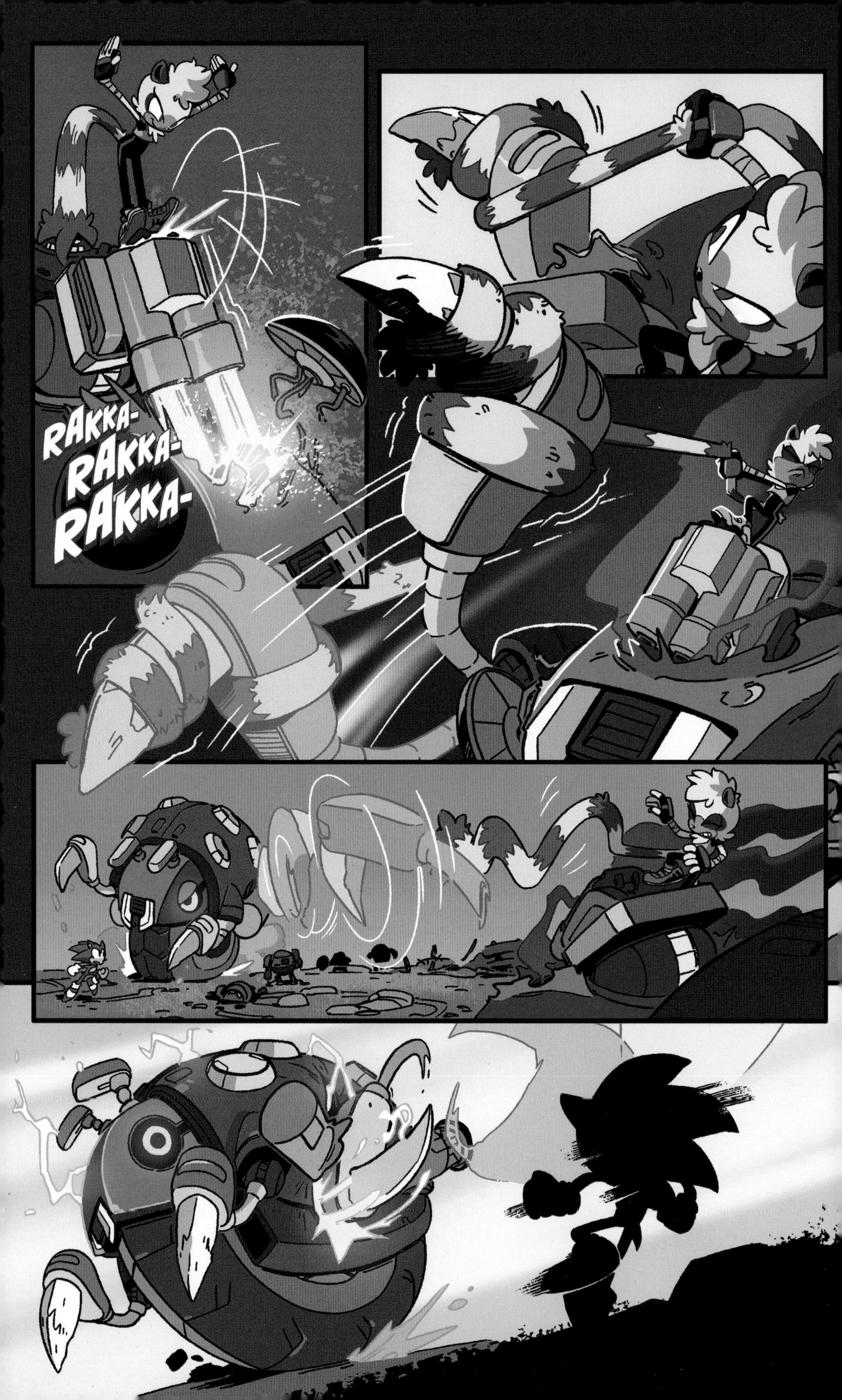
RAKKA-
RAKKA-
RAKKA-

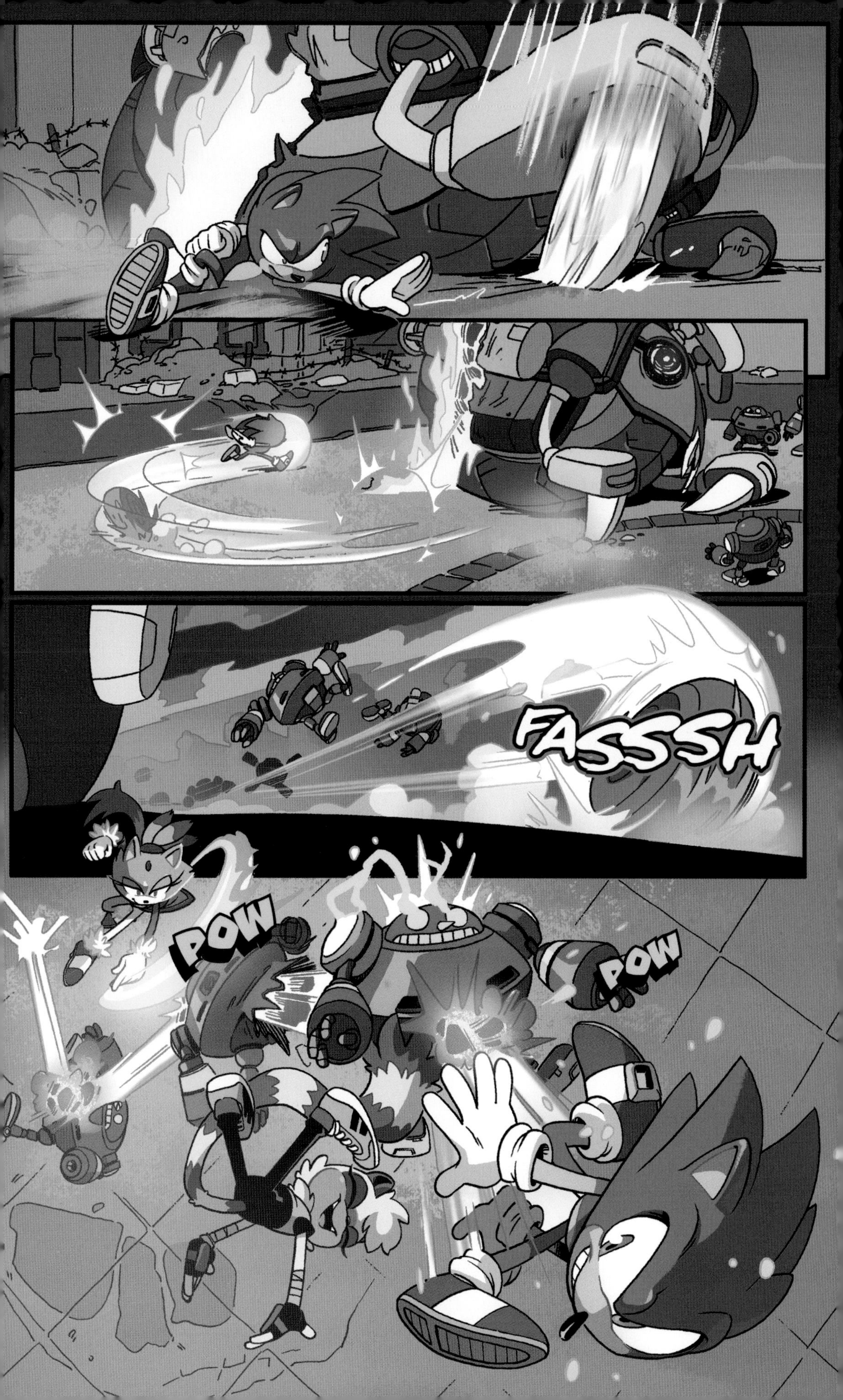
FASSSH
POW
POW

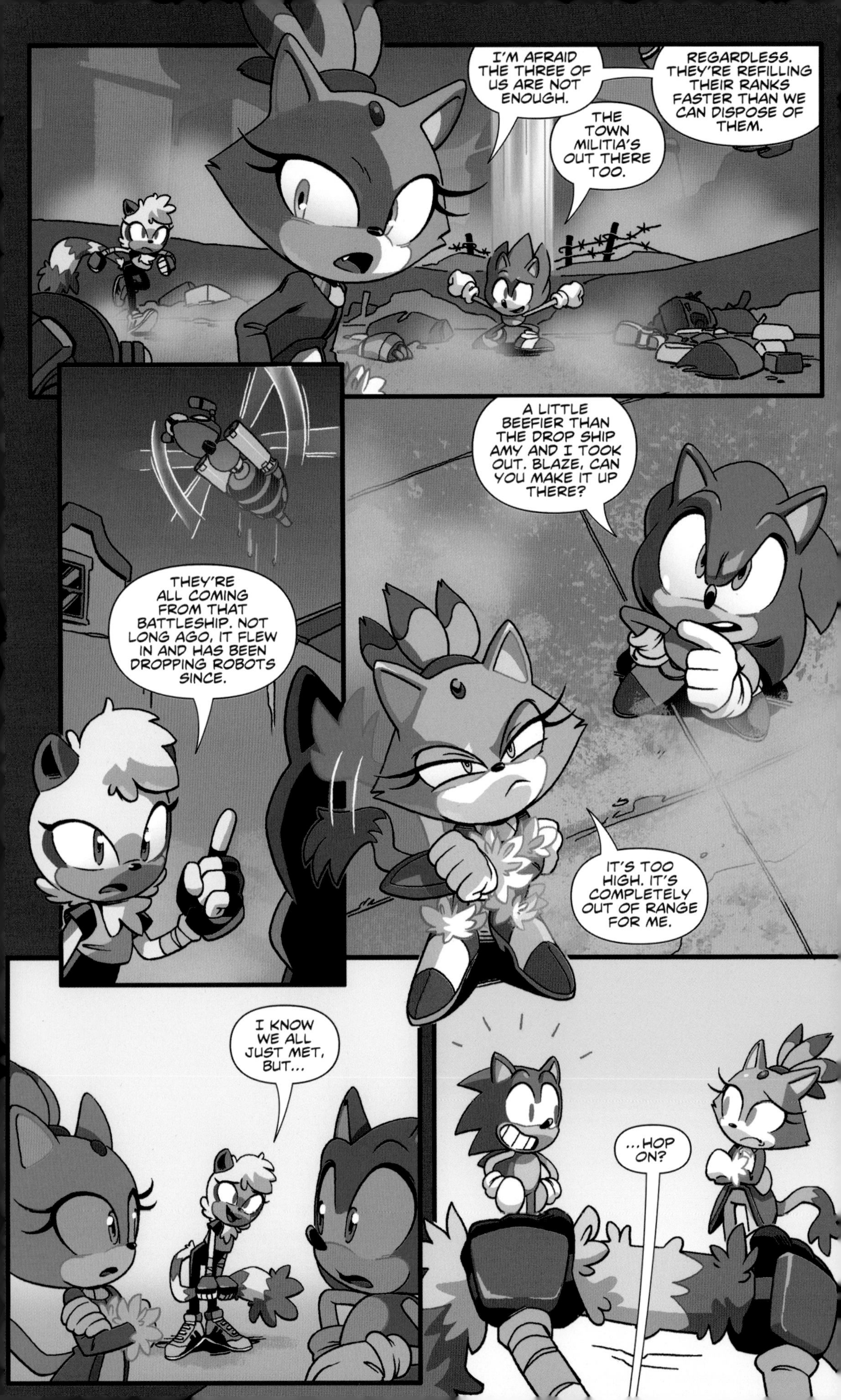

I'M AFRAID THE THREE OF US ARE NOT ENOUGH.
THE TOWN MILITIA'S OUT THERE TOO.
REGARDLESS. THEY'RE REFILLING THEIR RANKS FASTER THAN WE CAN DISPOSE OF THEM.
THEY'RE ALL COMING FROM THAT BATTLESHIP. NOT LONG AGO, IT FLEW IN AND HAS BEEN DROPPING ROBOTS SINCE.
A LITTLE BEEFIER THAN THE DROP SHIP AMY AND I TOOK OUT. BLAZE, CAN YOU MAKE IT UP THERE?
IT'S TOO HIGH. IT'S COMPLETELY OUT OF RANGE FOR ME.
I KNOW WE ALL JUST MET, BUT...
...HOP ON?

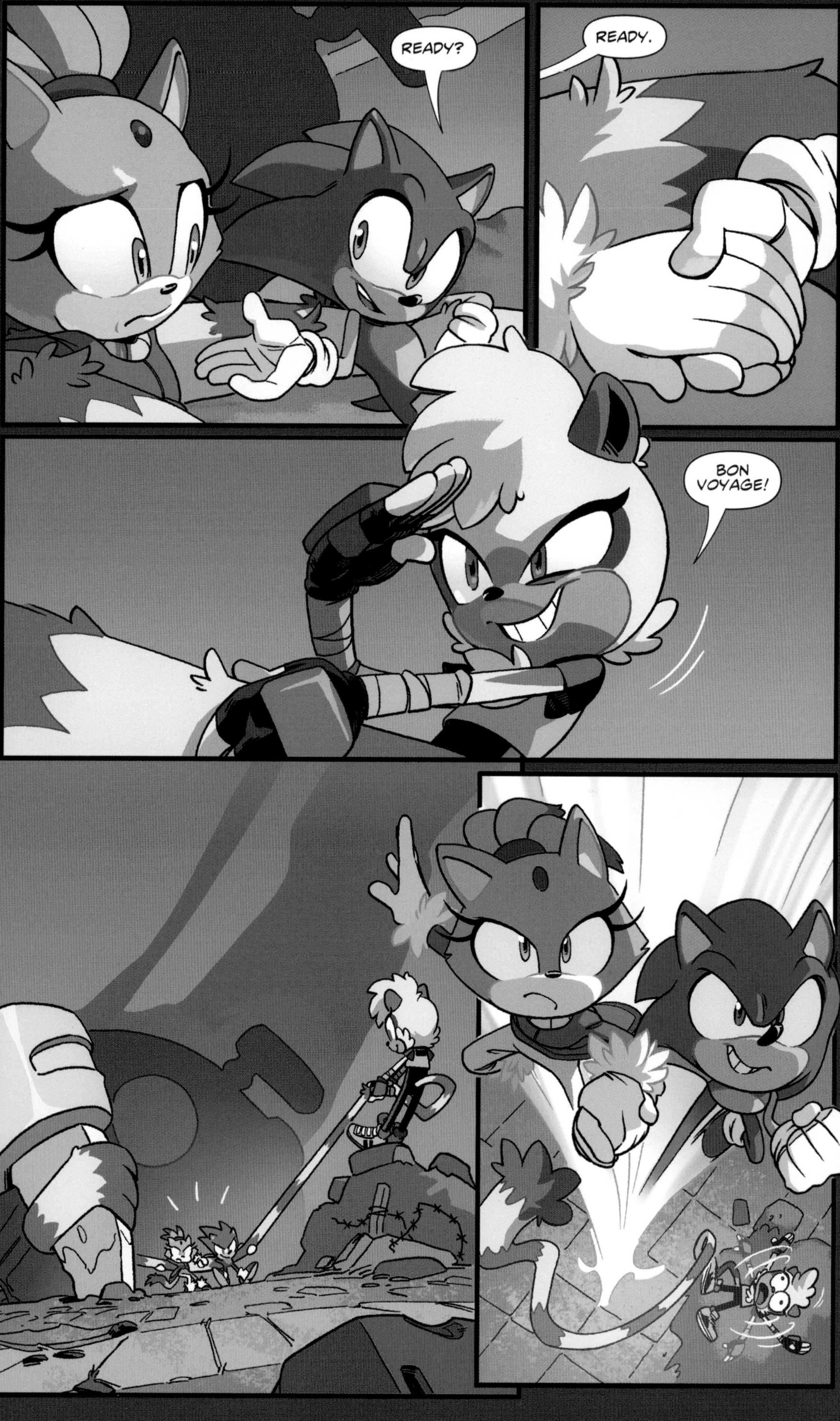
READY?
READY.
BON VOYAGE!

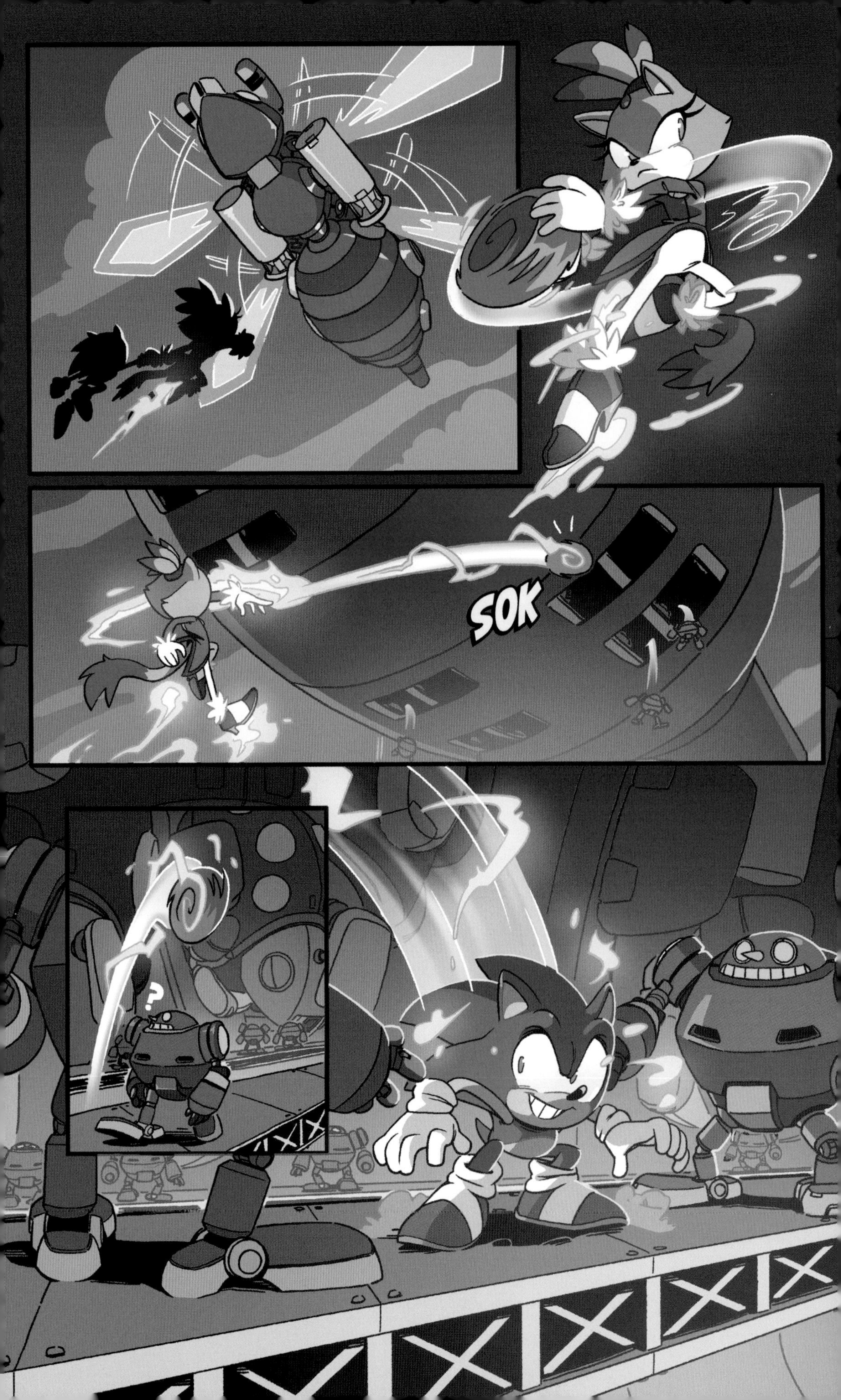
SOK
?

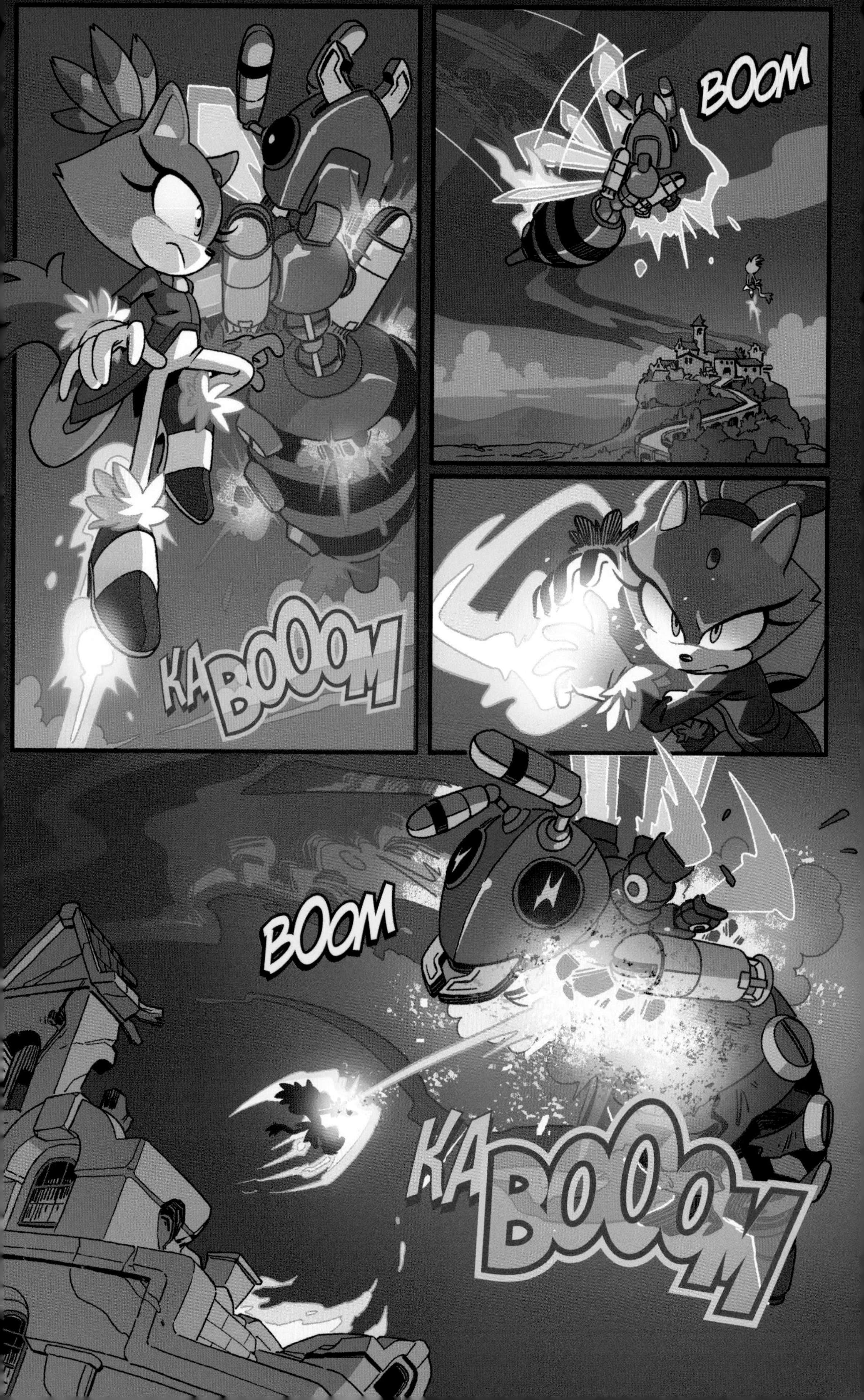
KABOOOM
BOOM
BOOM
KABOOOM

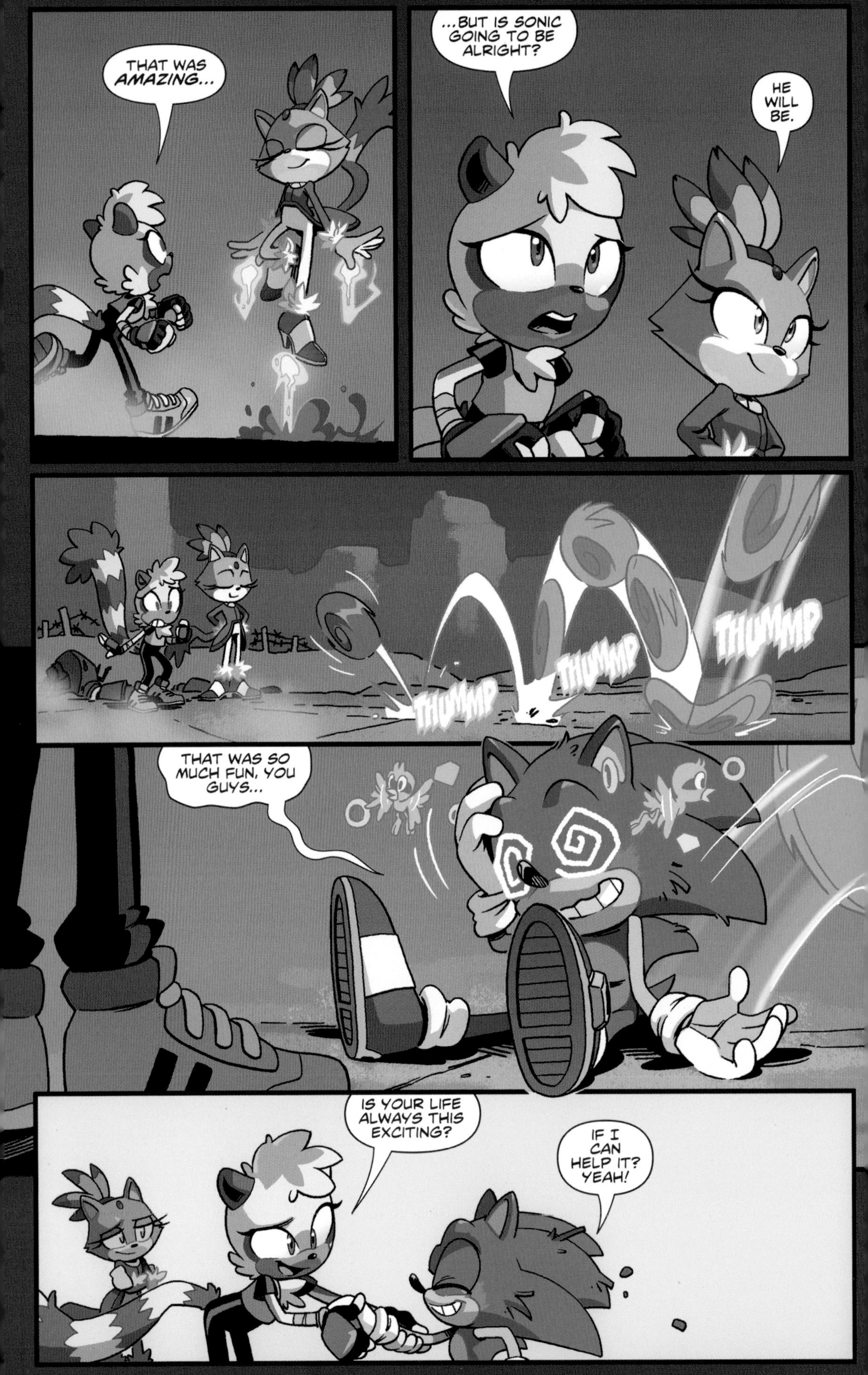
THAT WAS AMAZING...
...BUT IS SONIC GOING TO BE ALRIGHT?
HE WILL BE.
THUMMP
THUMMP
THUMMP
THAT WAS SO MUCH FUN, YOU GUYS...
IS YOUR LIFE ALWAYS THIS EXCITING?
IF I CAN HELP IT? YEAH!

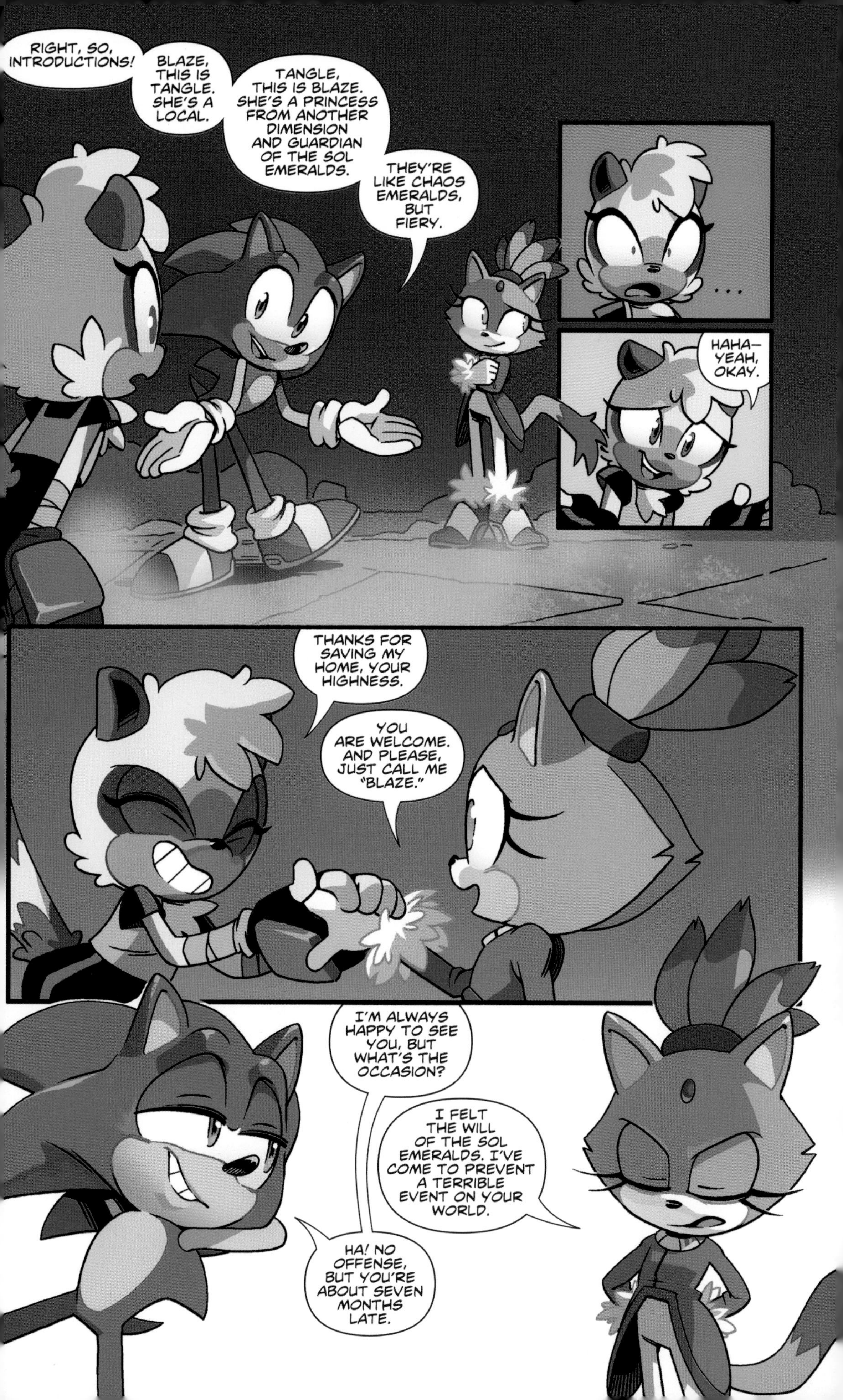
RIGHT, SO, INTRODUCTIONS!
BLAZE, THIS IS TANGLE. SHE'S A LOCAL.
TANGLE, THIS IS BLAZE. SHE'S A PRINCESS FROM ANOTHER DIMENSION AND GUARDIAN OF THE SOL EMERALDS.
THEY'RE LIKE CHAOS EMERALDS, BUT FIERY.
...
HAHA—YEAH, OKAY.
THANKS FOR SAVING MY HOME, YOUR HIGHNESS.
YOU ARE WELCOME. AND PLEASE, JUST CALL ME "BLAZE."
I'M ALWAYS HAPPY TO SEE YOU, BUT WHAT'S THE OCCASION?
I FELT THE WILL OF THE SOL EMERALDS. I'VE COME TO PREVENT A TERRIBLE EVENT ON YOUR WORLD.
HA! NO OFFENSE, BUT YOU'RE ABOUT SEVEN MONTHS LATE.

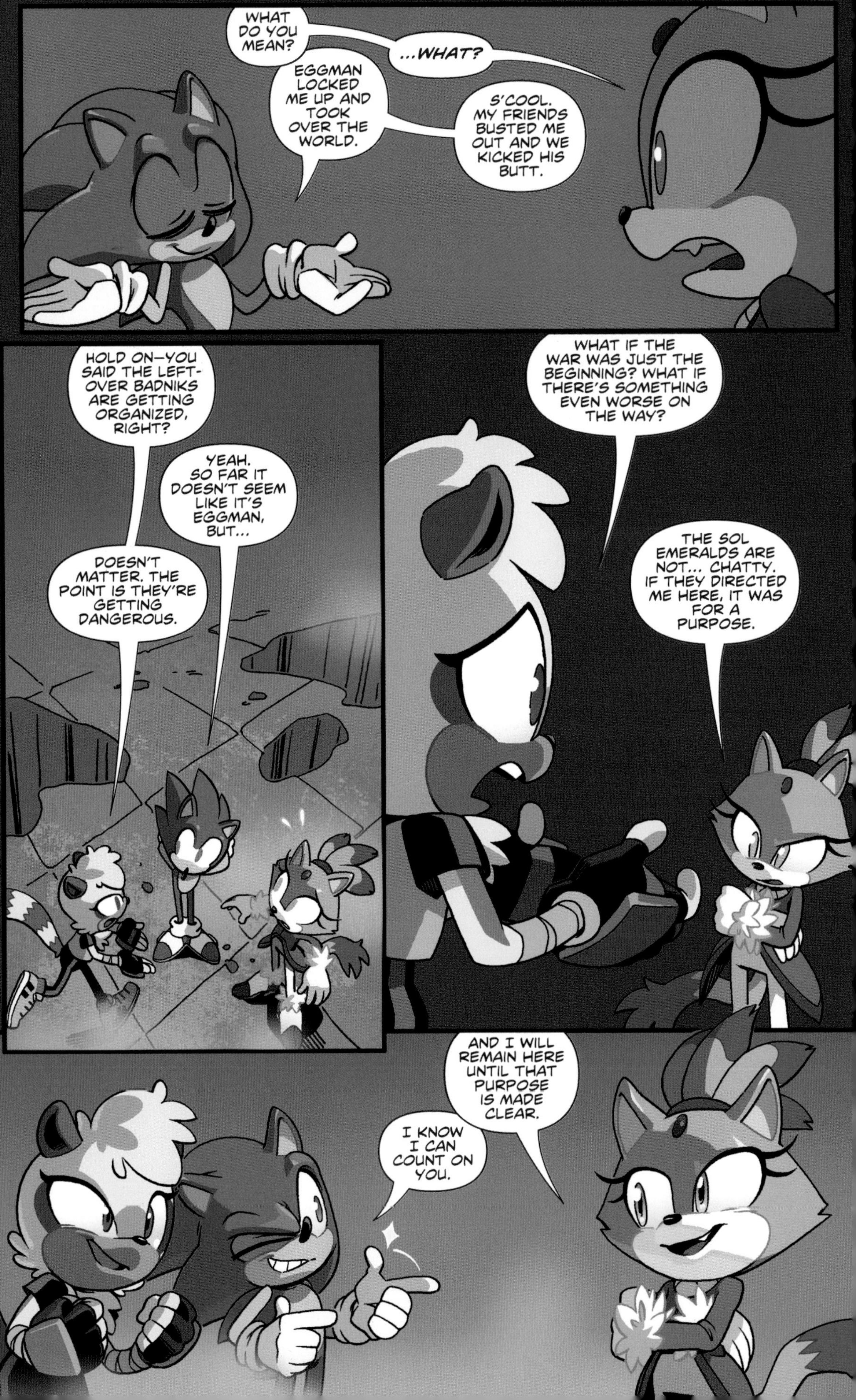

WHAT DO YOU MEAN?
...WHAT?
EGGMAN LOCKED ME UP AND TOOK OVER THE WORLD.
S'COOL. MY FRIENDS BUSTED ME OUT AND WE KICKED HIS BUTT.
HOLD ON—YOU SAID THE LEFT-OVER BADNIKS ARE GETTING ORGANIZED, RIGHT?
YEAH. SO FAR IT DOESN'T SEEM LIKE IT'S EGGMAN, BUT...
DOESN'T MATTER. THE POINT IS THEY'RE GETTING DANGEROUS.
WHAT IF THE WAR WAS JUST THE BEGINNING? WHAT IF THERE'S SOMETHING EVEN WORSE ON THE WAY?
THE SOL EMERALDS ARE NOT... CHATTY. IF THEY DIRECTED ME HERE, IT WAS FOR A PURPOSE.
AND I WILL REMAIN HERE UNTIL THAT PURPOSE IS MADE CLEAR.
I KNOW I CAN COUNT ON YOU.

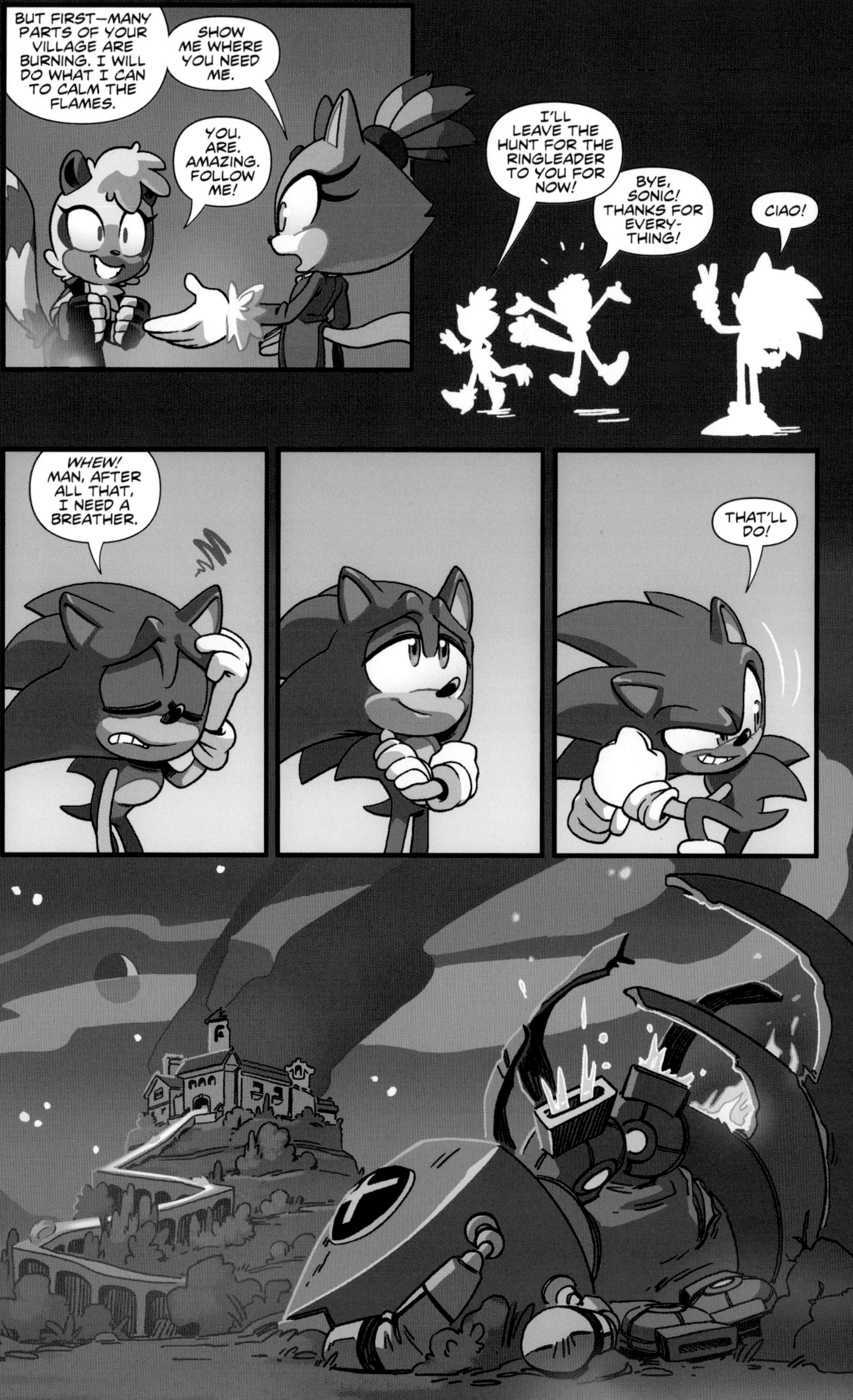
BUT FIRST—MANY PARTS OF YOUR VILLAGE ARE BURNING. I WILL DO WHAT I CAN TO CALM THE FLAMES.
SHOW ME WHERE YOU NEED ME.
YOU. ARE. AMAZING. FOLLOW ME!
I'LL LEAVE THE HUNT FOR THE RINGLEADER TO YOU FOR NOW!
BYE, SONIC! THANKS FOR EVERY-THING!
CIAO!
WHEW! MAN, AFTER ALL THAT, I NEED A BREATHER.
THAT'LL DO!

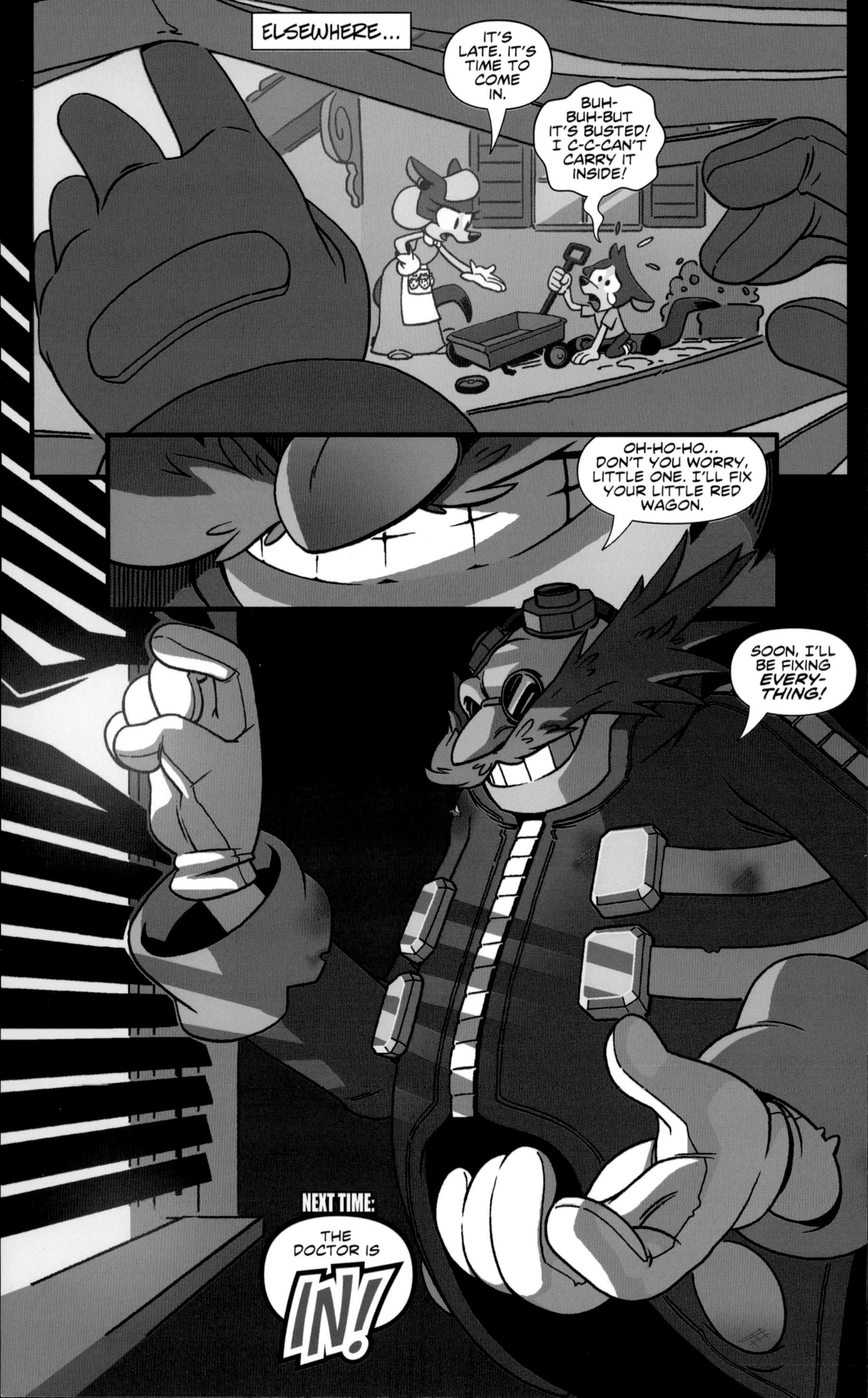
ELSEWHERE...
IT'S LATE. IT'S TIME TO COME IN.
BUH-BUH-BUT IT'S BUSTED! I C-C-CAN'T CARRY IT INSIDE!
OH-HO-HO... DON'T YOU WORRY, LITTLE ONE. I'LL FIX YOUR LITTLE RED WAGON.
SOON, I'LL BE FIXING EVERY-THING!
NEXT TIME:
THE DOCTOR IS IN!

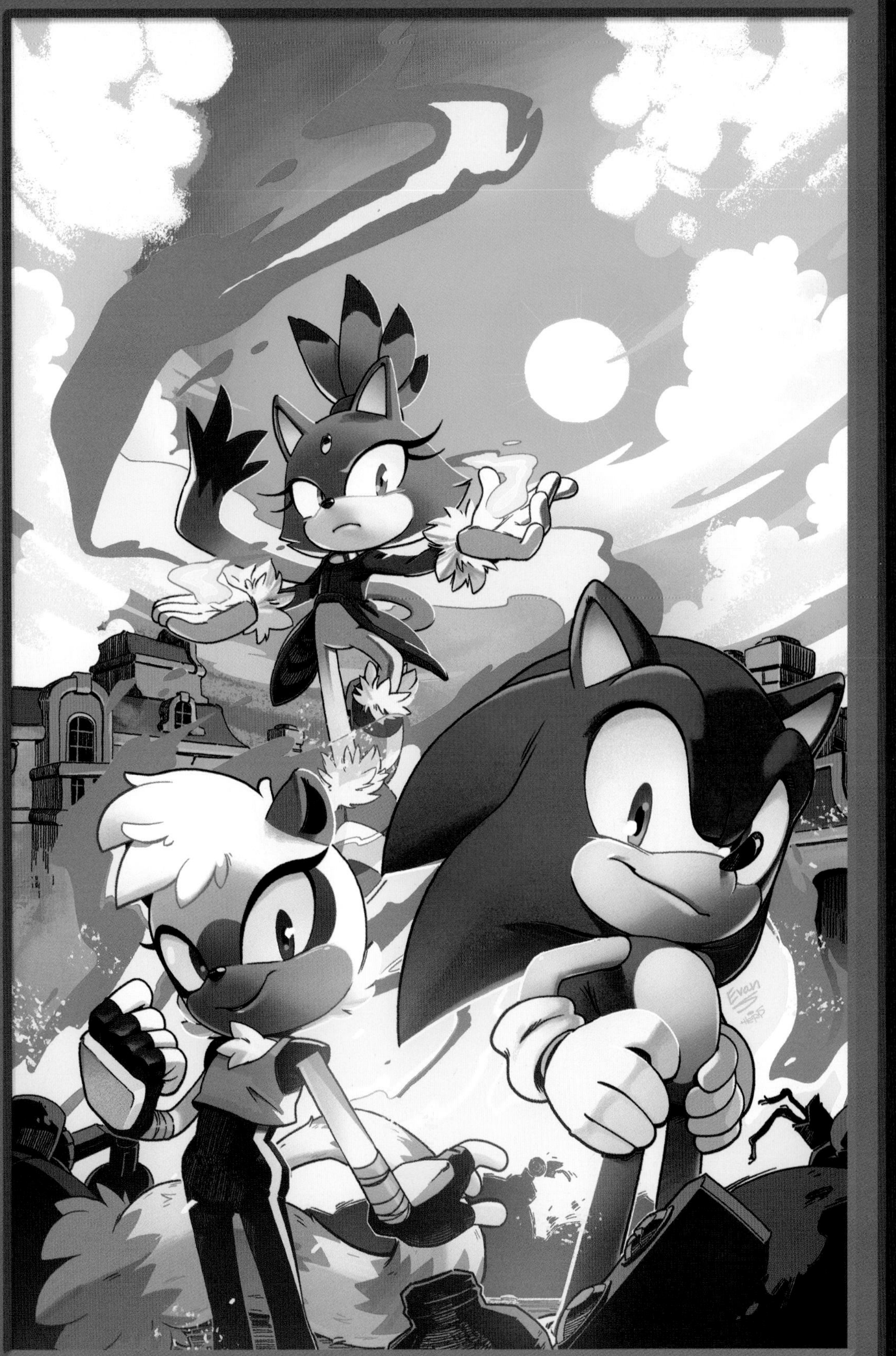
Evan

ART BY **EVAN STANLEY** COLORS BY **MATT HERMS**

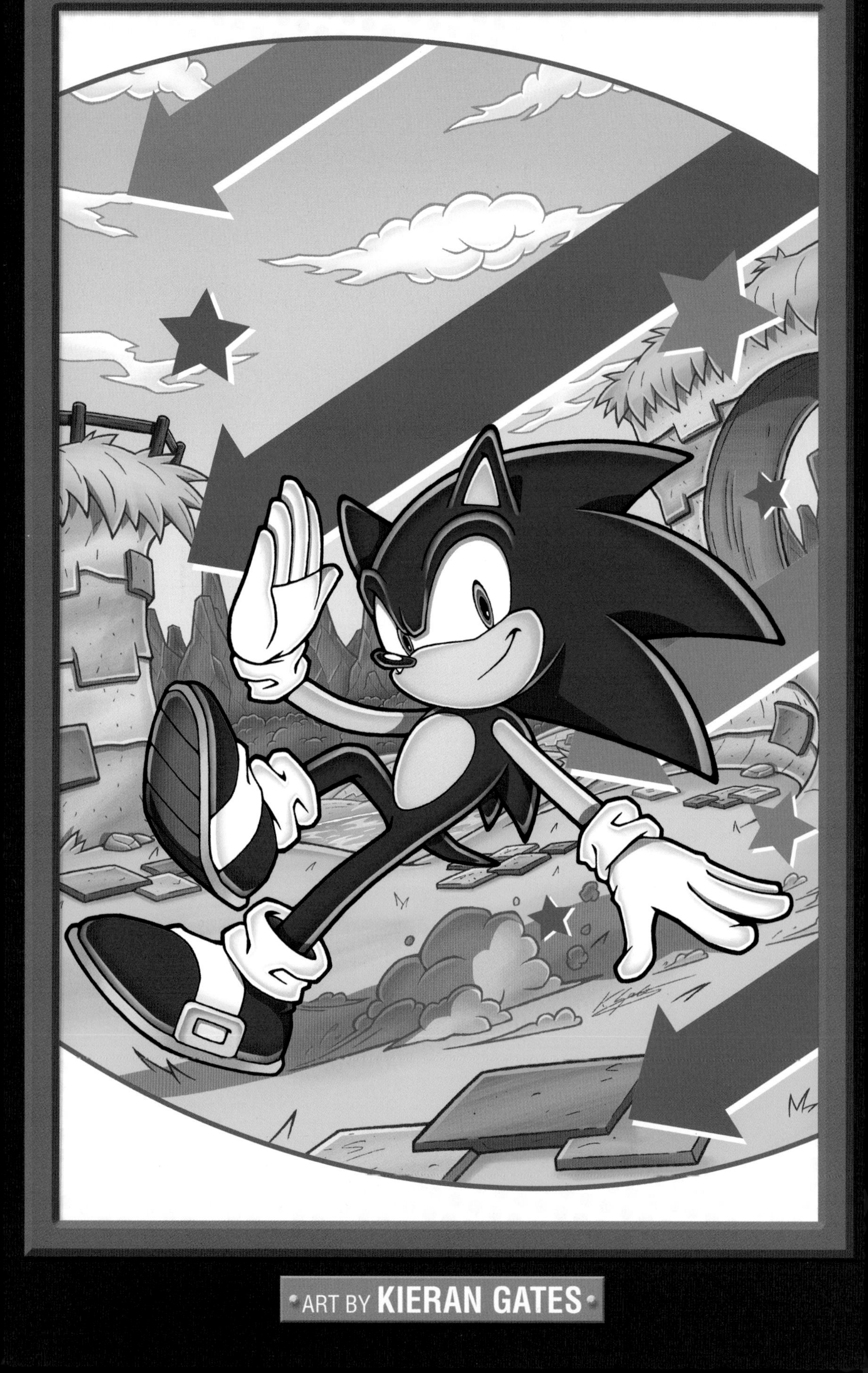

ART BY **KIERAN GATES**

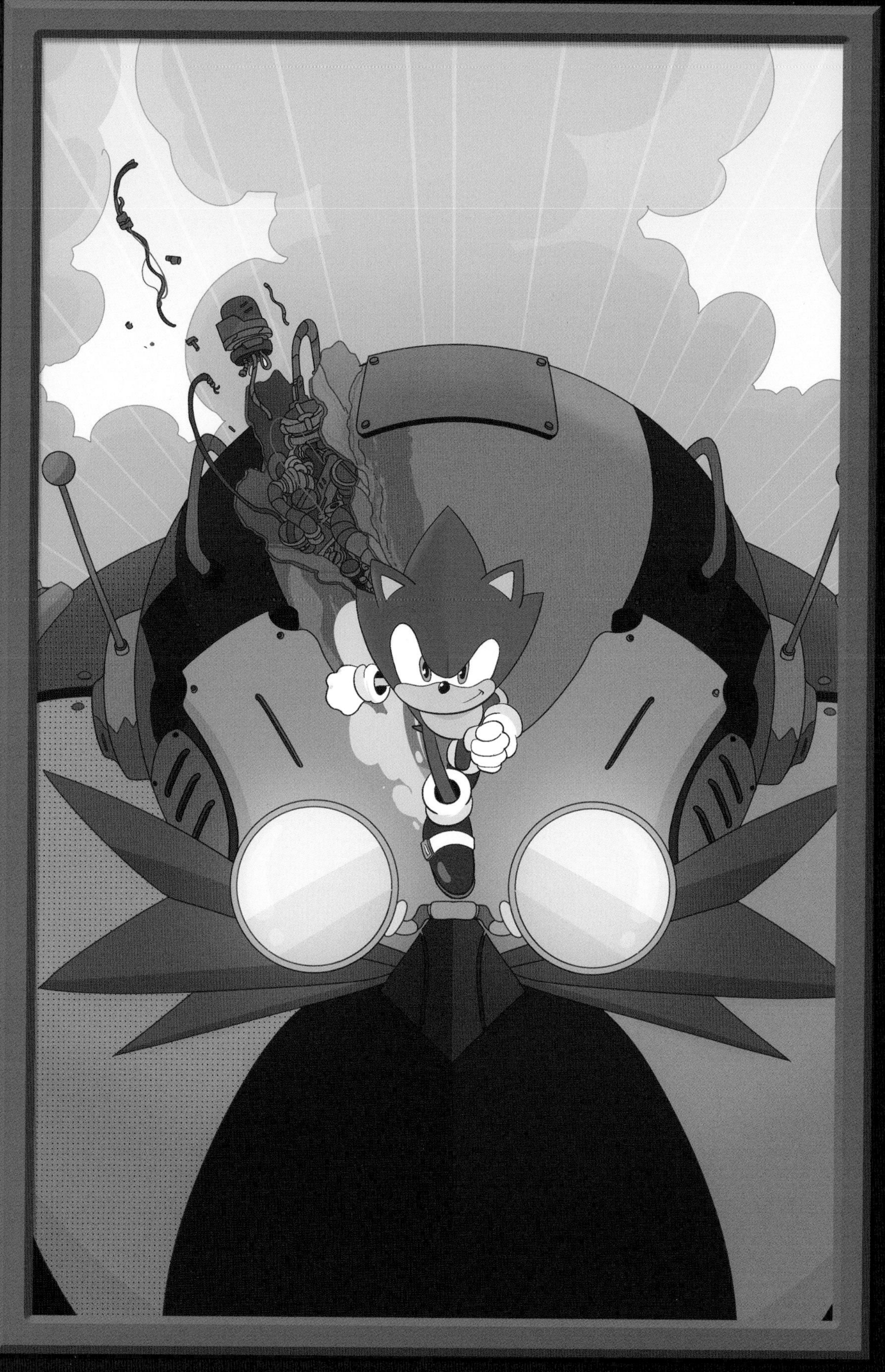

ART BY **DEVIN KRAFT**

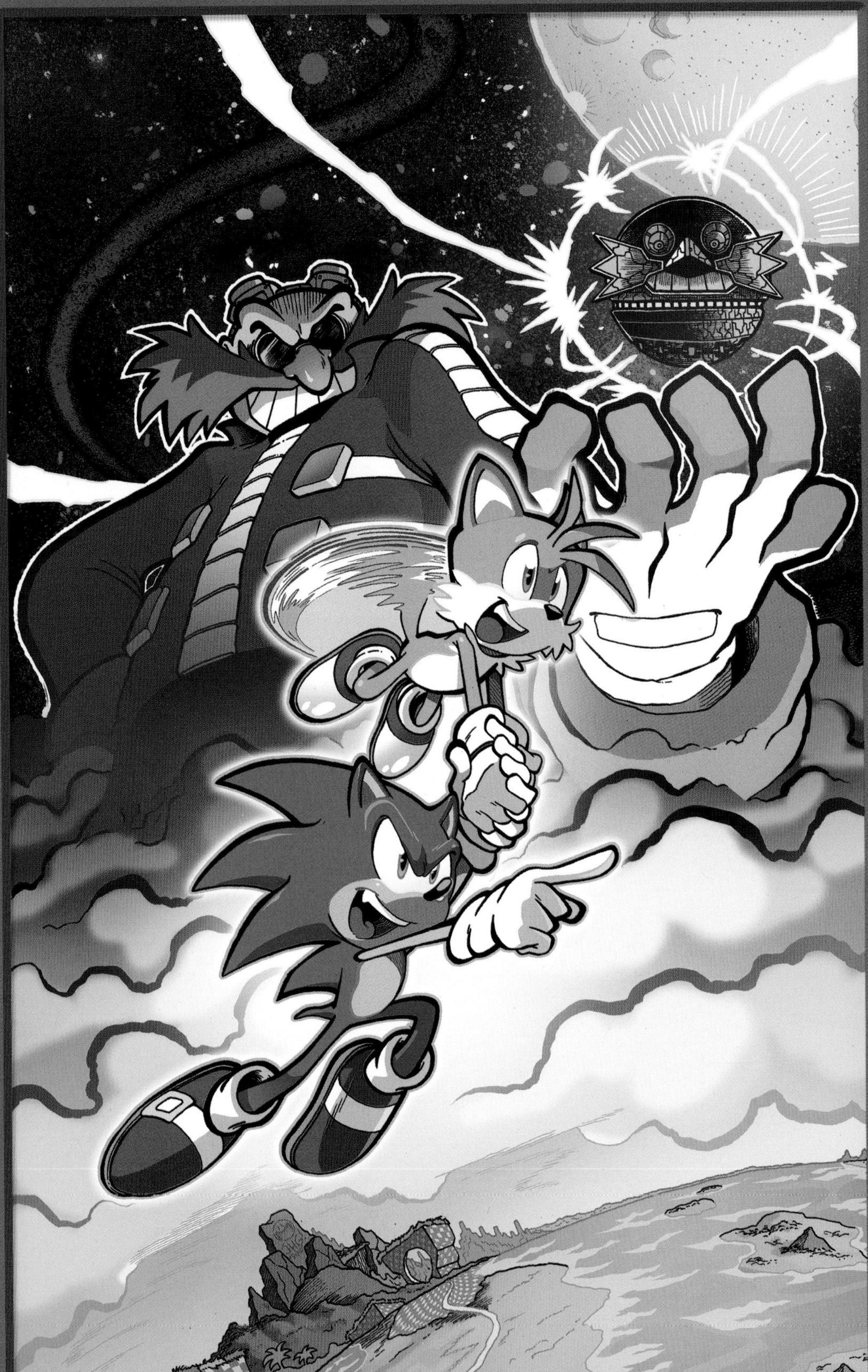

ART BY JONATHAN GRAY COLORS BY MATT HERMS

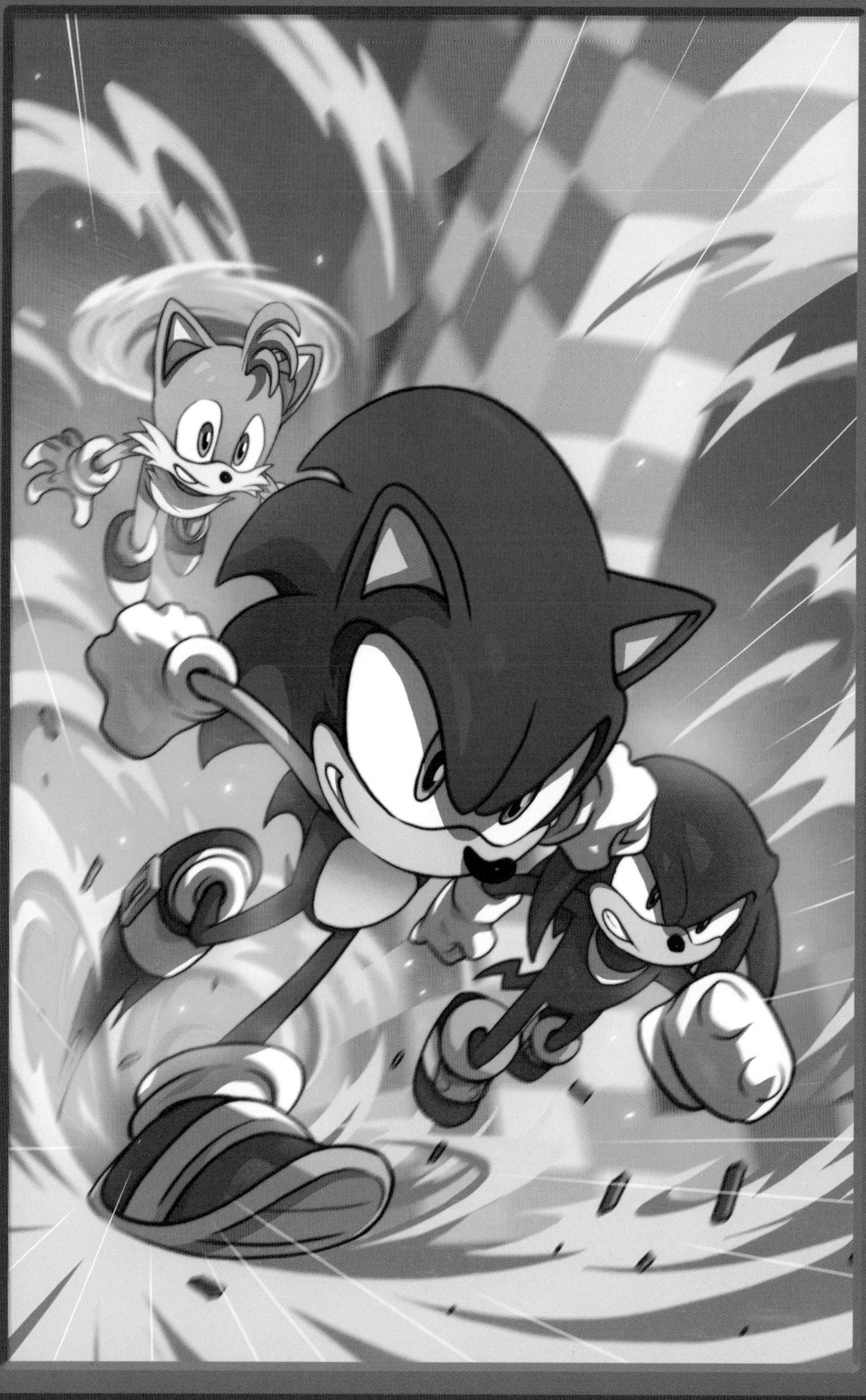

ART BY **EDWIN HUANG**

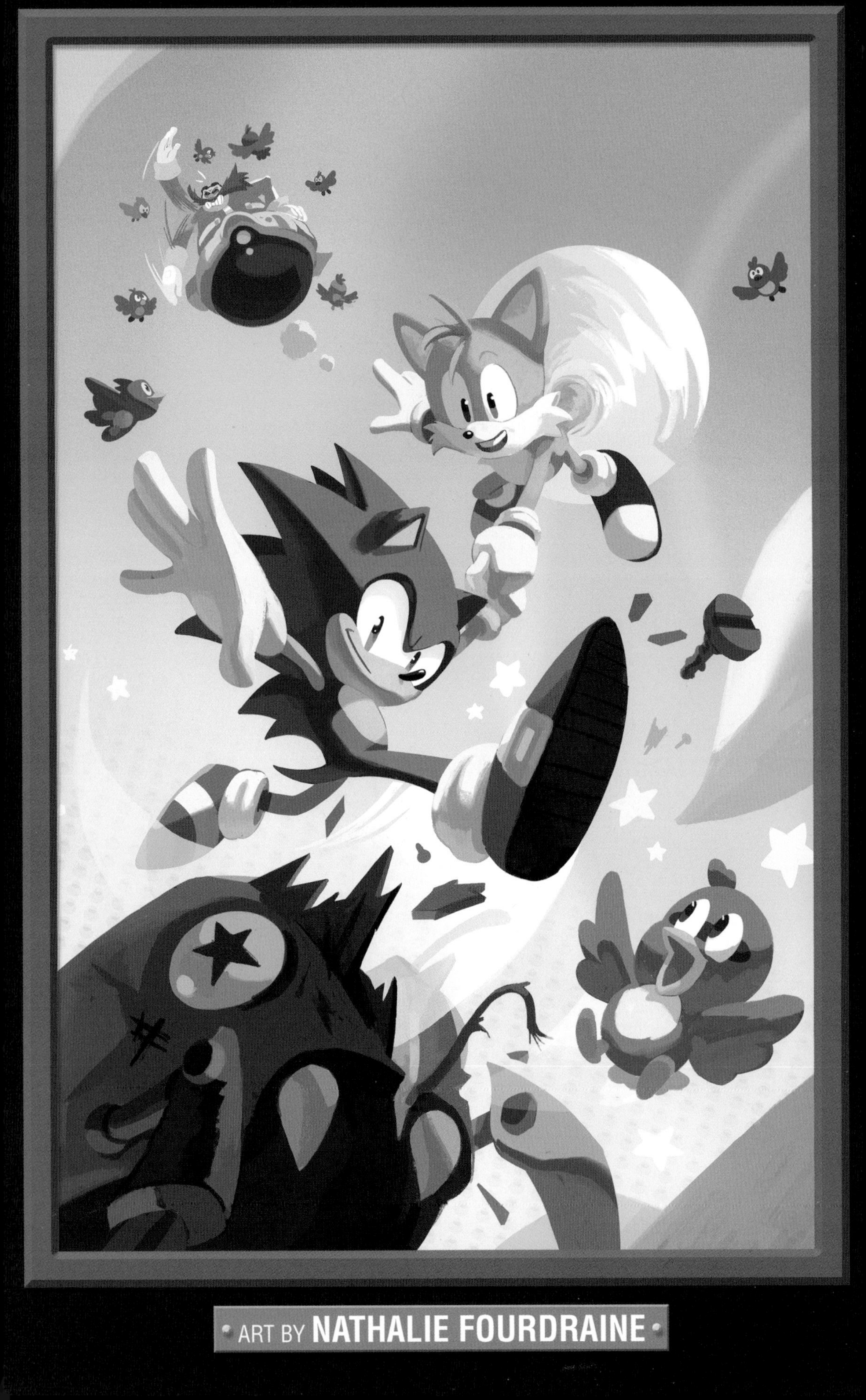

ART BY **NATHALIE FOURDRAINE**

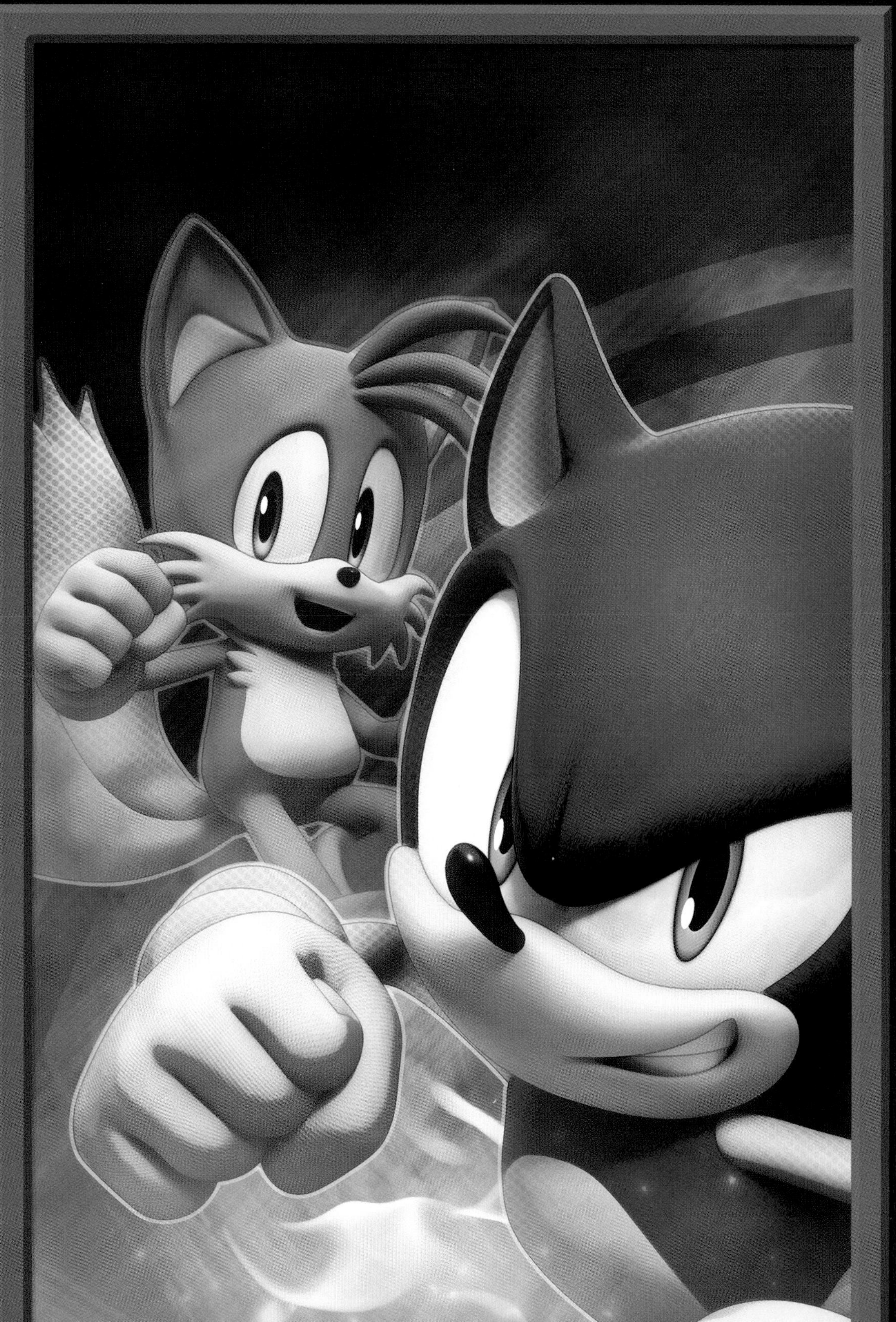

ART BY **RAFA KNIGHT**

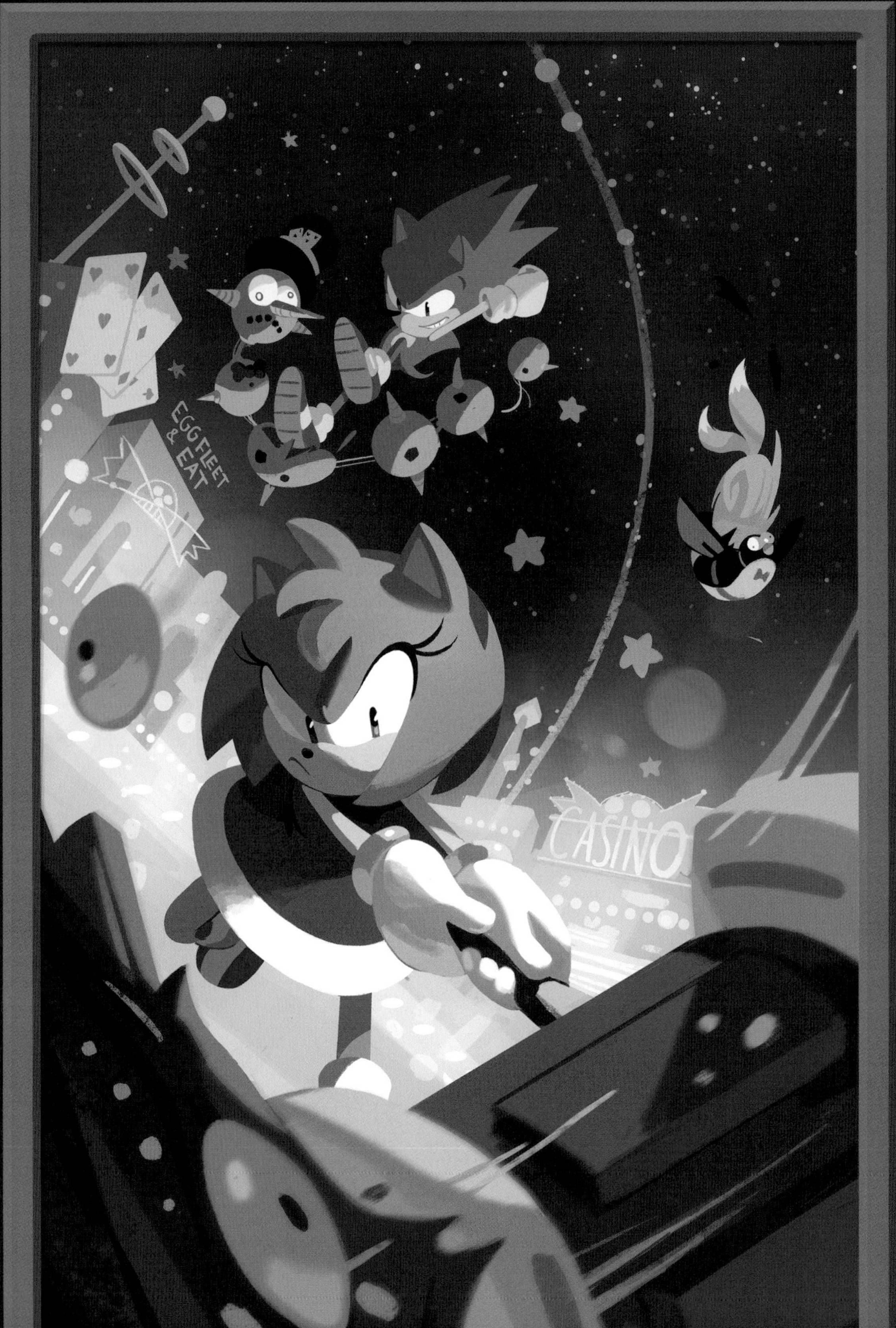
EGG FLEET & EAT
CASINO

ART BY **NATHALIE FOURDRAINE**

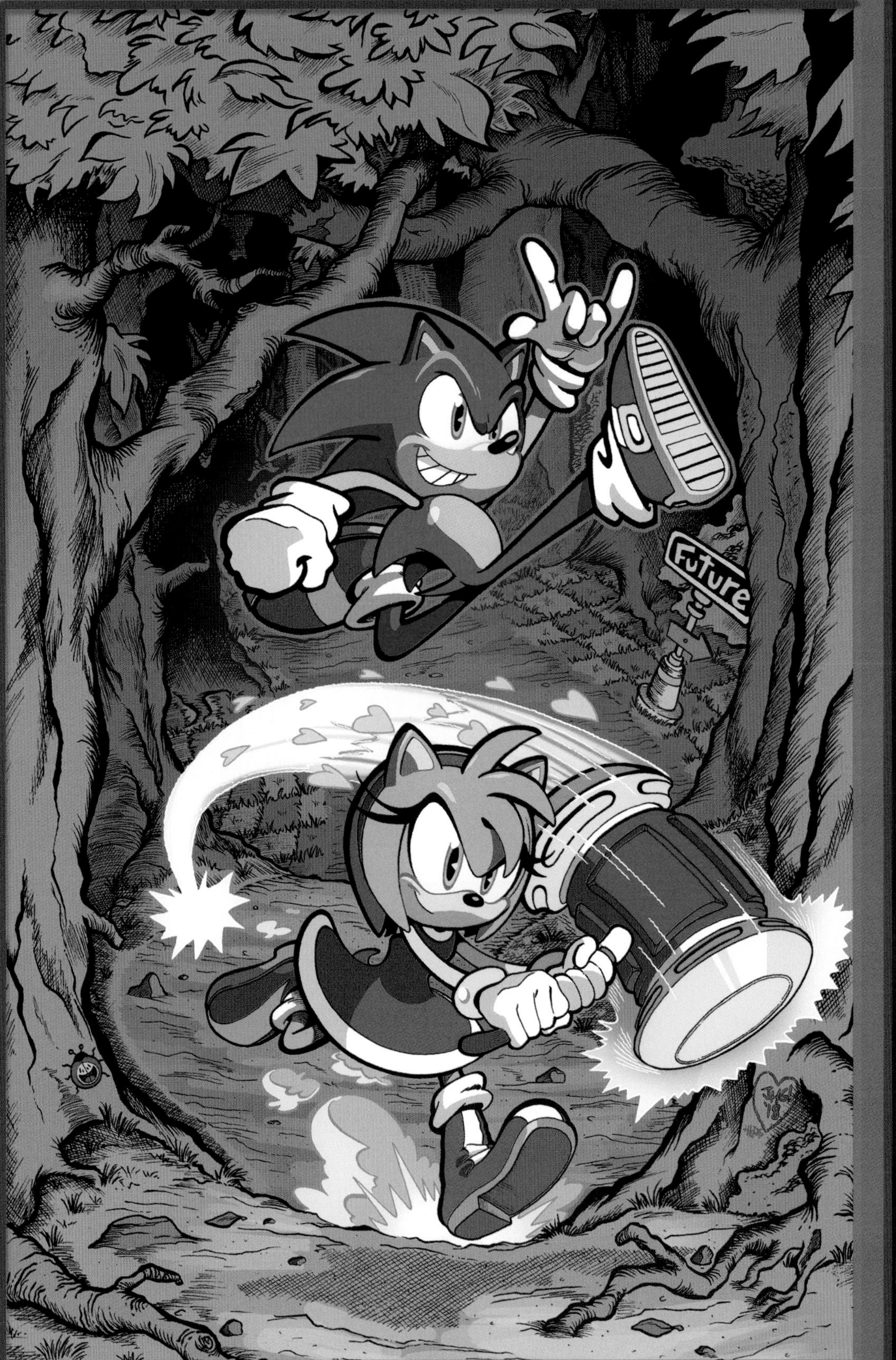
Future

ART BY **JONATHAN GRAY** COLORS BY **MATT HERMS**

ART BY **NATHALIE FOURDRAINE**

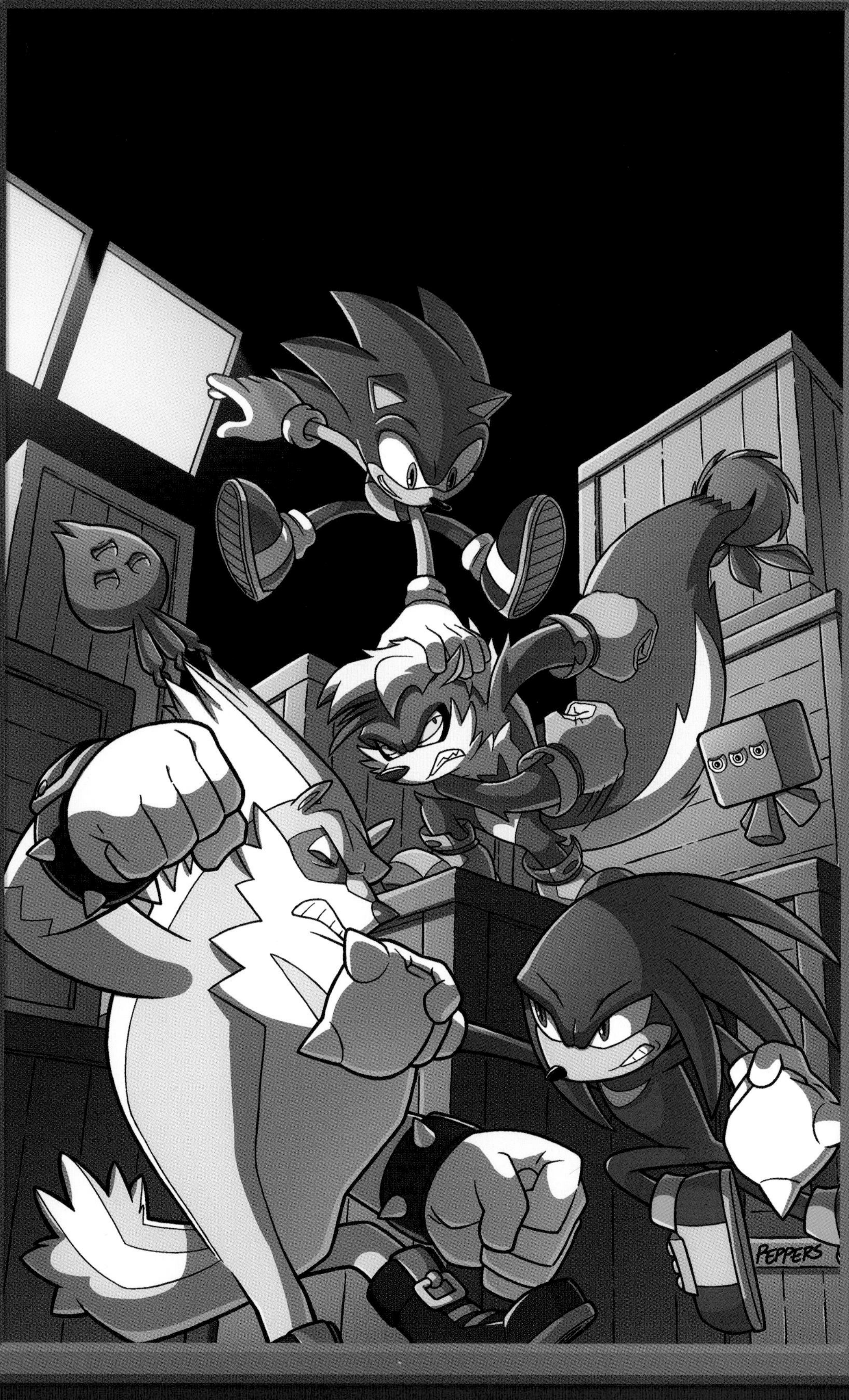
PEPPERS

ART BY **JAMAL PEPPERS** COLORS BY **HEATHER BRECKEL**

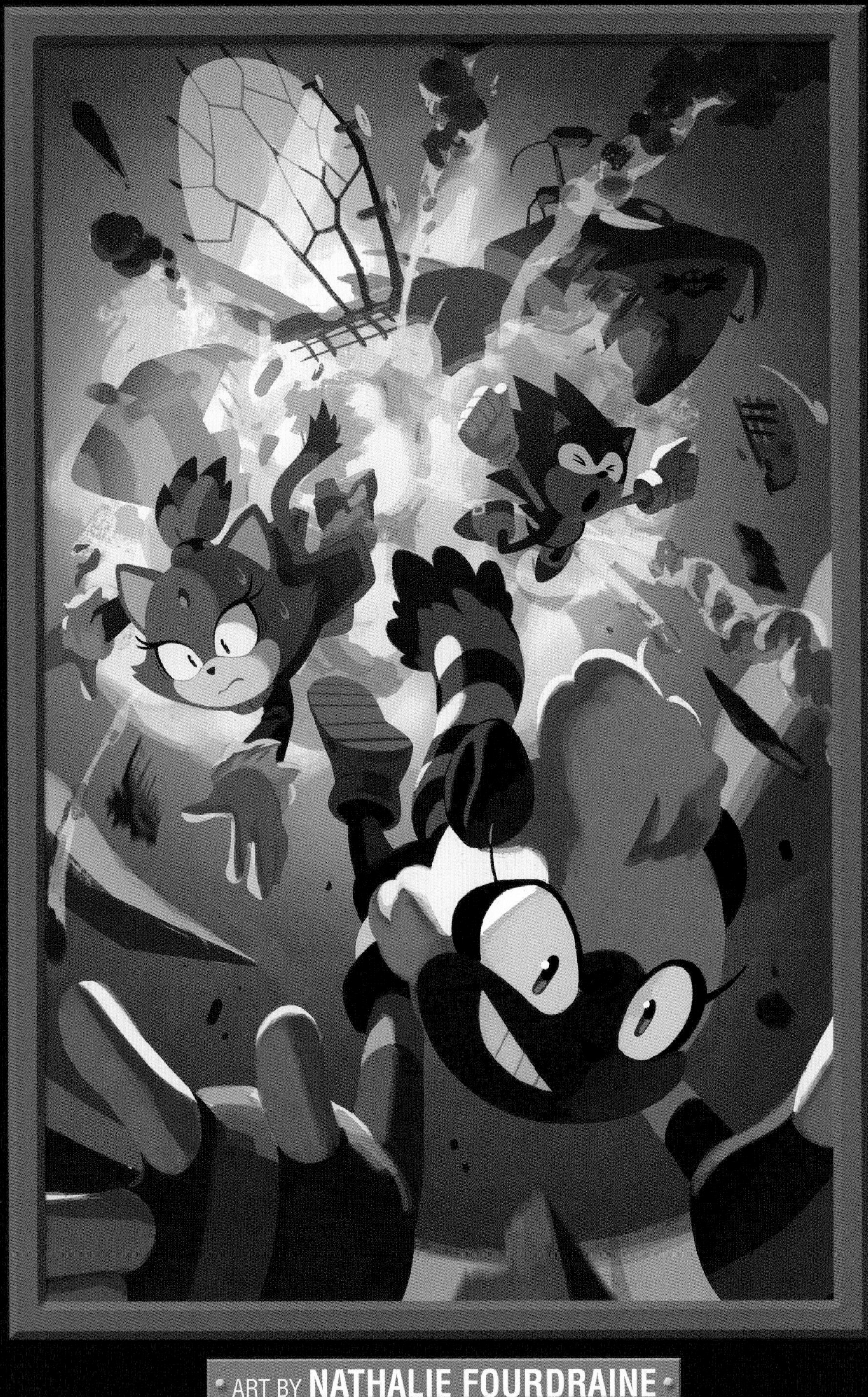

ART BY **NATHALIE FOURDRAINE**

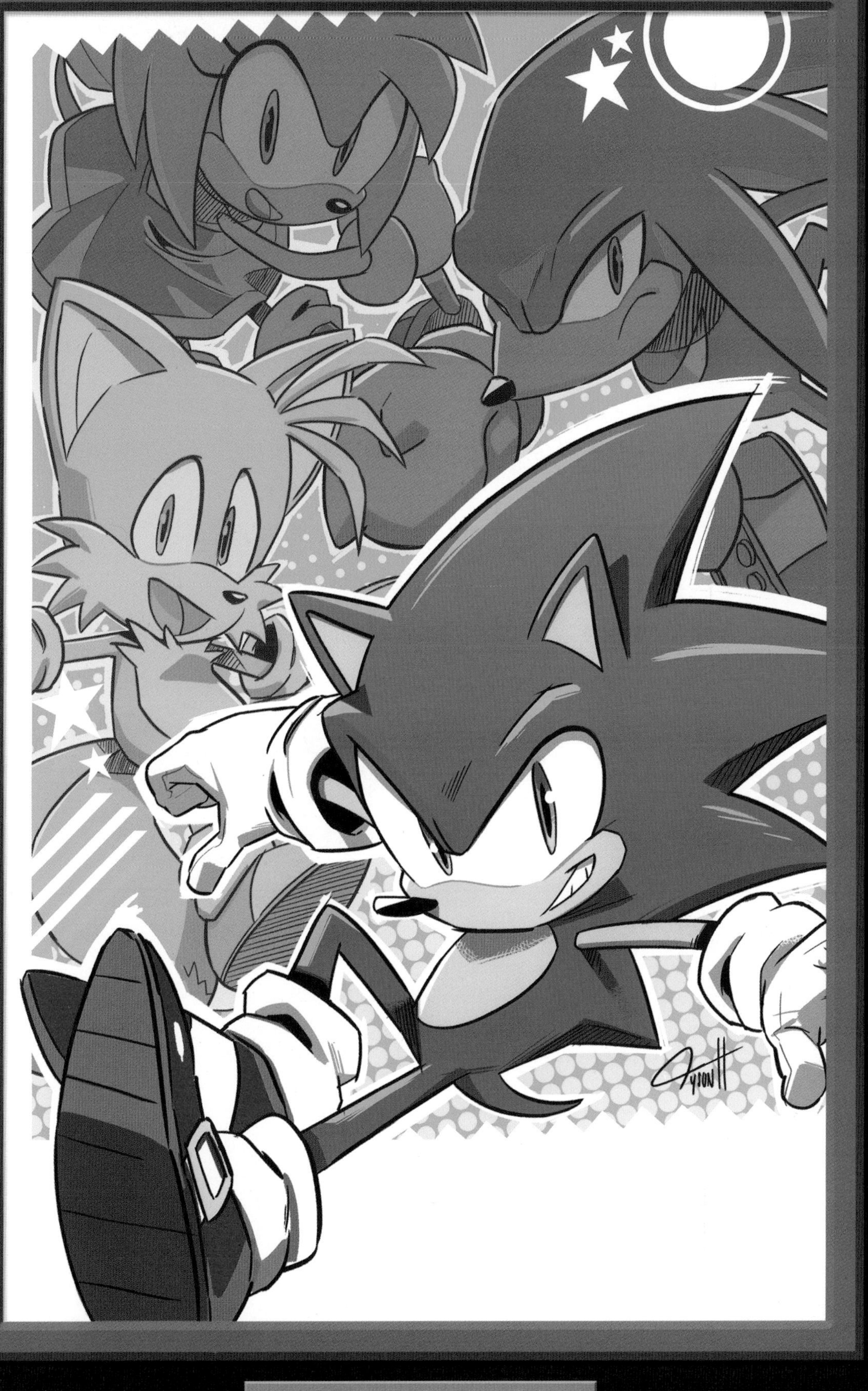
TYSON H

ART BY **TYSON HESSE**

SONIC™

THE HEDGEHOG

SEGA®

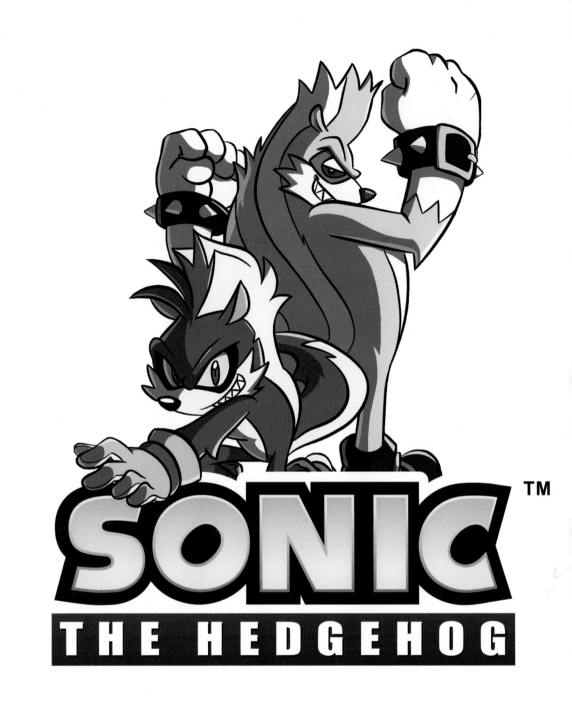

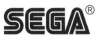